ALSO BY DL HAMMONS

TWIST

Taggart McGill YA Series
PRICK
JERK
TOOL (2026)

Silent Sleuth Investigations Series
Knight Rise
Fallen Knight

Copyright © 2026 by DL Hammons

All rights reserved.

No part of this publication may be reproduced, distributed, or transmitted in any form or by any means, including photocopying, recording, or other electronic or mechanical methods, without the prior written permission of the publisher, except as permitted by U.S. copyright law. For permission requests, contact [include publisher/author contact info].

The story, all names, characters, and incidents portrayed in this production are fictitious. No identification with actual persons (living or deceased), places, buildings, and products is intended or should be inferred.

Book Cover Design by Christian Storm

ISBN: 979-8-9890231-7-2 (paperback)

First edition 2026

This is for all of us who are still afraid of the dark.

"F-E-A-R has two meanings: 'Forget Everything And Run' or 'Face Everything And Rise.' The choice is yours."

— Zig Ziglar

Prelude - Part One

Oklahoma City - Summer 1979

After two years of residency at Mercy General, Ginny Alverez could finally envision a promising future ahead of her. There were times when she still felt overwhelmed, but she no longer dreaded her shifts. Instead, she was excited about the challenges each one brought. It was gritty, fast-paced, exhausting, and often heartbreaking. It was also deeply gratifying. Whatever doubts she had about her career choice were fading day by day. Now, she embraced the madness and dove in headfirst, outlasting more than half of her male classmates, which she took way too much pleasure in. The people she typically treated weren't always the most well-adjusted members of society, but she had developed an earned respect and affection for each of them.

On Tuesday, Ginny's day was going like so many others until she stepped into an emergency room observation bay to find a woman sitting on the table, holding her arm against her chest with a large man standing beside her. A quick glance at the woman's admission paperwork listed her as the same age as Ginny, but the woman's appearance caused Ginny to double-check the dates. The woman looked much older. Her hair was matted, cheeks withdrawn, and sunken eyes that were cherry red. She had either been crying or she had spent an extended evening inside a cigar bar. Even though it was late afternoon, the woman was still wearing a light-blue sleeping gown, and her feet were dirty and bare.

The mountain of a man, who Ginny surmised must have been the woman's husband, stood off to the side facing the wall, his broad back to the room. He was an enormous brute, twice the size of the woman, and he took up much of the free space in the examination area. At first, Ginny thought the man was whispering to himself, but when he turned around, she could see he was holding a small boy in his arms, probably three or four years old.

"I'm Doctor Alvarez. You must be Vera?" Ginny asked as she approached the woman. It was her standard greeting.

When the woman didn't respond, Ginny looked at the man.

"Yeah, this is my wife, Vera," the man responded with a deep, husky voice. "I'm Jake, Jake Coulson, and this is our son, Teddy." Ginny smiled at the small boy, who did not return the gesture. She returned her attention to Vera.

It didn't take Ginny long to determine that the arm Vera was holding against her chest had a nasty break in both the radius and the ulna bones. The fracture had to be causing the woman no small amount of discomfort, but Vera sat placidly on the examination table, staring straight ahead, not making a sound. Not a whimper or moan. Normally, Ginny would have suspected shock, but Vera's blood pressure was normal, as was her breathing, and her skin wasn't clammy. Outside of general appearance, and without her initial examination revealing the break, Ginny was hard-pressed to find any outward signs of distress. *Is she drugged?*

"So, what's the story here?" Ginny asked using a casual tone.

Vera didn't respond other than to cut her eyes toward her husband. Ginny looked at the husband again.

"I'm not sure," the man said. His body language was sending Ginny conflicting signals. He seemed tense, fidgety, but also apprehensive and confused.

"You're not sure?" Ginny responded, unable to keep the surprise from her voice.

"All I know is when I got home from work, she was in the kitchen getting dinner ready. That's when I noticed she was having trouble holding onto the bowls and utensils. When I looked closer, I saw her arm looked funny. She didn't say anything when I asked her what happened to her, so I grabbed Teddy, and the three of us rushed right here. I didn't bother to look around the house for clues."

Ginny returned her attention to Vera, but the woman didn't seem to be paying attention to the conversation. Her eyes were unfocused and looking straight ahead. Ginny was convinced that something else was going on.

"Is she on medication, or did you give her something?"

"No, nothing."

"Has she been unresponsive the entire time?"

"Yeah. She fussed a little when we walked through the hospital doors, that's all."

Ginny's spousal-abuse radar was going off. She had unfortunately seen her fair share of abuse victims in the emergency room, and this looked like a textbook example. She'd seen the aftermath of what people could do to one another, and it always drained her. The hospital tried to train its residents to keep their emotions in check and be cautious about how they dealt with situations like these, but it was a tall order. The key was figuring out if the woman would file a criminal complaint, but this woman wasn't saying anything. The whole thing felt weird. The husband just stood there holding his son as if somebody was going to rush in and snatch him out of his arms, staring at his wife like she was some stranger he was doing a favor for.

"I'm not sure you're telling me the whole truth. Your wife looks like she's been crying for some time and shows signs of borderline malnutrition."

"Her red eyes are because she's been having difficulty sleeping… I think that's affecting her appetite as well."

"Is there a reason she's not getting enough sleep?"

Jake seemed to consider his answer. "We moved here from New York a week ago and… well… she really hasn't been herself since. She's been obsessed with this odd box and…well…it's just been a lot."

Ginny still didn't feel comfortable about the situation. She stepped out of the room and called for a nurse. She arranged for him to pull the husband aside to answer some insurance-related questions so she could get Vera alone. It was the hospital's standard procedure for potential abuse cases.

When Jake was out of sight, Ginny asked the woman directly, "Ma'am, did your husband do this to you?"

There was no response.

"Honey… all you have to do is say the word, and we can have the police take him away and see that he never does this to you again. Is that what you want?"

Still nothing. Vera's blank expression had Ginny reconsidering the possibility of shock. But she wanted to give it one last try before allowing Vera to return to a possibly abusive husband. She needed someone to help her get through to the woman, someone who was maybe a little older and "fatherly". Mercy General always had an active pastoral presence, especially in the emergency room.

"Maybe you'd prefer the priest speak to you?"

Vera's gaze instantly became clear and focused, locking onto Ginny's eyes. The woman's face seemed to change, unnerving Ginny and causing her to take a step backward. She recalled seeing videos of vicious animals being threatened in the wild, how their ears went back, their skin drawn tight, and razor-sharp teeth seemed to dominate their face. She was seeing the same thing now on Vera. Ginny felt like she was staring into the eyes of a feral creature. She had experienced plenty of odd behaviors working in the ER. Patients strung out on PCP, people who were otherwise deeply disturbed, and all manner of humans in various states of distress. But this was different.

Vera smiled. Large, toothy, and even predatory. Ginny had a hard time likening it to any smile she'd even seen before. It was the most disturbing thing Ginny had ever seen in her life. The eerie grin and penetrating eyes continued to grip Ginny's attention. She was too afraid to move, petrified.

Vera's mouth opened wide, and strange noises, emanating from deep within her chest, came out. To the ear, it sounded like a stream of grunts and groans, guttural, but somehow Ginny understood it was a kind of language, though not one she had ever heard before. In her head, she understood perfectly what was being said.

"If you call anybody, especially a priest, I will end you. I will adorn these walls with your intestines and bathe the floor in a river of blood. This family is mine. Move on. There is only sorrow here."

Ginny lurched backwards as if someone had let go of a rope she'd been tugging against. She bumped into a countertop, sending a tray of implements clattering to the floor.

Jake rushed back into the room, and when he did, his wife returned to a listless stupor.

Seeing the terrified expression on Ginny's face, he blurted, "Is everything okay?"

Ginny opened her mouth to reply, but instead bolted from the observation room. She rushed through the ER, ignoring her name being called behind her. She burst into the break room, gathered her possessions from her locker, and fled the hospital without looking back.

Later, she vaguely remembered driving home and checking to make sure every door and window was locked once she arrived. She consumed an entire bottle of Jack Daniel's that evening and passed out.

She slept for two days straight.

On the third day, she turned on the TV and watched a handsome news anchor inform her that a young woman, her arm in a plaster cast, had stabbed her husband and child to death while they slept and then slit her own throat.

That's when Ginny left her apartment and bought a bible.

Prelude – Part Two

Ft. Smith, Arkansas - Last Week 2026

"Are those restraints really necessary?" the priest asked.

The orderly continued strapping the wide leather belt around the woman's waist without indicating he heard the question. His ill-fitting uniform, consisting of matching white pants and a short-sleeve shirt, suffered from a terminal case of wrinkles and did a poor job of concealing his massive girth, with a pink strip of stomach bulging from below the orderly's shirt. The laminated hospital ID clipped to his uniform pocket flapped around like a cowboy holding on for dear life atop a bucking bronco. Working without a sound, he finished tightening the leather girdle, and then guided the woman's listless body into the chair opposite the visitor. A small metal table separated them.

The priest, a big man himself, was dressed in a dark gray suit with a black clergy shirt and white clerical collar. He studied the orderly without comment and a frown grew on his face as he watched the man treat the woman like a side of beef, maneuvering her roughly back and forth, oblivious to her own will.

The room he had been waiting in was brightly lit, which he understood enhanced the view for any observers on the other side of the room's two-way mirror, but the intense lighting also accentuated the dust and grime. From the layer of film covering the various surfaces, it was obvious the cleaning staff hadn't concerned themselves with this part of the hospital for quite some time. A musty smell of neglect and a faint hint of stale sweat and urine, which assaulted his nose as soon as he entered the room, had put him in a foul mood. The orderly's inhumane actions only deepened it.

The priest had taken the seat on the far side of the table, putting the mirror covering most of the back wall behind him. On the wall to his left rested an old metal radiator, fed by a pipe that ran along the baseboard and onto the floor next to the lone entrance. The only furniture in the room was a table and chairs, all bolted to the concrete floor.

The woman offered no resistance throughout her manhandling, flopping around like a rag doll, her distant eyes providing no hint that she was even aware of the orderly's actions. Grabbing the bulky chain hanging from the rear of the belt the woman was now wearing, the orderly secured it with a lock to a loophole at the base of the chair. He gave it a quick yank, jerking the woman back in her seat. Only then did he step back and look at the priest.

"They said you wanted to talk to her alone," the hulk finally answered with an ugly twist in his mouth. He had a deep voice that matched his appearance, his pronounced Adam's apple bobbing as he spoke. "Alone means she gets the belt. No belt, then I hafta stay."

"Surely, you can't still consider her a threat?"

The orderly's bushy eyebrows rose, and his beefy right hand came up to pinch the tip of his chin. "Hmmmmmm... maybe we should ask her husband and children that question? Oh, wait, we can't. Because she KILLED them!" He dropped his hand and leveled a stern gaze back at the priest. "Rules are rules."

The priest looked at the woman's face to see if the man's biting comment registered at all, but there was nothing. "Thank you," he replied, his tone clear that he considered it time for the hourly employee to leave.

The orderly turned and grabbed the door handle, pausing to look back over his shoulder at the priest.

"Aren't you burning up in that getup?" the orderly said. "It's gotta be over a hundred today. Don't they let you guys wear short sleeves or nuthin?"

The priest glanced down at his coat sleeves and tugged on the ends of the shirt.

"I'm fine, thank you."

"You know, you don't look like any priest I've ever seen. I bet that white hair scares the bejesus outta the kids."

The priest's ponytail of long white hair shifted across his back as his gaze casually moved from his hands to the orderly.

"Son, I don't imagine you've seen very many priests in your lifetime."

A scowl flashed across the orderly's face. "I won't be far. I have a feeling this is going to be a quick visit. This bird ain't saying much," he said, then closed the door behind him with a clang.

The priest studied the woman across from him. Although he knew she was in her late thirties, the deep lines running through her pale complexion and sunken eyes outlined by dark circles made her appear much older. Her unkempt black hair with streaks of premature gray hung loosely in front of her face like an organic hoody, shrouding her from her surroundings. The maroon scrubs she wore, faded from years of use and too much salt content in the laundry detergent, appeared to be two sizes too large. They hung off her shoulders like a bedsheet being used for a last-minute toga party.

"How are they treating you here, Mrs. Cole? Do you need anything?"

The woman did not respond and gave no sign that she was aware of his presence.

"Do you know who I am, Mrs. Cole?" the priest asked using the soft tones he's learned could soothe the most timid of people.

Still nothing. The officials had told him she was on medication but could still interact... if she chose to.

"Mrs. Cole... Evelyn... may I call you that?"

Still nothing.

"Evelyn, my name is Wilfred. I told them I was your family priest, but you know that's not true, don't you?"

Evelyn Cole still did not move. Her breathing was so shallow that Wilfred thought holding a mirror under her nose to tell if she was alive would be inconclusive.

The priest leaned forward in his chair and slowly slid his hands across the table until they were in the woman's line of sight. "I had to tell them I was your priest. I had to lie, so I could see you today. Do you know why I had to do that?"

Somewhere in the room, a fly buzzed as it desperately searched for an escape. The priest watched the woman's eyes through her mass of hair.

"I came because you are an incredibly special person, Evelyn. Very special indeed. In fact, you are truly one of a kind."

A muffled rumbling preceded a blast of cold air that spilled out of the air vent above, falling across the back of the priest's neck.

"I would have come sooner, but I needed to be patient. I hope you understand I couldn't risk coming to see you earlier — too many prying eyes… but I'm here now, and I need your help."

The priest paused, choosing his words carefully.

"Evelyn, you have survived something nobody else in recorded time has survived. It is that which has drawn me to you, to find answers to some very important questions."

The sound of the fly stopped, almost as if it were now listening in on the conversation.

"I need you to tell me about... *the box.*"

Mrs. Cole's eyes blinked several times.

"You know what I'm referring to, don't you?" The priest's coaxing voice was barely a whisper now. "The parts of your story that nobody would believe?"

The woman's head tilted such a minute amount that if the priest hadn't been so intently focused on her he would have missed it.

"I realize what you've been through these past months. I surely do. In fact, I'm probably the only person who does. Nobody wants to listen, to hear a truth they can't comprehend. Instead, all they'll do is say you must take responsibility... accept what happened as the result of your actions... or else their treatment cannot help you. And I suspect your only recourse has been to withdraw into what I see before me now. This shell. The one place where you can still deny their truth and cling to your innocence."

The hands of the priest inched closer, stopping just short of touching the woman.

"But, it happened, Evelyn. As horrendous as it is to remember, it happened precisely how you remember it. And unlike everyone else, I'm here to listen so I can help others."

Mrs. Cole's breathing was now very noticeable, her shoulders rising and falling. For the first time, she lifted her head and looked directly into the priest's eyes. The look in her eyes was both pleading and fearful.

A raspy voice that cracked from lack of use replied, "You... know?"

"I know it's real, that you weren't making it up. I know where it came from. And I know what was inside."

The woman's eyes filled with tears.

"But none of that matters right now. Both of us know that. What I need you to tell me is something I don't know. Tell me about the book."

Evelyn Cole replied, her lips trembling as she spoke. "What?"

"Let's back up and start with what happened when you opened the box. How did it make you feel?"

In the far corner of the room, the fly fell to the ground. Dead.

Without warning, the woman's hands shot out and grabbed hold of the priest's wrists. Her eyes had enlarged to the size of fifty-cent pieces, and the veins in her neck popped out. Her one-word response was scarcely a hiss through her bared teeth, its hideous sound sending chills down the priest's back.

"Consumed!"

One

Present Day

Knox

I watched helplessly as the box hit the ground at just the right angle, splitting the seam and forcing the cardboard sides to burst wide open. Dozens of paperbacks scattered across the hardwood floor in every direction, taunting me with the images of big-breasted women with long flowing hair embraced by men with glistening pecs and washboard abs.

"Shit!" I let slip, my sudden anger boiling over. That was the third time I had tripped on that damn step. It might have been partially my fault because I was daydreaming about starting at yet another high school on Monday. But what idiot house designer would place one step leading down from the foyer into the sunken living room, but two steps up into the adjoining study? That was the one I kept catching my foot on. I stood there looking at the damage long enough for my anger to change into worry. I needed to get this mess picked up before anyone else came across it, especially my stepmom, Lorna. She would claim I'd intentionally dropped the box, since it contained her romance books. I wasn't supposed to be carrying any of her boxes, anyway. I forgot to check the label before I picked it up, so sue me for being extra-helpful.

I couldn't let this ruin today. It was important that everyone see I was trying to be useful.

The box was a complete loss, so I hurriedly searched for something else to throw the books into. I knew there wouldn't be any empty boxes yet; that wasn't how things were done in my family. All the boxes had to be unloaded and placed in the right room before we opened a single one, but surely there had to be something. Then I remembered carrying in my laundry hamper filled with winter clothes. I spun on my heel and sprinted back through the living room, across the foyer, and into the bedroom I shared with my younger brother, Travis.

The hamper was just inside the door against the outer wall. I gave it a flip when I grabbed it, dumping out my sweatshirts and jeans on the ground.

"What are you doing?" came a voice from the other side of the room.

Startled, I turned to find Travis partially hidden by a stack of cardboard boxes. He had backed his customized solid black wheelchair with fire-engine red spokes into the corner to gain a better view out of the window. The box on top of the stack next to him was open.

"You know you're not supposed to open the boxes yet," I pointed out, purposely dodging his question.

Travis nodded towards his ferret, sleeping peacefully in the cage on the floor next to him. "I had to get Bowzer's food. Besides, I think those rules don't really apply to me anymore."

A wave of sympathy... and guilt... swept over me. I dealt with it the only way I knew how. I ran.

Darting back across the foyer, I spotted one of my older sisters coming up the porch steps carrying a pair of smaller boxes. I knew if she discovered the busted box, it would be game over. I skidded to a halt, reached back, and pushed the front door closed, making sure she couldn't see me. When it clicked shut, I heard her muffled voice from the other side. "Hey!"

I dashed through the empty living room to the scattered books, tripping yet again on the second step between the living room and study.

"Frak!"

As quick as I could, I scooped up and threw all the smutty paperbacks into the hamper, wishing I had thought to grab a pair of latex gloves. Once finished, I gripped the basket in one hand and the busted box in the other. I headed back to our room, ignoring the pounding on the front door as I passed by.

In my room, I returned the hamper to where I found it, threw some of my disheveled clothes on top to cover the books, then tossed the empty box at the base of my brother's wheelchair. I would come back later when there were plenty of empty boxes available to transfer the books into and move them back to the study undetected.

"Just go with it, okay?" I said, answering Travis's confused look.

My brother shrugged his shoulders. "Okay."

I stepped into the foyer and casually opened the front door. Lindsey stood there, her foot drawn back to deliver another blow while still holding her boxes, face red and teeth clenched. Of my two identical sisters, Lindsey has always been the more ill-tempered, running a tad hotter than Jadie. Jadie, on the other hand, is more dramatic when she gets angry, but that happens less often.

When I say identical twins, I mean down to the number of freckles on their noses. It's a source of irritation in our family that Mom and I were the only ones who could always tell them apart. Now that mom was gone, I kept the secret of how to tell them apart to myself. That especially irritated Lorna, my stepmom, which I guess was the point.

Today, it was easy to tell them apart as they were wearing different clothes for the move. Lindsey wore an old blue t-shirt and faded jeans, Jadie a white tank and shorts. Lindsey had tied her shoulder-length brown hair back in a ponytail, allowing me to see her glowing red ears, which always looked that way when she was really pissed.

"Why did you lock me out?" she spat.

I put on my best innocent face. "I didn't lock you out."

"Chace, it was you. You're the only one in the house."

"Not so. Travis is in here with me. And how many times do I have to tell you my name is Knox now?"

If she didn't have her arms full of boxes, I could imagine one hand going to her hip and the other grabbing the jewelry around her neck. That was her default arguing posture.

"No, it isn't. It's Chace. When are you going to stop playing these stupid games?"

I put my hand on the doorframe and leaned against it. Although I was two years younger than my sisters, at five foot nine, I was a couple of inches taller. "I promise I didn't shut the door, Lindsey. Maybe Dad opened the back door, and the cross-breeze pulled this one shut. Want me to take those for you?"

The offer of aid took my sister by surprise, which I knew it would. Right now, she was asking herself why I would bother to lock her out and then turn around and offer to carry her load? Unable to come up with a suitable answer, she'd decide not to look a gift horse in the mouth, and my distraction would be complete. I knew both my sisters well — at least I used to.

"Um... sure," she replied hesitantly. "These go in Dad and Lorna's room."

I flashed my most innocent smile as I reached out and took the pair of boxes from her.

Disaster averted.

As I made my way up the stairs with Lindsey's boxes and into the first room on the right, I could already feel the heaviness seeping back into my heart from its momentary distraction. This new house wasn't ideal. The main-floor bedroom was obviously intended to be the primary bedroom, but Travis's condition forced us to share the downstairs room. That meant Dad and Lorna had to sacrifice by squeezing into one of the two second-floor bedrooms, both of which were much smaller than the master. Even worse, it forced them to share a bathroom with my twin diva sisters. All because of the pile of medical bills they were dealing with, limiting the size of the house they could afford. I had overheard Dad and Lorna discussing it before our move. A single-story with more bedrooms would have fit our family better. But Dad said they got a real good deal on this one. It had an unfinished basement that would eventually become another bedroom and bathroom, so he said they should consider themselves fortunate. I couldn't help but chuckle at that one. On one hand, I'd hardly consider us fortunate, and on the other, my dad rarely finished his projects.

I placed the boxes on top of another stack and turned to look around their room, filled with furniture, boxes, and an unassembled bed. It wasn't that there was a lot, just that the room was that small.

What had my therapist said? I should expect ripples of guilt-induced despair to pop up from time to time, reminding me of what my actions had brought about. He had a point, but the reality of it all was a lot higher on the suck scale than he let on. Ripples would assume there'd be some space between the times I felt like crap. And the gap between each wave would eventually widen. But that hasn't been my experience. I felt like I was drowning beneath a rising tide of sadness. It surged into our lives when mom died, turned into a tsunami after my brother's accident, and now it has engulfed our entire family. The worst part was that it all fed off me, and no matter how I tried, I couldn't find my way back to the surface or calm waters. The best I could do right now—according to the doc—was weather the storm. Was there even an umbrella that big?

The sound of someone coming up the stairs shook me from my thoughts. Stepping back into the hallway, I saw Lorna heading my way, carrying a large oval mirror covered in bubble wrap.

"Need any help?" I asked.

"I got it, thanks," my stepmom replied, flashing me a thin smile lacking warmth. Lorna and Dad had only been married a couple months, and I could tell her attitude towards me was even more tense than usual, not that I cared that much. My brother Travis thought her recent chill might be more about this move and the anxiety it was causing. But I had a pretty good idea it was more about me insisting on going by my middle name immediately after she and Dad were married.

I stepped out of the way to allow her into the room, where she placed the mirror against the wall directly inside the door. As she stood up, she wiped her brow with her forearm, being careful not to let her work gloves dirty her face. The tan Hard Rock Cafe T-shirt she was wearing was now covered in dirt and dust bunnies, with a couple of specks embedded in her short, black hair as well. If there was one thing to admire about her, begrudgingly, it was that our move had proved that she was a hard worker.

My stepmom's eyes lingered on the two boxes I had just brought in.

"Chace, I thought we agreed—"

"Knox," I corrected.

Lorna gave me another bitter smile. "I mean Knox... you agreed you wouldn't carry any of the boxes belonging to your father or me."

I let my shoulders drop. "Lorna, I won't do anything. I promise. Lindsey was having a tough time with them, so I offered to help, that's all." Now I was really glad I had hidden the busted box and books.

Lorna looked at me like she was waiting for me to say something else.

"Okay," she finally said. "Your sister's dresser needs to come up next, so you should probably get your dad to help."

Eager to escape the uncomfortableness, I turned and bounded down the stairs, out the front door, barely avoiding my sister Jadie coming up the steps with another load of boxes. I swerved to the right, vaulted the porch ledge and prickly bushes on the other side, and landed next to the cube.

This was the first time our family had used the Cube-Move service to relocate. It was also the first time we were paying for it out of our own pockets. I understood Cube-Move meant savings, but it also meant a lot more work. The company had placed the 16 x 7 x 7 cube container in front of our old house, the family loaded it up with all our stuff, the Cube-Move service transported the cube here, and now we we're unloading it. Easy-peasy. Of course, there was more work to go around now that we were short one pair of helping hands. That thought spurred yet another depressing ripple.

Out on the street, a couple of seven or eight-year-old kids rode their bikes past our house on their way to some unknown adventure. The neighborhood was a lot different from the typical military housing we'd lived in when my dad had been in the Navy. The homes were all average-sized, all two-level, but not squished together like square footage was at a premium. There were plenty of trees and bushes, with well-kept lawns everywhere. I liked the change.

I walked past the cube towards the backyard when a movement out of the corner of my eye caught my attention. The house next door was approximately the same size as ours, but situated closer to the street, which gave it the extra room needed for the pool in its backyard. It was two floors, like our house, with three windows on each level facing our direction and a basement, which you could see by the pair of rectangular windows right above ground level.

It was at one of those basement windows that I saw a curtain being pulled to the side. When I turned my head to get a better look, the curtain dropped back into place.

The neighbors were obviously curious… and maybe even a bit creepy.

Shrugging it off, I turned the corner of the house and found Dad on the patio measuring a piece of wood laid across a pair of sawhorses.

"Whatcha doin?"

My dad was still sporting his military haircut, even though he mentioned he might let it grow out before we left North Carolina. He was somewhere in his upper forties, but had the body of someone much younger, which wasn't a surprise considering his rigorous workout schedule. His youthful appearance could just as easily result from him working on his endless list of uncompleted home projects. At fifteen, I was a few inches shorter than him, but he probably weighed twice what I did. It was my mom's side of the family that I got my lean stature from.

Dad answered without looking up. "Building some ramps so your brother can move in and out of the living room."

Was there no question I could ask, or topic to talk about that didn't lead back to my brother… and my guilt?

"Lorna said Lindsey's dresser needs to go up next, and you should help me."

From somewhere above us, Lorna's voice called out. "David, when you're finished helping your son, I could use your help in the bedroom."

"Will do," Dad yelled back, looking up to the second-story window. He tossed the measuring tape onto the wood. "Let's do it then."

As we headed back towards the cube, I could tell that Dad was looking at me carefully.

"How are you doing?" he asked me.

I resisted the temptation to let out a heavy sigh. "I'm good."

"You'd tell me if you weren't, right? The doctor said this was going to be a stressful time for all of us, and we needed to discuss our feelings openly. I want to make sure you remember that. Stop me and we'll talk."

I knew I should probably tell Dad about how I felt like I was treading water and failing at it, and how my ripples were turning into tidal waves. But I knew that wasn't what he really wanted to hear, any more than I wanted to talk about it.

I flashed him my patent smile and lied. "I will, Dad."

MOVING FEAR

Two

Lewis

Lewis ignored the discomfort in his feet for as long as he could. They ached from standing on his tippy toes for so long. The basement windows were situated high on the wall, and the chair he'd positioned underneath was a tad too short, not providing him the height he needed to peek outside. Instead of taking the time to find something different to stand on to gain those few extra inches, he ignored the discomfort for as long as he could until it forced him to rest.

He had just pulled back the white sheet covering the window, stretching himself to look outside again, when the boy next door burst out of the house and performed an acrobatic jump off the front porch, soaring over the holly bushes and making a perfect landing without the hint of a stumble. The boy was walking around the side of the house and into the backyard when he stopped dead in his tracks and looked in Lewis's direction.

Lewis dropped the sheet as he recoiled. His right foot missed the edge of the chair, and he fell over backward, arms flailing, eyes closed as he braced for the inevitable impact. The overstuffed beanbag on the floor directly behind him prevented his slight frame from taking a more severe spill.

Thank goodness he'd thought to place it there. What he didn't expect was his left arm slamming against the floor, where no amount of carpet padding could shield him from the concrete foundation underneath. Nor that his leg would become entangled with the chair back as he tipped over, causing it to knock down a small bookcase filled with DVDs.

"Shit… shit… shit… shit," Lewis said under his breath. Any louder and his mother and her parabolic hearing would detect his profanity regardless of where she was in the house. She'd ignore whatever racket he might occasionally cause, like an overturned bookcase, but let one curse word slip and she would be all over him. Although his arm was throbbing and causing him to hold his breath, he was more upset about being caught spying by his new neighbor.

Lewis straightened his glasses, then rolled off the bean bag onto his knees, pulling his left arm against his chest and using his other to steady himself. He climbed to his feet and looked back up at the covered window. It took all of his willpower to fight the urge to return.

The boy is probably still standing there, waiting for me to peek out again.

It really didn't matter now, anyway. Lewis had already found out what he needed to know.

Righting the overturned metal chair, he maneuvered it back in front of the bench at the rear of the dark room. He had purposely left the lights off so nobody would see his shadow in the window, but now he reached over and switched them on. The fluorescent bulbs flickered to life, illuminating an old kitchen table covered with an enormous battlefield made entirely out of Legos. Over the battlefield, suspended by pieces of black thread attached to the ceiling, were several versions of airborne Lego assault vehicles. Underneath the table sat a large radio-controlled drone.

He righted the toppled bookshelf and began putting the movies back in order, making sure each DVD was in its proper place. He made a mental note when he slid the Night

Stalker—Season One set back into its spot to watch that one again soon. It had been a while.

As he stood up to leave, the voice of a bellowing Wookie emanated from the cell phone on his hip. He snapped it out of its holster and put it to his ear without looking at the caller ID.

"Hey, Brodie," he said flatly, already anticipating the disappointment in her voice.

"So, what's he like?" said the excited female voice on the phone. "Have you met him yet?"

Lewis plopped back down on the beanbag, a spike of pain shooting up his arm and forcing him to suppress a moan he didn't want Brodie to hear. He stared up at the covered window.

"No, and I'm not going to either."

"Why not?" she asked, disappointment evident in her tone. "You promised me you'd try to make friends with him."

"He's a jock, Brodie, a stupid jock. You should see him bouncing around all over the place. He's wearing a Chicago Bears t-shirt for chrissakes!"

"So, you're not even going to try?"

"I don't think we'd have much in common."

"But you promised."

"I only promised because you wouldn't let it go. But now that I've seen him, I'd have better luck making friends with George Lucas."

There was a slight pause before the voice on the line continued. "Okay, I understand it might be a challenge, and I'll give you that. We knew that could be a possibility. But I also think you're just looking for excuses not to try. Remember, this could work to your advantage. He's a jock who's new to town and has zero friends. You don't know what his interests are, so don't go assuming. If you get to know him and he gets to know you before school next week, he could be a perfect ally."

Lewis pressed his eyes shut and shook his head. "Or he could turn on me as soon as he's assimilated by the collective. I could end up being a convenient way to practice his wedgies."

"You know I would never let him do that to you."

"I know...I know. But I don't want you coming to my rescue all the time."

"Lewis, you're not giving yourself enough credit."

"And I think you're giving me too much."

A lengthy stretch of silence was his answer.

"So, what did you learn about them?" Brodie started in again, unfazed. "You said your mom knows the real estate agent who sold them their house, so you could probably find out more."

"Yeah, Ms. Blabbermouth Virginia Murphy is the agent. She's in my mom's church group. I made a point of being close by every time she came over. My mom says that woman never met a secret she couldn't spread."

"Lewis, be nice."

"Well, it's true. Anyway, the family moved here from North Carolina. The dad just got out of the Navy and is going back to college to finish his degree. The mom, or rather, the stepmom, is going to be working at our school. She's a nurse. There are four kids, jock boy is our age. There's a set of older twin-sisters who are seniors and a younger brother who's in a wheelchair."

"Awwwww. How come?"

"I don't know the specifics, but I understand that it's kind of recent. Blabbermouth didn't talk much about that, although she was worried they wouldn't take the house because of the wheelchair thing."

"So why did they move to Ox-Bow?"

"They have family here. The kids have a grandmother who lives by herself out on Hwy 5. She's a retired doctor or something."

"Interesting. Anything else?"

"Want to know their credit rating?"

"Be serious. What does the boy look like?"

"I think he's kind of short, but with the wheelchair and all—"

"Stop stalling. You know who I mean."

"He's your typical jock model. What does it really matter, anyway?"

"Lewis, we agreed. This will be good for you. Just tell me you're going to go over there and introduce yourself. Don't force me to come over there and make you."

"Mom has been baking cookies all day, so whether I want to or not, I have a feeling we'll be paying them a visit after church tomorrow."

"Why not this afternoon?"

"She'll want to wait until she's all dolled up."

"Good for your mom. Call me afterward."

"Will do."

There was another long pause, so much so that Lewis wondered if Brodie had hung up.

"Lewis... if you end up going over there, keep your hands in your pockets."

Lewis paused before responding. "I'll try."

"I'm serious, Lewis. Promise me you won't mess this up. Let him get to know you first."

"I promise. Bye, Brodie."

"Bye, Lewis."

He slipped his phone back in its holster, glanced back up at the covered window, then made his way to the stairs. At the top of the steps, he flipped off the basement lights at the same time he opened the door that led into the kitchen.

The aroma of chocolate chip cookies engulfed him.

His mom was sitting at the table, her back to him, mixing another batch of cookie dough while her cell phone was pinned between her shoulder and cheek. Lewis swiveled quietly away from her and then up another set of stairs to his bedroom. Safely inside with the door shut he went to the window. The shades were down so he could stand in front without fear of being seen. He leaned in carefully and used his right hand to inch down the slats.

Nothing moved in the yard next door. The cube was still open, but there was no other activity. He was about to step away when the boy and one of his twin sisters, the one in the white tank top, walked out of the front door together. Knowing he'd probably be grilled about it later, Lewis paid more attention this time. The boy's disheveled hair was much lighter than his sister's, with a tinge of curl in it. Their facial features were similar, with pronounced cheekbones, wide chins, and thin, closely set eyebrows. The boy's nose was pudgier than his sister's, though.

He probably could have done a better job describing him to Brodie, but he felt uncomfortable describing another boy in that much detail. What was the point, anyway?

As Lewis spied on them, he noticed the sister seemed to be more playful, trying to goad her younger brother. But the boy seemed reluctant to play along. In fact, Lewis couldn't recall seeing the boy smile once all day.

A moody jock with a poor attitude. How could Lewis ever hope to be friends with someone like that?

Three

<u>Knox</u>

Being constantly uprooted and moved from city to city played a big part in my life. I hated it. Absolutely despised it! However, having a dad in the Navy meant lots of it — twelve times in sixteen years, to be exact. We moved more than most because my dad had one of those jobs that was in high demand. Great for him, not so much for the rest of us. Despite what seemed like an eternity of fighting against the inevitable relocation, even going so far as to sabotage moving plans (which was really the reason for my situation of not being trusted), I had to admire the efficiency with which my family moved into their new housing.

    I've listened to stories from other families, even military ones, who took weeks or months to settle into a new home. With our family, the cube was dropped off midday on Friday; we unloaded it by midday Saturday, and now, on Sunday morning, I have carted the last of the empty boxes out to the street. Completely settled in under forty-eight hours. Military efficiency at its finest. Moving so many times had obviously given us a lot of practice, but it also helped that doing it so often meant we accumulated very little. Everyone made do with a minimum of possessions and furniture. Goodwill was a recurring beneficiary of a Giddens family purge ahead of a move.

Supposedly, that was all history with Dad's promise that this would be our last move for a good, long time. Still, the pessimist in me couldn't help but wonder how long it would be before we needed those boxes again. Old habits die hard.

Jamming the last of my clothes into the bottom drawer of my dresser, I turned around and surveyed our new space. Travis and I have always shared a room, but we've never had one this big, and the added space was a welcome change. Plus, it was so much brighter than what I was used to. Lorna had already put a shade on the one window looking out over the front porch, and I pulled it up to let in the late-morning sunlight. I allowed the warm rays to wash over me, relishing a moment of comfort in the light. On the adjacent wall, both of our twin beds had a window beside them, with Travis's dresser in between the beds. The combination of the three windows gave the room an open, airy feeling I was unaccustomed to, but it certainly felt good right now.

At the front of our room sat my three-drawer dresser, side-by-side with the plain desk Dad had given us when we moved up to high school. Our gaming equipment, which was technically mine but I shared with Travis, sat on top of my dresser.

Having a bathroom that we didn't have to share with Lindsey and Jadie was another big plus. This benefit came with a condition, though. I had to share the responsibility of caring for Travis. The previous owners must have had someone with a disability, as many fixtures were already in place. Dad had installed extra support bars and railings in both the bathroom and our bedroom, including a heavy-duty chain that now hung from the ceiling at the edge of Travis's adjustable bed. A triangle bar at the end of the chain was there to support him when he maneuvered in and out. This was all to help my brother be as independent as possible. I knew there would still be times I would have to help. Lots of times. That was okay; a penance I felt obligated to pay.

I spotted Bowzer peeking out from behind my monitor. Travis's ferret was out of his cage for another tour, investigating his new surroundings. His excursions were getting longer in both time and distance before he hopped back to the safety of his pen on top of Travis's dresser. I liked how his long, slender body, covered with brown and white fur, glistened whenever the sun from the windows fell on him. What I didn't like was the stench—nothing quite like living with a musky-smelling varmint.

"Better not let Lindsey or Jadie see him out of his cage. They'll go ballistic," I said.

Travis looked up from the posters spread out on his bed. "He's not going anywhere. Lindie can just deal with it."

Lindie was Travis's mash-up name for our sisters, which they both despised. What surprised me was my brother's open defiance of house rules. Growing up, Dad had forbidden us to own pets, telling us they made moving more difficult. After Travis's accident, he made an exception. Travis could get any pet he wanted... which turned out to be Bowzer. The twins almost lost it, despite understanding why Dad allowed it. To them, a ferret was nothing more than a long rat, and no one could convince them otherwise. The only way to restore order was for Travis to agree to a strict set of rules, one of which was that Bowzer would be confined to his cage when either of the sisters was home.

I thought about pointing out the obvious rule violation, but considering I was trying to keep a low profile and it was his battle anyway, I kept it to myself. I was about to offer to hang Travis's posters when a shadow moved past the front window. A moment later, I heard a knock, then footsteps from the kitchen moving towards the front of the house.

"Who do you think it is?" Travis asked.

I shook my head, then took a step so I could better see the driveway from the front window.

"No cars. Must be a neighbor."

The door to our bedroom leading into the hallway was closed, but I could hear the front door open, followed by an exchange of muffled voices. Shortly after that, I heard Lorna's raised voice calling both our names. As usual, she first called me Chace and then immediately corrected herself. She was adapting to the change pretty quickly, and I wasn't sure how I felt about that.

I waited until Travis rolled toward the door in his wheelchair, then moved in behind him. His wheelchair lacked handles to push with, which was how my brother wanted it because he didn't enjoy being helped. I watched as he pulled open the door, then followed him out into the foyer.

Waiting for us were Lorna and a thin, slightly older woman. The woman wore a bright yellow dress and black high heels, holding a Bible in one hand and what looked like church programs printed on plain white paper in the other. Next to the woman stood a boy who had the biggest nose I had ever seen in person. A pair of black, thick-rimmed glasses sat perched on top of the nose. He looked about my age, wearing tan slacks and a plaid shirt buttoned all the way up to the neck.

"Knox, Travis, these are our neighbors, Mrs. Bonvillain and her son, Lewis. They live in the house next door, the one with the pool, and they brought us this wonderful plate of cookies." Lorna held up a plate overflowing with chocolate chip cookies, wrapped in plastic.

Travis and I meekly said hello in unison, but my eyes were firmly fixed on the plate of cookies.

"Our daughters, Lindsey and Jadie, went with their father to the store, but they should be back soon."

To me, Mrs. Bonvillain's skinniness bordered on the unhealthy, and her complexion was pasty, but she possessed a smile that really lit up her oval face. Abruptly, her smile disappeared, then it was back just as quickly. Then it was gone again… then reappeared. I was wondering if her smile batteries were running low or if there was a short in her happy circuit.

"We just had to welcome you to the neighborhood by bringin' you these cookies and introducin' ourselves," Mrs. Bonvillain said, her deep Southern accent sounding almost like a foreign language because of the speed at which she spoke. I always thought that southerners were laid-back and talked really... really... slow... but our neighbor was quickly trashing that myth. "We also wanted to be the first to invite you to our church."

Mrs. Bonvillain handed a program to each of us. "We have a popular youth group you might be interested in. I'm so glad to see more children your age move into the neighborhood. Lewis could sure use more playmates."

The grimace on Lewis's face at the mention of playmates didn't go unnoticed. Otherwise, he just stood there with his hands jammed deep into his pockets, staring at the floor and avoiding eye contact. I guessed that the two of them had come directly from church. At least, I hoped that was the reason he dressed that way. He was a bit on the scrawny side, but not soft. More like the look of a long-distance runner.

The kid also looked as awkward as I felt, which was fine with me. I wasn't interested in making friends yet, hadn't been for a very long time, and I especially didn't plan on making one who stood out like he did. I could just imagine the amount of abuse he took at school. Signing up for a front-row seat for that wasn't for me.

"Bonvillain," Lorna repeated, almost as if she was trying it on for size. "That's an unusual name for these parts, isn't it?"

Our neighbor's smile dimmed again. "Lewis's father was originally from Nawlins."

I found it strange how she referred to her husband only as her son's father.

"Oh. Well, this is so very nice of you," Lorna said, taking the plate of cookies. "Knox, why don't you and Travis show

Lewis your room and get to know one another? Mrs. Bonvillain and I —"

"Jules," the older woman interjected.

"—*Jules* and I are going to talk a bit."

Before I could object, Travis started rolling himself backward and said, "Come on."

Lewis shot his mother a concerned look. "Are you sure you don't want me to stay with you?"

Mrs. Bonvillain glanced at Lorna, then back at her son. Her smile had returned, re-energized. "I'll be fine, Lewis. You go have fun with the boys."

With the reprieve snuffed out, I turned around and followed Travis back into the room, our new next-door neighbor trailing behind. Travis wheeled over to his spot alongside his bed and spun around like a pro. I tossed the church program Lewis's mom had handed to me onto the desk, then sat down at the end of my bed. I considered motioning to the chair in front of our desk for the kid to sit in, but decided he could figure it out for himself if he were tired.

"Is there something wrong with your mom?" my brother blurted out.

Lewis looked up from the floor. "Why do you say that?"

"You sounded worried about her being alone with our stepmom, that's all," Travis answered.

Lewis opened his mouth to answer when Bowzer suddenly darted out from under my bed and leaped onto Travis's lap. The ferret's appearance elicited a shriek from our neighbor.

I covered a smirk with my hand.

"What is that?" Lewis asked, taking a couple of steps back towards the door. He pulled his hands out of his pockets and jammed them under his armpits.

"This is Bowzer," Travis said, stroking his pet. "He's my ferret."

"Does he bite?"

"Only twins," Travis said, smiling.

Lewis dropped his hands but stayed where he was.

"So, what's the deal with your mom?" Travis asked again.

Lewis turned his attention back to the floor. When he spoke, his words came in spurts. "She has problems with strangers... or people she doesn't know very well... or someone she hasn't seen in a long time."

Lewis then looked directly at me. "She kind of has problems with people."

"It can't be that bad. She goes to church, right?" I said.

"She throws up every Sunday morning before we go. She's fine once we get there. It's just that she gets anxious. I heard somebody at church call her high-strung once."

I didn't know what to say to that. I'd look like a jerk if I agreed, and a liar if I disagreed. Ultimately, I opted for silence.

"I wouldn't be too keen about eating those cookies we brought you."

Travis and I exchanged looks.

"Why not?" Travis asked.

"She means well, and she tries really hard, but she doesn't always pay very close attention to what goes into the mixing bowl before she bakes them," Lewis explained.

Great, we moved next door to the Addams Family.

"Don't worry, she'll like Lorna," Travis said. "Lorna makes friends with everybody."

I couldn't argue the point, as much as I wanted to. In my book, she was too friendly.

Lewis turned to Travis and smiled. He seemed to relax a bit.

"How long have you been in your wheelchair?" Lewis asked nonchalantly.

Right away, my defense radar went up.

"Almost two years," Travis answered just as casually. "But I should start getting some feeling back in my legs any day now."

I purposely looked away, so Lewis... and Travis... wouldn't see the frown on my face. When I looked back, Lewis was nodding and looking around the room.

"Your mom doesn't know your name?" Lewis asked while continuing to scan the room.

"Huh?" I said.

Lewis met my eyes. "I heard her call you Chace. Then she changed it to Knox."

Travis chuckled in his chair as he stroked Bowzer's back.

"I recently started going by my middle name, which is Knox, so she forgets sometimes." I didn't bother to add that the change was an act of defiance prompted by my dad's hasty marriage to Lorna. I certainly wasn't going to explain that my mom picked Knox as my middle name because she said it represented the impenetrable love she had for me... like the vaults of Fort Knox... and I used the name change to signify to Lorna that she could never break that bond and replace my mom.

Lewis nodded and continued his assessment of our room. "You guys sure moved in fast."

"We've had a lot of practice," I said.

"Our house is laid out kind of the same way. You guys are lucky that you get to share the big bedroom."

I thought about asking my brother if he felt lucky, but decided to let that comment pass. I followed the boy's gaze to my desktop, where my journal lay open, surrounded by some of my baseball trading cards.

"You write?" Lewis asked.

I shifted position, suddenly uncomfortable.

"A little."

"That Chipper Jones rookie card is worth a pretty penny."

"You like baseball?" I asked, surprised.

Lewis shook his head, his gaze continuing to move through the room. "No, not really. I just spend a lot of time on eBay and have a pretty good idea of what collectibles are worth."

It figures. "Do you play any sports?"

Lewis took the chair at the desk, turned it around so it faced the room, then sat in it. "Are you kidding, with a snoz like this? It's a ball magnet, and I'd be begging for a broken nose. What size hard drive do you have in your PS5?"

I glanced at my PS5 resting on top of my dresser, next to the 27-inch monitor. "One hundred twenty Gig. You have an PS5?"

"Three of them. Two older models, one is modded, and the newest version as well. All of them have two-hundred-fifty gig drives in them. What games do you play?"

I was becoming more interested in this conversation now. "Mostly shooters: Call of Duty, Modern Warfare, those types."

"I have all those. Ever try role-playing games?"

"I have a little," Travis chimed in.

"Like I said, I'm mostly a shooter," I replied. "Do you play online?"

"All the time. What's your call-sign?" Lewis asked.

"Browncoat2011."

Lewis leaned forward in his seat and pushed his glasses up on his nose. "You're kidding. I think I've played against you in a deathmatch before."

"No joke? What's your call sign?"

"B space I space T space E space space M space E."

Now it was my turn to lean forward. "B I T E M E?! That's you? I remember you. It was on a Black Ops map. You were fantastic."

"Thanks. Same goes for you."

I wondered if I had underestimated this guy. He definitely had skills when it came to online gaming, and if I remembered the right player, he was quick-witted with a sharp sense of humor as well.

"Hey," I blurted as a thought came to mind, "is your wireless network cajun64?"

"Yeah, why?"

"I was scanning for networks last night and came across it. Our parents have locked us out of the internet. Maybe I can hook up to yours?"

"They locked you out, Knox, not me," Travis corrected.

"Whatever. How about it? What's your WEP code?"

Lewis shook his head. "I don't think so. You'll bog down my bandwidth and make me lag."

"Dude, I won't slow you down, and we'll be able to play against one another."

"If you want to do that, you can come over to my house and we'll play. Anytime."

Maybe I did peg him right, after all.

"Whatever," I replied.

The room fell silent.

"What's that?" Lewis asked.

I followed Lewis's eyes to the far corner of my dresser. Wedged in between the furniture and my laundry hamper was a box I hadn't seen before. Something was wrong. When you move around as much as I do, every single item you own, its shape and the boxes you move it in are immediately recognizable. Yet, here was a completely foreign box. It was square, roughly three feet by three feet, not made of cardboard, and pitch black.

I looked over at Travis. "Where did that come from?"

My brother's answer was a blank stare.

I got out of bed and walked over to the box for a closer inspection. Picking it up, the cube had a heft to it. Not heavy, but well-constructed. My first guess was that it was made of wood, like balsam wood, because it had some give. Covering the surface were strange etchings, wrapping around the sides and spilling over the top. Odd pictographs were everywhere. It wasn't like anything I'd seen before. Similar to Hieroglyphics, but different. The images were too...

aggressive. I couldn't find a seam, and an opening wasn't plainly visible. All in all, the box didn't belong in Travis's and my room.

"This isn't one of ours. I have no idea how it ended up in here. I didn't carry it in," I said.

"Neither did I," Travis said, smiling. The extent of his involvement during the move, per Dad's orders, was supervising.

"Why don't you open it and see what's in it?" Lewis asked.

I studied the odd-looking box, debating. It was in our room, and even if it wasn't ours, opening it might help us find out who it belonged to.

But...

I stood up and walked towards the bedroom door. "We'd better tell Lorna. She and Dad are kind of anal about their stuff."

I called Lorna's name, then returned to my seat on the bed. A minute later, she appeared at the door with Lewis's mother in tow.

"There's a box in here that's not ours," I announced, pointing to the dark cube. "There's no label, either."

Lorna's eyebrows pinched together in confusion as she stepped farther into the room to see what I was pointing at. When she saw the box, she stood over it with her hands on her hips, staring down at it. Her back was to me so that I couldn't see her expression, but when she turned around, suspicion was all over her face.

"Chace!" my stepmom said, restrained anger right below the surface.

"My name's Knox," I responded calmly.

"Dammit. What are you up to this time?"

I sprang to my feet. "This isn't me. I swear. We just noticed it, and we don't know where it came from. Tell her, Travis."

"It's the truth. I don't remember seeing it earlier, but suddenly there it was."

"I mean, look at it," I continued, defending myself. "There's no way I could have hidden that during the move."

Our new neighbor cleared her throat.

"Um... well... I can see Lewis and I have worn out our welcome," Mrs. Bonvillain interjected, gesturing for her son to join her at the doorway. "We'll let you get on with your settling in. You just make sure you come knock on my door if there's anything you need."

Lorna gave the neighbor an embarrassed smile. "Thank you for stopping over and for the cookies."

"You're most welcome."

I watched as Lewis followed his mom out of the room, stopping momentarily at the door as if to say something, then deciding against it. Instead, his eyes met mine, and I thought I saw something in them that caused me to rethink my opinion of him... sympathy.

Four

Knox

The bizarre black box sat atop the coffee table in the middle of our living room, surrounded by my entire family. I had chosen to sit in the recliner, while Lindsey and Jadie sandwiched Dad on the couch, with Lorna next to them. Travis was in his own chair in front of the dark television. We all had our eyes glued to the strange container.

I couldn't shake the odd sensation I'd felt ever since we discovered the box. It was mesmerizing, hypnotic, almost trance-inducing. Every time I looked away, I felt this strange tug, almost magnetic, pulling my attention back to it. It was like a lingerie model had taken a seat in the middle of the room, and I was helpless to look away. Except this model was old and wrinkled in places that she shouldn't be.

"So, let me get this straight: no one remembers bringing this box in from the cube?" Dad asked all of us.

Heads shook side to side around the room, mine included.

"It kind of sticks out," I said. "I think we would have remembered it."

"That means it couldn't have accidentally been left inside the cube by the previous renters. It must have been in the house before we started moving in," Dad concluded.

Lorna shook her head again. "David, we went through this house room by room before we signed the papers. It wasn't here."

"Maybe somebody was in the house and left it after you did your walk-through?" Jadie asked.

"That's a possibility, but only the real estate agent had a key to get in. And why would she leave a box here?" Dad said.

"Call her just to make sure," Travis suggested.

I shifted my weight in the chair. "You know, those agents always leave a key in lockboxes on the front door. Any agent could have gotten in. Or maybe somebody else got the key out of there?"

"Stole the key, broke into the house, just to leave this odd box? Why would they do that?" Lorna asked.

Everyone fell silent, and our attention returned to the box. Although it was now dusk outside and all the living room lights were on, the room was dimmer than I remembered it the previous night. I couldn't shake the feeling that the box was absorbing the light in the room. I felt goosebumps forming on my arm.

Jadie clapped her hands together. "I say we open it up. It's got to have some clues inside. Maybe they can help us find out who it belongs to?"

My stepmom shook her head again. "I'm against it. We shouldn't open it until we find out who it belongs to, or we've at least tried everything we can. How would you feel if somebody went through your possessions?"

Typical Lorna. She always plays it safe.

Jadie turned her head to address Lorna directly, a hint of attitude in her response. "If opening the box helped return my things back to me, I'd be okay with that."

Way to go, Jadie.

"What if it's just an old box somebody left behind? We might never know who it belongs to. What then?" I asked.

"Then we'll open it. But we're not crossing that bridge until we've exhausted everything else," was Lorna's answer.

"Is it heavy?" Travis asked.

"No, not very," Dad said.

"Did you shake it?" my brother continued.

"No, but I could feel something shift around inside when I moved it out here," Dad answered.

Jadie leaned forward in her seat. "What do you think those markings are all over it?"

"Don't have a clue. Definitely not your typical moving carton," Dad said.

Until that moment, Lindsey hadn't said a word, but then she suddenly stood up and put one hand on her hip. Her other hand grasped the ring hanging from a silver chain around her neck, a sure sign she was agitated. The small band was a mood ring my sisters had given our mom a long time ago, which was given to Lindsey after the funeral. She never took it off unless she wanted to play a trick and pretend to be Jadie.

"Why are we not asking the obvious question? I think we all know who's behind this," Lindsey said.

That's when everyone turned and looked at me. I was surprised it took so long.

"Wait a minute," Dad said. "This doesn't feel like that."

"I didn't do this!" I stated.

"Come on, Dad," Lindsey continued, "this is just more of the type of stuff he used to pull. Remember the time he blacked out all the descriptions on the boxes and we couldn't tell what went where?"

"Or when he mailed back the moving company confirmation with cancel written on it," Jadie added.

"Then there's the time he set off that stink-bomb in the moving van right before they started loading everything. We waited around for hours until that smell went away," Travis added.

"Read my lips. I. Did. Not. Do. This."

Dad continued to come to my defense. "Girls. Your brother has promised that all that behavior is in the past, and I believe him, so let's try to be constructive here."

Lindsey sat back down, her eyes still locked with mine. "Then I say we open it up and see what's inside. I bet it's just some trick Chace thought up."

"I said no. And to make sure nobody gets any ideas, we're keeping it upstairs in the bedroom with us tonight." Lorna looked past Lindsey to our dad. "David, help me out here."

Dad seemed torn between his own curiosity, supporting his wife's decision, and worrying about missing an episode of his favorite show if the discussion dragged on much longer.

He chose the safest route. "Lorna is right. We'll leave the box alone until we've tried everything we can to find out who it belongs to."

Frowns and groans came from everyone under the age of eighteen.

"Now, is everyone ready for school tomorrow?" Lorna asked.

The moods switched instantaneously, with Jadie speaking up first. "Almost. I still have to pick out my outfit." The perkiness in her voice was nauseating. "I can't wait."

Lorna smiled at Jadie's enthusiasm. *Best buds again.* Then she turned her attention to the rest of us. "Travis? Lindsey? Knox? Do you have your backpacks ready?"

I had always found it irritating that Dad was the military man, supposedly the strict disciplinarian, but Lorna had become the taskmaster around the house. I wasn't sure if I was more upset with Lorna for always picking on us to do our chores or with Dad for being so willing to let her take control.

"No, not yet," Travis said, "but I can do it right now."

"Knox... Lindsey?"

"No," we answered in unison. It wasn't worth the argument to explain how I could pack in the five minutes before we left in the morning.

"Well, everyone better get to it then. Dinner is in—" Lorna checked her smartwatch, "—twenty minutes."

Everyone rose to leave.

"You're going to call the real estate agent about the box, right?" Lindsey asked before anyone could depart.

"I'm going to do that right now," Lorna replied.

I watched as my brother wheeled himself up Dad's newly installed ramp. When I started after him, Dad called out my name.

I turned to find Lorna and Dad still standing side-by-side in front of the couch.

"We need to talk to you alone for a moment, son," Dad said.

My heart sank, and I could feel the cords of my neck tightening. Despite my dad's support, given the way Lorna acted when she first learned of the box, I suspected the old saying, 'where there's smoke, there's fire,' would apply to me. Dad seemed to believe me, and Lorna had seemed less suspicious now, but deep down I knew how it appeared—another ripple.

I slowly sat back down, unable to meet either of them in the eye as they took their own seats.

"Son, I'm really trying to keep an open mind here. We believed you when you said you've changed, and we have seen plenty of evidence to support that... but this is our first move since Travis's accident and the first time you've really been tested. You've got to admit, this box really feels like some sort of trick."

I squirmed in my seat and rubbed the back of my neck. I felt trapped. What could you do when your word means so little?

As I spoke, I kept my head down. "I really, really, really have nothing to do with that box. I promise. I'll admit it seems like something I might have done before, but I don't do that anymore. I don't know where that box came from."

"Fair enough. We just wanted to give you a chance to speak up now, without repercussions, if it were something different. Because, in case it hasn't sunk in yet, after what happened to your brother, this type of shenanigan isn't funny, cute, or taken as simple acts of teenage rebellion. They are very, very serious."

At the mention of my brother, I looked up at the two of them.

"I've learned my lesson. I live it every single day. But what I can't do is..." my voice trailed off, and I let my head dip down again. But then I snapped it back up and turned to Lorna. "It's like you said with the trust cup you told me about, Lorna. How one lie will tip it over, and years and years of trust can be gone in an instant. And how it takes a very long time to fill that cup up again. Well, it's like my cup leaks. I can't seem to gain any traction, to raise the level at all in your eyes. I'm not lying about the box, but you can't see that."

The longer I talked, the more confident my voice sounded, and I saw Lorna searching for truth in my eyes.

"It's hard, Knox. There's nothing in this world I would love more than to be able to trust you again." She continued staring into my eyes until finally she turned to my dad. "I think we should believe him," she said.

Dad nodded. "Okay. I'll call the real estate agent, Lorna can finish dinner, and you can get your backpack ready for school tomorrow, young man."

I smiled. As I rose from the chair, I paused to look at the black box again.

It was a pain in my ass I did not need.

Five

Knox

I awoke the next morning to the Atomic Razorblades blasting heavy-metal chords from my phone next to my bed and the sound of my brother calling my name.

"Leave me alone," I moaned without bothering to pull my face out of my pillow. Insomnia had been a constant companion of mine recently, so when sleep found me, I fought to hang onto it.

"Knox!" my brother repeated, louder and with more urgency.

I rolled over onto my left side and picked up my head, my eyes still closed.

"What?"

"Look."

I pried open my eyes and tried to focus in the dim morning light. As my vision adjusted, I could make out my brother in his sleeping t-shirt, sitting on the edge of his bed with his legs dangling limply. His left arm was pointing towards something at the front of our room.

I raised myself on an elbow to get a better view, and what I saw sent a chill down my spine.

Next to my dresser, in the same spot it had rested the day before, was the black box.

"What the hell?"

I threw the covers back and sat up. Looking at Travis, I asked, "Did you hear Dad or Lorna come into our room last night?"

"Nope," he replied.

A quick succession of questions went through my mind, each more unsettling than the previous as my mind spiraled downward. Why would Dad or Lorna return the box to our room? Could they be giving me a taste of my own medicine? If not them, who? Lindsey? Jadie? Why? Surely not to get me in more trouble—neither was mean-spirited that way. Or were they? Or maybe nobody moved it because it moved *itself*.

I shook my head. *Get a grip*. I was ashamed of the growing sense of foreboding I felt. Nothing made any sense. What should I do? I wanted to put it out by the curb with the other boxes. Still, that wouldn't solve my situation, and besides, I didn't really want to touch it. I either needed to return the box upstairs or just act innocent, which I was.

The decision was made for me when a knock on the door preceded its opening. Lorna stepped into the bedroom and flicked on the overhead lights. She was wearing one of her colorful flowery scrub tops that was part of her school-nurse uniform.

"Let's get going, guys. I have to go in early, so your father—" she paused when she caught sight of the box.

I swear it was like a death ray coming out of her eyes when she turned to face me. She was so stiff, radiating so much extreme dislike. It reminded me of Carrie going ballistic at the prom. If this were that movie, my head would explode at any moment.

"Get ready to go. We'll talk when your father and I get home tonight," Lorna snapped, then turned around and stormed out of the room.

I had briefly considered asking her what she wanted to do with the box before she left, but ultimately decided it was better not to bring further attention to it.

My hands went to the back of my head, and the fingers interlocked together. "I'm so screwed."

"But you didn't do anything," Travis said.

"I know, bud. Let's get ready before we get in any more trouble."

I didn't think it possible for anything to distract me from worrying about the first day at a new school, but the dread I felt towards the black box and the brewing trouble it was causing at home was doing a darn good job of it. I got ready for school in a mental fog, my mind continually returning to a worrisome question. What was in that box, and who moved it? The ten-minute commute to school felt more like an hour-long ride in a hearse.

I've been to plenty of new schools. Plenty. This one was going to be different because it wasn't butted up against a military base —a first for all of us —which meant there wouldn't be as many kids transferring in and out as at the schools I was used to. It was possible I would be the only new kid in my class and stick out like a sore thumb.

Starting a new school in the middle of the year meant two things: first, all eyes would be on me since I was the new kid. Second, the packs, groups, or cliques — whatever they called them here in Ox-Bow — were pretty much set. I had seen it repeatedly in different schools. At the beginning of the year, the packs from the previous year would re-form and discard old members who dared to develop outside interests. Then they'd go about hunting for new meat to replenish their numbers. By the middle of the school year, the cliques were now solidified. There was a good chance I might be left alone, which would be a relief.

In the past, just about every group at school would seek me out to join their ranks. I realize that sounds conceited, but I see it as a brutal reality. I'm athletic and can play on any sports team if I choose to, so the preps or jocks want me. The way I dress, my tendency to stick to myself, and my taste in music would have the emo kids after me. My 3.8 GPA and interest in the occasional chess game, combined with the fact that I'm constantly writing in my journal, put me on the nerd radar. The only groups I rarely drew interest from are the Goths, drama kids, or druggies.

Regardless, I avoided them all.

The only positive aspect of repeatedly moving from city to city and school to school was this: you learned friends were temporary and fleeting. If there were such a thing as a genuine friend, they wouldn't care what clique you hung out with. So, I kept to myself, answered only those questions directed at me, concentrated on my schoolwork, and poured myself into my writing.

After registering and being handed my schedule, I made my way to my new locker to stash the extra notebooks and supplies Lorna had forced on me. As I was transferring it all from my backpack, my journal slipped out and landed on the corridor floor. I snatched it up and returned it to my pack, making sure I shoved it deeper.

I had been filling my journals with short stories, other story ideas, random thoughts, memories, or simple observations since Mom gave me the first one after I graduated from Kindergarten. Mom told me I should use it over the summer to practice what I learned during that first year, so it would be fresh in my mind when I started first grade. She was always telling me how imaginative a storyteller I was, which unfortunately, I showed off during some of our moves. She prodded me to explore the unknown with my stories. I experimented with it at times, but it wasn't until mom died that I really started taking it seriously. It proved to be an excellent way for me to vent my anger, confusion, and loneliness during that time. Now it serves as a way to deal with the fallout I've brought upon myself and the heartache I feel from missing her. Who knows, maybe someday I'll be a writer and all this gibberish will be worth something. For now, all I do is think of her every time I open its cover.

Making my way around the crowded corridors, taking in all the unfamiliar faces, the feeling of déjà vu returned. Boyfriends trying to sneak kisses from their girlfriends, the disinterested trying to avoid the overly interested, the pranksters targeting the self-involved. I experienced this at every new school I attended. Everybody seeming so familiar. Interchangeable pieces playing the same roles over and over again.

The only difference was Travis.

I spotted my brother in the hallway, and he seemed to be fitting in just fine. More than fine, actually. He already had a small group of kids following him around, which shouldn't have surprised me. Like both my older sisters, Travis was a social butterfly and adapted effortlessly with each of our moves. His disability hadn't changed that. As much as I despised being uprooted so often, the rest of the family, especially Travis, thrived on it. Lindsey and Jadie viewed it as a way to reinvent themselves and try new looks, new personas.

Biltmore Marion High was on the small side compared with our previous schools. I was used to overcrowded classrooms and congested hallways, but Biltmore was a welcome departure. In my first three classes, the number of kids in each was under fifteen. But I wasn't complaining. That meant fewer classmates I had to ignore.

I was amped when fourth period rolled around because it was gym. My previous school hadn't offered PE, and a good game of basketball, volleyball, dodge ball, or even badminton in the middle of the day was exactly what I needed to avoid the mid-afternoon yawns. I followed a stream of other guys past the lunchroom, which fronted the gymnasium, and made my way down an adjacent hallway to a door labeled *Boys Locker Room*. The other kids entered and went immediately to the closest open lockers, but I continued to the last row, where I deposited my backpack on the bench between the two sets of cages.

Over the years, I've grown accustomed to the sights, sounds and smells of various schools, but the one scent I found to be universal to every school was the gym locker room.

The stench of the BMH locker room had definitely reached mid-year potency. The scent of a mile run and the odor of fifty pushups hung heavy in the air. Some boys emit a type of corn chip smell following strenuous exercise, and others are more like a rotten egg. Here in Ox-Bow, the dominant smell was one of my all-time favorites, a cross between sour milk and damp socks, mixed with a dozen different body sprays.

I laid out my shorts, t-shirt, and sneakers from my backpack on the dark green bench and lifted my hiking boot to untie its laces. That's when I heard a raised voice coming from the showers off to my right, which seemed odd, since I wouldn't expect anyone to be in the showers at the beginning of class. I paused, but when I heard nothing else, I pulled off my boot. I had just started on my other boot when the voices started up again. Now there were at least two emanating from the showers. The voices grew louder, one of them definitely more aggressive than the other, and I thought I recognized the timid one.

Curiosity got the better of me, and I shuffled towards the shower entrance. As I approached the end of the bench, I peered around the corner and saw a large, fully clothed boy with shoulder-length hair standing in the middle of the room. He was facing my direction but looking off to his left, pointing a finger at someone who was still out of my view. The bully was wearing a pair of faded jeans and a gray sweatshirt with the sleeves torn off and the school logo imprinted on its chest.

"—tell you again, *Villain*. I want my AirPods back. And if you don't give them to me, I'm gonna take it outta ya ass," the long-haired kid was saying.

"I'm going to be late to fourth period," I heard the other boy say.

"You're gonna be late for the whole rest of the year if you don't fork it over. Uh-huh, you ain't going nowhere and your girlfriend won't be bailing you out in here either."

"I don't know how many ways I can say it, Tug. I didn't take your AirPods."

I suddenly knew where I had heard that other voice. It was my next-door neighbor. Lewis Bonvillain.

I turned my back on the two of them and walked back to my locker, grabbed the front of my hoodie, and started pulling it over my head—then stopped. *Why am I hesitating? Go ahead... get undressed,* I told myself. *Why am I stalling?* I stared into an empty locker, unsure of what to do. I never get involved in these situations. That was one benefit of shunning friends, a social inoculation from peer pressure and feeling responsible for everyone else's well-being. It sure beat the alternative, losing friend after friend as your family traipses around the country. After a while, you figure out there wasn't a point to making friends.

So why was I standing frozen here now? The kid could very well deserve what he was getting. But all I could think about was the sympathetic look he had given me when he walked out of my room yesterday. Maybe I could just say something.

The sharp sound of a slap from the other room made up my mind.

When I strolled confidently into the shower, I found Lewis down on one knee, holding the side of his face, his glasses missing. The boy Lewis called Tug was standing over him.

"There you are, Lewis. Mrs. Salerni sent me to find you," I said.

Tug and Lewis both seemed surprised to see me standing there.

"Who are you?" Tug asked, stepping back from Lewis.

I let him have my patented smile. "Name's Knox. I'm Lewis's neighbor."

Tug glanced down at Lewis, then back at me. "Well, *Knox*, you interrupted an important conversation. We really need to finish, so if you don't mind, you can tell Mrs. Salerni that Lewis will toddle along to class shortly."

Lewis slowly stood up, his hand still on the left side of his face. Without his glasses, his nose stood out like a big toe.

"Sorry, Tug, conversation's over now," I said, smile still intact. "Lewis is coming with me."

Tug had a couple of inches on me and maybe fifteen pounds, with muscle tone in his arms that I'm sure had been earned via a close relationship with a dumbbell. He turned his attention away from Lewis and faced off directly against me. I watched as he gave me the once-over, smiling when he saw my socks.

"You're new here, right?" Tug asked.

"I am."

"Are you sure you want to start out walking around with a bruised face?"

I was still as a statue, refusing to acknowledge Tug's aggressive stance. Slowly, I replaced the smile on my face with a deathly serious stare.

"And *you* don't want to meet my stepmom on my first day, either."

Tug laughed loudly, taking a couple of steps backward to shoot a look at Lewis, then quickly taking on an expression of disbelief.

"Oh, that's sweet. You're really going to run to your mommy?"

I let the hint of a smile return to my face. "She's the school nurse, you ignoramus."

The humor melted from Tug's face like butter in the sun.

"Should I go?" Lewis asked.

Without taking my eyes off Tug, I asked, "Did you take his AirPods?"

"No."

"Then shut up and stay put. What's it gonna be, *Tug?*"

The stare-down between the two of us went on for what seemed like an eternity. I'd been in these types of confrontations lots of times over the years. No matter how hard you try to fly under the radar, there's always someone who feels they have to put the newcomer in his place. We studied it in biology once: an Alpha Male establishing dominance. Although it made sense in a primitive sort of way, it still pissed me off. There's something else I learned—it's hardly ever about who's the biggest and strongest.

It's mostly attitude. And I have that in spades.

We continued our staring contest until Tug shot a brief glance over at Lewis, then another.

"This isn't over, Villain," he finally barked as he stormed out of the shower.

I drew in a deep breath and glanced over at Lewis. I watched as he located his glasses and put them on.

"You're late for class," I said, then turned and walked out.

Six

Lewis

Lewis looked up from his lunch when he heard someone approach. Brodie's smile quickly turned into a frown.

"Holy crap! What happened to you?" Brodie asked as she slid into the lunch-table seat next to him. She plopped her backpack into an empty chair.

Lewis's hand instinctively went to the left side of his face, partially covering a sprawling red splotch on his cheek. "Where have you been? Lunch is almost over."

She pushed aside Lewis's hand, then took his chin in her hand, turning his head slightly to get a better view. "I was talking to Mr. Bland about my essay. What happened to your face?"

"Is it still red?"

"Duh. It looks like you've been rubbing it with sandpaper."

Lewis dropped his hand back onto the table. "Tug Dempsey. He cornered me in the locker-room shower and accused me of taking his AirPods."

Brodie's light blue eyes darkened. She pushed up the sleeves on the untucked plaid shirt she wore over a gray tank top. "What? Why would he think that?"

Lewis shook his head, then shoveled another plastic fork full of green beans into his mouth. His mother had outdone herself with his lunch today: Meatloaf, green beans, and cornbread.

"I don't think he does," he answered while chewing, not bothering to cover his mouth as he spoke. "I doubt that he even owns a pair. He probably heard the stories and figured he could intimidate me into giving him a set."

"Did you?"

"What?"

"Give him a set?"

"No way."

"And he let you go with just a slap? You're lucky he didn't tear you to shreds. The guy's a friggin' troglodyte. Just wait until I get my hands on him."

Lewis watched Brodie squirm in her chair, getting worked up just as he knew she would. He scanned the surrounding tables, making sure none of Tug's "crew" were close by and could overhear their conversation. The lunchroom was buzzing with activity, filled with the clattering of utensils on plates and loud voices, making it hard to distinguish anyone except those close by. None of it mattered much. Lewis knew Brodie wasn't afraid of Tug Dempsey, or anyone else at the school. It was the thing he both admired and worried about the most. She was like a five-pound miniature poodle going up against a one-hundred-pound pit bull until it gets eaten. Her fiery temper and aggressiveness didn't match her slight frame.

"I had some help," Lewis said. "From my new neighbor, Knox."

Brodie froze, then the twinkle in her eyes returned. She leaned forward on the table with her elbows. "You're kidding."

"Stood up to Tug and didn't budge an inch. It was impressive." He could feel himself flushing and imagined his entire face had turned the color of his injury. It still bothered him that he asked Knox if he should leave during the confrontation, but in his defense, Brodie told him to 'get outta here' whenever she stood up for him.

"But why? I thought you said the two of you didn't really hit it off."

"We didn't, so I'm not sure why he did it. But I've seen him a couple times today, and he doesn't behave like I thought he would. He keeps to himself a lot. And I found out yesterday he's a gamer and likes to write, so maybe I misjudged him. I tried to call and tell you about it."

"I had my phone turned off," she said, popping a chip in her mouth. "I had to finish that essay."

"Well, it turns out he's not your typical jock."

Brodie half-raised out of her seat and scanned the lunchroom. "Does he have lunch this period?"

"No, I already checked. His brother does. He's over there by the Ram."

Brodie turned her head towards the metal statue of the school's mascot positioned right inside the doors to the parking lot. A boy in a tricked-out wheelchair with bright red spokes was sitting at a table surrounded by a swarm of girls.

"He must be nothing like his brother, the social magnet, then. So maybe there's a chance the two of you could be friends?" she asked as she sat back down, smiling from ear to ear. "This is what we hoped for, Lewis. A solid friend... a guy friend who could have your back when I'm not around. And, like I told you, next-door-neighbor friends are a special kind of friend. This is so great."

Lewis flashed her a half-smile, then reached a hand into his backpack. He pulled out a baseball card in a transparent plastic sheath and laid it in front of her. His smile had disappeared.

Brodie sat back in her chair, the smile on her face slowly fading as well. "Tell me that's not what I think it is."

"Chipper Jones rookie card. I took it yesterday when I was in his room."

The look of disappointment on Brodie's face was painful for Lewis to bear. He lowered his gaze to what was left of his meatloaf.

"Oh, Lewis."

"I promise I really tried."

"I know. I know." She picked up the baseball card from the table and slid it into her backpack. "Anything else?"

Lewis shook his head, still looking down at his food. "I'm sorry."

Brodie busied herself by picking up the trash in front of him and closing up his lunch box, but Lewis knew her well enough to know she only did it to avoid scolding him.

"We'd better be heading to class," was all she said.

It was a short walk to Mrs. Allen's Language Arts class, with Brodie quieter than usual as they navigated their way through the congested corridors.

Lewis enjoyed Mrs. Allen's class for two reasons: the room was located on an outside wall, where the windows brightened the space on sunny days, and it was one of the few courses he shared with Brodie. They entered through the door at the head of the class. Lewis spotted his new neighbor sitting at the back of the room. Knox's chin rested on his chest, and he appeared to be dozing.

"Brodie," Lewis whispered to his friend.

When she looked up, Lewis flicked his head in Knox's direction. "Knox," he mouthed.

She twisted her body around, following Lewis's head motion, and stayed that way for several moments. When she faced forward again, her expression had changed, making it hard for Lewis to read. Her skin was flushed.

The stream of students entering fell off to a trickle. Mrs. Allen entered the room and was about to close the door behind her when Tug Dempsey squeezed his way in with a playful smile. The long-haired athlete strutted to his seat in the first row next to the window, winking at Lewis as he did.

"Seats, everybody," Mrs. Allen stated with a commanding voice that Lewis was confident would frighten small children. "Take your seats and let's get started. I hope everyone had a wonderful weekend and is well rested for the week ahead. First on the agenda, we need to welcome a new member to our class. Mr. Knox Gidden has joined us today. Are you here Mr. Gidden?"

Lewis, along with the rest of the class, looked over their shoulders and watched as Knox raised his hand and offered a crooked smile. When their eyes met, Lewis spun back around.

"Your arrival is most fortuitous, Mr. Gidden. Today, we will divide up into groups for our projects."

Mrs. Allen was somewhere around five feet tall, at least a couple hundred pounds, and when she wore a dress, she showed off calves that put half of the linemen on the football team to shame. But despite a decidedly nononsense approach, they also knew her to be one of the kindest teachers at MBH. She was simply a powder puff stuck inside a brick house of a body.

"Many of you have asked for weeks what the special projects will be. Today you find out. This assignment is going to test your creativity, your writing proficiency, your storytelling ability, and your performance skills. You will write, produce, and perform an original radio episode, ten to fifteen minutes in length."

"What do you mean by radio episode?" Valerie Eaton asked.

"We talked about them a couple of weeks ago. Dick Tracy, Little Orphan Annie, Hopalong Cassidy, Amos &

Andy, Radio City Playhouse. Comedy, drama, mystery, western; it's totally up to your group. But let me emphasize, this must be original material, written only for this assignment."

A rumbling of unease spread throughout the room, and Lewis understood where it was coming from. This didn't sound like an assignment he would particularly enjoy. He looked at Brodie and she was smiling ear-to-ear, as usual. There wasn't an assignment created that could dampen her resolve.

"You'll have to record your audio show and have it ready to present in class two weeks from today. I'll allow you to work on it in here on Tuesday and Thursday each week, but the rest of the work will be done on your own time."

Mrs. Allen walked over to her desk in the corner and picked up a single piece of paper.

"Now for the teams. Mostly, I assigned these teams randomly, with a few key adjustments made to keep things properly balanced. And thanks to the arrival of Mr. Gidden, there will now be an even four students per team."

Lewis listened as the names of four of his classmates were called out. His fingers on both hands were crossed underneath his desk, hoping that Brodie ended up on his team.

After she announced the second round of names, neither his nor Brodie's had been called yet. Glancing at Brodie again, it pleased him to see that her fingers were crossed as well.

"Team three. Lewis Bonvillain, Brad Dempsey, Brodie James, and Knox Gidden."

Lewis was in shock. The dread of being forced to work with Tug Dempsey offset his elation at having Brodie on his team. And then there was Knox. He didn't know how to feel about him yet, but at least maybe he'd keep Tug in line. That and Brodie the five-pound poodle, that is.

Brodie was squeezing his arm now, and he realized that no matter what else might happen with their team, they were going to get an A. Brodie James never settled for anything less.

Mrs. Allen had finished reading the list of teams and was once again using her powerful voice to ask for quiet.

"We have forty minutes left today. Use that time to get started on your projects; go ahead and move the chairs around to form your groups. But please keep your voices at a reasonable level."

Since he and Brodie were already so close together, Lewis expected the other two would come to them. At the rear of the room, Knox was already standing, his backpack over his shoulder, moving in their direction.

"Hey," Knox said when he walked up.

"Hey," Lewis mimicked. "This is Brodie. Brodie, Knox."

Brodie looked at Knox with the same facial expression and flushed skin she had when Lewis first pointed out his new neighbor to her.

"Hi," she muttered softly. Lewis had never known Brodie to be embarrassed about anything, but that's how she was acting.

The three of them turned towards the front of the room near the windows and saw Tug still sitting in his seat, smiling at them, showing no sign of moving.

Lewis exchanged looks with Brodie and Knox, then grabbed his backpack from his seat back and shrugged. The three of them walked to the front of the room and slid empty chairs around Tug to form a circle.

They all sat there without saying a word. One minute turned into two. Not even Brodie was willing to break the ice.

"I'm already failing this class," Tug finally broke the silence. "So, I hope you don't expect me to do anything for this candy-ass assignment."

MOVING FEAR

Seven

Knox

I turned the dial to the final number and lifted the handle, opening the locker door easily. With the door open, I reached down and unzipped my backpack, but not before I caught sight of a wheelchair rolling in my direction.

"Got your text," Travis said as he glided to a stop beside me. "You have an after-school meeting already?"

"It bites, I know. Tell Lorna or Dad to pick me up in an hour."

"Ten-four. See you at home." Travis did an about-face and wheeled off.

I started pulling books from my backpack to store away in my locker.

"We need to talk!" a female voice from behind commanded.

I finished transferring the last book before turning around to find Lewis's friend Brodie standing in the middle of the hall. Her arms were holding a notebook tightly against her chest, and she seemed oblivious to the other kids hurrying past her for the exit door.

"Uhhhh... don't we have a meeting in... like... five minutes?"

"I told Lewis and Tug that I remembered I had something else planned for after school, so we'd have to work on the project some other time. It's just the two of us."

I pushed my locker door shut. "Why did you suggest a team meeting after school if you had something else planned?"

Brodie moved closer. "I have nothing planned. I want to talk to you alone, without Lewis knowing about it."

"What do you need to talk to me for?"

"Can we go somewhere a little more private first?"

That sounded more like an order than a question as Brodie moved back towards the rear of the school without waiting for an answer. I thought about blowing her off and running to catch up with my brother. Normally, I would have, but curiosity made me reconsider. Grabbing my backpack off the ground, I ran to catch up to her.

This Brodie girl was a complete mystery. She was one of the cutest girls in the school, and that was saying a lot, but she downplayed her looks. Her clothes were tomboyish, though she didn't appear to be overly athletic. She wore no makeup, and she tied her hair back in what I thought was an unflattering ponytail. Even her mannerisms differed from those of the other girls I was used to. I could tell from the brief time we spent together in class that she was smart, but I'd been around intelligent girls before. Brodie had something else—a straightforward, no-nonsense approach that could be both intimidating and irritating. I found it refreshing.

But there were a couple of other things that struck me as odd: one—she wasn't constantly staring at her cell phone like other girls did, and two—I hadn't seen her talking to any boys, except Lewis, nor were there any hovering around her. Most girls with her kind of looks always had an entourage, but not her.

Brodie James could definitely be a puzzle worth solving.

Maybe she was gay, but even then she'd still likely have a group of girls around. Such a puzzle.

Turning left at the main hallway, she led me into the cafeteria and then to a table on the far side of the empty room. She plopped her backpack into a vacant chair. She took a seat opposite me and laid the notebook on the table in front of her.

"So, what's this about?" I asked as I sat down and dropped my backpack on the ground next to me.

"It's about Lewis," Brodie answered. She was giving me the same look she'd given Tug during Language Arts class, and it wasn't friendly.

"What about him?"

"I need to make sure you won't take advantage of him or mistreat him."

I threw up both my hands. "Whoa! We're just neighbors. I barely know him."

"You helped him today with Tug, right?"

That took me by surprise, and suddenly I felt uneasy. She was trying to pin a hero badge on me, but she didn't know the whole story. How I hesitated beforehand and almost walked away.

"Yeah... well... I don't like to see bigger kids throw their weight around."

I watched as the intensity in Brodie's face softened, and I took the time to really look at her. She had expressive eyebrows, big puppy-dog eyes, and flawless skin. Each of those was in contention as her most outstanding feature.

"Well, it meant a lot to Lewis," she said. "And me. I know him better than anyone, and now because of what you did, if you asked him to jump off a cliff, he probably would."

"Listen, he seems like a nice guy and all, but really—"

"Lewis isn't like everyone else," she blurted out, her intensity turning into something else. Something more... vulnerable.

"What do you mean? Is he gay or something?" Now I was more confused than ever. Were the two of them gay friends? It wouldn't matter to me one bit if he/they were. It was just the only thing I could think of based on what she was saying and how she was acting.

Brodie turned sideways in her chair, partially facing away from me. She bit her lip and toyed with her disheveled ponytail. I could tell she was struggling with something.

She must have made up her mind because she swung back around to face me and put both her hands on the table.

"Promise me you'll keep this to yourself and won't tell Lewis I told you any of this."

It had been my experience that in the long run, promises were always broken. Maybe not on purpose, but the truth always seemed to come out somehow, and you were kidding yourself to think you could keep it bottled up. But she had me hooked, and my curiosity would only allow one answer. "Sure."

Brodie nodded, but then almost a minute passed, and she still said nothing else. Maybe I wasn't convincing enough with my answer, or she changed her mind?

"Okay, here's the thing. When Lewis was six years old, his father abandoned him and his mother. Just woke up one day and decided he wanted a different life, so he ran off with another woman and left Lewis and his mom penniless. Lewis's mom had a fragile personality to begin with, and when her husband took off, she kind of lost it. I mean, completely shut down. It got so bad that she needed to be hospitalized, and they made Lewis a ward of the state because they couldn't locate the dad, and there were no other family members to take him in. He spent two years in the foster care system while his mom was straightening her life out, but those two years were very hard on him."

Brodie paused briefly, bringing her hands together and interlocking her fingers. Her eyes were glistening.

"Lewis has never told me the details of what he experienced during those two years. Even today, he won't talk about it, but it really left him kind of... damaged."

"Damaged how?"

Brodie reached into the backpack and handed me something plastic. It was a sheathed baseball card.

I stared at the face of Chipper Jones on the trading card, not understanding at first. Then I made the connection, and heat radiated from my collar. "Hey! Is this mine? Did he steal this from me?"

"He can't help himself. He sometimes takes things that interest him, usually small things, but he is getting much better."

"He's a kleptomaniac?"

"Well, it's not technically stealing. He feels horrible after he takes things, so he gives them to me, and I return them for him. Think of it more like extreme borrowing."

"Extreme borrowing? Are you kidding me?"

"He can't help it," she snapped, a wisp of her own temper showing. "It's a condition he developed after going through what he did and then having to learn to trust his mother again. Listen, I make sure everybody gets their stuff back. You have your stupid baseball card back. Nobody is really hurt. And he only does it when he's stressed."

I could see she was getting irritated, and for some reason, that bothered me. Surprisingly, I cared more about her thinking poorly of me than I did about having my baseball card stolen, and that was uncharted territory for me, a self-proclaimed loner. Now, more than ever, I felt unsure of myself. I softened my tone.

"How else is he… and I don't mean to sound insensitive… *damaged*?"

My change in attitude seemed to work as Brodie relaxed. "His therapist says he has periods of extreme anxiety and difficulty relating to others, especially men. And he has panic attacks sometimes and trouble carrying on conversations, which makes him come off as blunt."

"I actually prefer blunt."

I turned the baseball card over and over in my fingers. I thought my issues were a lot to handle, and they were, but Lewis's problems were enough to make me stop and think.

When Brodie spoke again, her voice was almost pleading. "Please understand, despite all that, Lewis is a wonderful person. I've known him since he started attending public school again, and he's by far my best friend."

"Which makes me wonder... why? The way you look out for him and the protectiveness, you act more like a sister than a friend. How did the two of you become so close?"

She took a moment to contemplate her answer.

"Let's just say that, at first, I owed him. But once I got to know him better, I saw a person anyone would be glad to call a friend. I do what I can to make school bearable for him. His mom had him tutored at home until last year, when he decided he wanted to go to school like everyone else. High school is hard enough for the rest of us, but for Lewis—"

Brodie turned her head away as if she were about to sneeze, but I could see that she was overcome with emotion again. She recovered quickly and continued.

"He's been steadily getting better, and I've been encouraging him to make friends and engage, but it's not been easy for him. I don't know you, or really if I can trust you or not, but Lewis thinks you're best-friend material, so here I am."

"Let him get to know me a little. He'll change his mind pretty quick."

"Well… that's up to him. I just know that if we let it slip about the money, the other kids would be all over him. That's no way to make friends."

"What are you talking about? What money?"

Brodie looked down at her inter-connected fingers.

"I kind of left out one more thing about Lewis you should probably know."

"And that is?"

Brodie glanced around the cafeteria to make sure no one was close enough to overhear.

"He's sort of a millionaire."

MOVING FEAR

Eight

Lewis

"Lewis! Do you know where the plunger is?" Jules Bonvillain called out.

Lewis got up from his desk and walked to the top of the stairwell. "It's underneath the sink." The downstairs bathroom had been backing up lately, and the plunger had become a regular decoration there.

"It's not there," his mother yelled back.

"Why don't you call the plumber? It's not like we can't afford it."

Lewis's mom appeared at the base of the stairs, wearing a pink sweatshirt and matching pink sweatpants, and holding a wet towel. This was the first he'd seen of her since he got back from school, and he went straight up to his bedroom.

"You know I don't enjoy spending money on things we are perfectly capable of taking care of ourselves," she called up to him.

Lewis shook his head. "Did you look behind the door?"

His mom smiled up at him and disappeared. After a brief pause, "Got it."

"Want me to come down and plunge it?"

"I can do it, honey. Finish your homework."

Lewis smiled to himself as he made his way back to his desk, knowing he had already finished his homework thirty minutes ago. He detoured on his way back to the window so he could look next door.

Since being home, he'd been compulsively peeking out of the window every couple of minutes. He had seen the twins return home twenty minutes ago and then Travis and his mom ten minutes behind them, but Knox wasn't with any of them. Lewis watched as the dad pulled up, but still no Knox. He was beginning to wonder whether his neighbor hadn't gotten the word that Brodie had canceled their after-school Language Arts team meeting and was still at the school.

Lewis forced himself to return to his desk and stare at the three 24-inch side-by-side monitors. The screen on the far left displayed a virtual chessboard with a match in progress between him and Pocketrocket12 from somewhere in the Ukraine, on the right was an eBay webpage he pulled up last night tracking a bidding war for a Chipper Jones rookie card, and the one in the center showed the results of a Google search for the name Chace Gidden.

Dammit... why did I steal that baseball card he kept asking himself, even though he knew the answer. He winced when he thought about what would happen when Brodie returned it. Knox was going to know who took it, for sure. Even if she slipped it into his locker, he'd still know. Lewis was confident he and his mom were the only strangers who'd been in Knox's house, so the suspect list would only have one name on it.

This morning, he hadn't felt as bad as he did now. Yes, he always regretted it when the compulsion caused him to do something he knew was wrong. But until Knox stood up to Tug, there was little hope the two of them could be friends, and now he had ruined that. Anyone willing to do that for a near-stranger was someone he wanted to call a friend.

If not for that damned baseball card!

Lewis desperately tried to think of something that might make up for what he did. He thought about buying Knox a larger hard drive for his PS5, or maybe a couple of rare baseball cards to add to his collection, but then he remembered what his mother's financial adviser was always cautioning her about... money didn't solve problems, just hid the symptoms.

Unable to resist the temptation, he got up from his desk chair and walked back over to the window again. With the slats pulled down, the window had a perfect view of both the front and side of the Giddens' house. Their driveway ran between the two houses all the way to the backyard garage, putting their home approximately forty feet from his. Lewis could see into two of the three windows in the room Knox shared with his brother, and had a partial view of the living room bay window. Upstairs, the bedroom closest to him was the parents', having seen them pop in and out of there when the shades were up, so Lewis knew that meant logistically, the other bedroom window on the far side of the house must have been the older sisters'.

Lewis could see flashes of activity inside the house, but still no Knox. More theories about why he hadn't come home yet kept popping into Lewis's head. Maybe Knox ran into some jocks after school, and they convinced him to go off pounding their chests or chase girls. Possibly he had an after-school job somewhere, but that seemed unlikely since his family had just moved here.

Maybe he was somewhere planning his revenge for the theft of his baseball card.

Lewis blinked and shook his head, realizing how stupid and pitiful he was acting. Then something caught his attention. Despite it being late afternoon on a perfectly sunny day, it had turned very dark in Knox's parents' bedroom. Like somebody had pulled down a pitch-black shade. He couldn't make out anything inside the room. His eyes darted down to the first-floor windows, and he noticed the same weird occurrence. A complete absence of light anywhere in the house.

Lewis grabbed the string hanging against the window frame and pulled hard, yanking the shades up out of his way. He leaned forward, holding his breath, then everything inside his neighbors' home returned to normal.

"What the hell?"

MOVING FEAR

Nine

Wilfred

Wilfred Jenkins smoothed his long white hair away from his scalp and pulled it into a ponytail. With his hair properly tied back, he made his way up the stairs and through the metal door onto the dock. He was debating whether to stay late and work a double tonight. He didn't want to, but he needed the money. The last trip had depleted most of his travel funds, and that made him nervous. Being prepared to move on a moment's notice was crucial, so being without money meant possibly having to trek across the country and sleep in his truck, and that just wasn't acceptable. His Dodge was rapidly approaching the too-many-miles-to-be-dependable mark, so it wasn't smart to leave anything to chance.

"Jenkins?" a voice called out from above.

Wilfred kept walking, wondering what today's work schedule would be like.

"JENKINS," the voice called again, louder.

Wilfred surfaced from the depths of his own thoughts. That was him. He sometimes forgot the name he was going by now. He looked up. "Huh... yeah?"

"Jesus, man, I think all that bleach you put in your hair has melted your brain," his skinny supervisor snarked. He was standing on the overhead platform above the receiving dock. The man was half Wilfred's age, with probably a third of his IQ. It often irritated him to put up with less-than-capable supervisors, but he kept telling himself that was the price he had to pay for the amount of freedom he required.

"Sorry, what did you say?" Wilfred asked the supervisor.

The man stuck his pen behind his ear and put his forearms on the railing. "I said I need your answer about working tonight."

"Yeah, sure. I'll work."

"Great. Don't forget to clock out after your shift here before you clock in on the other side. You'll be working for shipping tonight."

Wilfred gave the man a thumbs-up sign and watched as he made a beeline back to the supervisor's shack and the welcoming air conditioning. Wilfred walked back toward his station, enjoying the rush of warm air over his sweat-covered body as he passed in front of the dock fans. It had been a hectic day for a Monday, which didn't bode too well for the rest of the week, but it also meant more overtime was a good bet. But his body wasn't as young as it used to be, and long hours in these sweltering conditions were taking a toll.

He stopped at the cooler next to his workstation to pour himself a drink before heading back to his lift. The driver, sitting in a hard-plastic chair on the opposite side of the door, made a point of looking at his watch. Wilfred ignored him as he took a sip of cold Gatorade. Before he could swallow, his gut wrenched, and he blew the contents of his mouth all over his paperwork. As the pain in his stomach doubled him over, all the air left his lungs.

It's time again!

Knowing he had to get to the bathroom before what came next, he lurched towards the far wall. The truck driver was standing now, his eyes wide and mouth agape. Wilfred's vision was already blurring when he hit the concrete wall, feeling his way along it until he came to the bathroom door.

Stumbling inside, a wave of nausea hit him as he pushed his way into the first open stall. A stream of vomit erupted from his mouth, covering the toilet fixture and most of the wall behind it.

Falling to his knees, he managed to push the metal door closed behind him as the first searing pain shot through his temple. His hands went to his head, and he let out a moan as a white-hot poker of pain burrowed deep into his brain. When the convulsion came, it racked his body violently, causing him to fall against the side of the stall and forcing his shoulder blades to touch in the middle of his back.

As abruptly as they appeared, the symptoms were gone. Kneeling back on his legs and holding his hands to his temples, Wilfred's entire head felt bruised. He could almost see the beat of his racing heart against the back of his closed eyelids. The woozy, sinking feeling was still there, but the intense pain and spasms were gone. A loud roar in his ears replaced them, reminding him of the rushing wind from a car's open window.

Here it comes.

When he opened his eyes, Wilfred didn't see the inside of a bathroom stall. Instead, what he saw was some sort of home. Everything was hazy and distorted, but he could make out a living room with a couch and recliner. His vision wobbled as if the person whose eyes he was looking through stumbled, their gaze swinging around the room, pitching back and forth.

Concentrate. Look for clues. You don't have much time.

The vision was already dimming. There was a fireplace and a clock on the mantle.

Nothing useful yet.

Spinning to the right, he saw something odd at the base of the steps. Some kind of ramp. Whirling around back in the other direction now, then dropping, as if the person fell to their knees. There's a coffee table with a couple of magazines, a remote control, a half-filled bottle of water, a laptop, and a printed white flyer.

Then everything went black.

Wilfred closed his eyes, drew in a deep breath, and when he reopened them again, he was staring at his vomit on the bathroom wall.

He let himself form a small smile. Despite what he had just been through, he was more excited now than he could ever recall. All because of a few words printed in an obscure corner of the white flyer he'd seen in his vision.

Ox-Bow Methodist Church.

Ten

Knox

As soon as I saw my stepmom, Lorna, pulling up to the High School pickup area, the dread that I'd ignored most of the day came rushing back. I'd been sitting there for fifteen minutes with my back against the wall, writing in my journal about my new neighbor... and Brodie, his protector. The pair were an odd couple, but my thoughts dwelled on Brodie. Until now, I've done a pretty good job of ignoring girls, along with everyone else, but girls were especially easy because they were so tiresome and frivolous. Having twin sisters helped because I got to witness firsthand all the crap they put themselves through to be presentable. But Brodie seemed different. She was so self-assured, confident, and unaware of her own good looks. I was having a hard time thinking about anything... or anyone else.

Until my stepmother arrived.

I knew she was going to be all over me about the box — it was inevitable. And without Dad here to play referee, it was going to get intense. I could hear the questions now.

Why did you take it out of our room and move it, deliberately disobeying us? I didn't.

What's really inside of it? I haven't a clue.
What game are you playing? I'm not.
Do you not realize what these mischievous stunts have cost us? Yes, but this time it's not me.
Will you never accept me as your father's wife and part of this family?

When I slid into the passenger seat of her car, all I got was a polite "hello" and a perfunctory question about how my first day went. Then nothing else.

I didn't get it. Something was definitely different.

We rode in silence for ten minutes, which was highly unusual for Lorna. She had one of those personalities that never seemed to have an off switch. She was always carrying on a conversation with anyone within hearing distance, even strangers. It seemed to be her purpose in life to eliminate stillness of any kind. It could be really irritating, but now that she was sitting there wholly mute, it just seemed wrong.

Finally, I couldn't take it anymore.

"I thought you'd still be ticked about the box?" I blurted out.

Lorna kept her eyes on the road when she responded. "Your father and I discussed it, and we decided it was pointless. Maybe you're playing games with us again, maybe you're not—"

"I'm not!"

Lorna shot me a glance. "Please let me finish. Either way, confronting you would serve no useful purpose. This is our last relocation for quite some time, and you'll eventually adapt like you always do, so we just have to move past this, and we'll be okay."

I didn't quite know how to respond. To me, it sounded like they were still blaming me for using the box to throw a wrench into what was a near-perfect move, which bothered me a lot. On the other hand, they wouldn't be dogging me about it. In the end, I was getting what I wanted, which was to be left alone. However, the trust cup I was trying to refill wouldn't get any fuller.

If they can take an adult approach, so can I.

"I appreciate that, Lorna. But I want you to know that I have nothing to do with the box, and I'm going to do what I can to find out where it came from so that I can prove it to you."

My stepmom looked at me hard. When her gaze returned to the road, all she said was, "Fine."

I let that settle in for a minute, then pushed the issue even further.

"Did you find out anything from the real estate agent?"

"Not really. She spoke with the previous homeowners, and they say they're not missing anything."

"So, what do we do next?"

"I'm not sure. For right now, it can stay where it is in your room."

"Maybe it's time we open it?"

Lorna was silent for a moment before answering. "Maybe you're right."

We drove in a welcome silence the last five minutes to the house, pulling in the driveway and parking behind Dad's SUV. I grabbed my backpack and followed Lorna across the patio and through the rear door into the kitchen.

Inside, sitting on the stool at the serving island, Lindsey was staring at some documents that looked like the orientation papers they had given me at school.

"Lorna, can you help me with this? I'm thinking about changing my schedule," Lindsey asked.

"Certainly, honey," Lorna answered, dropping her purse and keys onto the island. "But why would you want to do that?"

"I'm just feeling overwhelmed and need a break, that's all."

"Okay, let me get dinner started."

"Have you signed up for the quilting classes yet?" Lindsey quipped upon seeing me.

"No, have you signed up for the Texting Anonymous twelve-step program yet?" I replied as I passed through to the hallway leading to my room.

"Groaner," she called after me.

"Moaner," I countered.

I was turning towards my bedroom when I noticed Dad sitting in the living room. What grabbed my attention wasn't the fact that he was sitting with his back to the hallway, alone, with no television on or music playing. It was because he was just sitting there, staring off into space.

"Hey, Dad."

My Dad turned to face me. "Hey, bud. What did you think of the school? Travis and the girls seemed to enjoy it."

What I wanted to say was *that my siblings are freaks who actually enjoy school*, but instead I replied, "It was alright."

"I bet already having a project to work on after school was a bummer."

"It actually wasn't that bad."

"Meet anyone nice?"

The image of a girl lecturing me about not stepping on her friend's feelings popped into my head, which caused me to smile. "Actually, a couple of people. It was an interesting first day."

Dad smiled back. "I'm happy to hear it."

I thought about heading into the bedroom, but remained stationary.

"What are you doing?" I asked.

"Me? I'm just waiting for an important phone call."

"Oh, okay. Well, I got homework."

"Then you'd better get to it," Dad said, and turned back around in his seat.

I walked into my bedroom and found Travis in what was becoming his usual spot next to his bed. He had his tray attached to the handles of his chair, providing him with a work area where a textbook and a notepad rested. Other books lay on the bed next to him. Bowzer was out of his cage again, violating Dad's rules, curled up on Travis's pillow.

Despite my attempt to avoid looking at it, my gaze fell upon the ominous black box, still sitting where we found it that morning. I felt a chill go down my spine. I know it was my imagination, but to me it looked bigger, and it was throbbing. Almost as if it were breathing. The longer I stared at it, the more it seemed to dominate the room. I could feel myself being drawn toward it. In my mind, I saw myself looking down through the open flaps, seeing nothing but emptiness. Then suddenly I was falling, engulfed.

I shook the crazy thought out of my head and turned back to Travis. "You could have used my desk if you needed," I said.

"This is okay," Travis said without looking up from the book.

I tossed my backpack on the floor at the foot of my bed, then dove forward, flipping over in mid-leap and landing on my back.

"It seemed like you were getting along okay today," I said.

He still didn't take his eyes off the book. "Yeah, I think I'm going to really enjoy it here."

I waited, but it didn't come. No ripple. No swell of self-disgust. Nothing. This was the point where I would typically grow silent and irritated. But not this time. Instead, I wondered what Brodie was doing at that moment. Probably homework. Or maybe she was helping her mother cook dinner. If she was helping with the evening meal, I bet she was the one directing who did what. That was her style. She had to be the one who —

Suddenly, I realized what I was doing, and I remembered my brother's last remark.

"You know what? Me too," I said, staring up at the ceiling.

Out of the corner of my eye, I saw Travis's head snap up and turn towards me.

"Don't shit or anything," I said, smiling with just one side of my mouth.

"Hey, did Lorna tell you about the weird thing that happened earlier?

"No. What are you talking about?"

"It was the oddest thing. It got really, REALLY dark in here. Like a nasty storm cloud passed overhead and blocked out the sun, or a solar eclipse, but it was only dark inside the house. You know what I mean? It was sunny outside, but dark inside, for no reason. It was freaky."

"For sure." My eyes returned to the black box. "I guess Dad and Lorna are going to leave the box in here for now."

Travis followed my gaze.

"Neither of them said anything to me about it. I wish they'd just get rid of it."

I sat up and continued staring at the box.

"How do you think it got back in here last night?" I asked.

"One of the girls, or maybe both. All those jokes you've played on them… they're probably getting payback."

"Maybe. I'm not so sure. Both are such goody-two-shoes, I can't see them doing something like that."

"Do you know what's strange about it?" Travis asked.

"I can name several things."

"Yeah, I know… but nobody has touched it since we found it this morning, right?"

"I guess so," I answered.

"Then why are some of the markings in different places now?"

I leaned forward. "What do you mean?"

"That symbol that looks like a starburst was near the bottom this morning, and now it's up at the top. And that symbol of a half-moon with a tail, that wasn't there at all."

I saw what Travis was talking about, but couldn't remember any specifics about the symbols from that morning. "Are you sure?"

He nodded. "It's odd, right?"

"I'll say."

Travis returned his attention to his textbook, but my eyes remained locked on the box. Dad and Lorna may not be giving me grief over it anymore, but I still had to find out where it came from and who was playing games with it.

I moved from my bed over to the desk chair and slid up closer to the box. I leaned over the top of it, then jerked back with a start.

"Travis," I called out.

"Huh?" he replied.

"The box is open."

MOVING FEAR

Eleven

<u>Knox</u>

Examining the creepy container more closely, I could see where its flaps once met at an almost invisible seam, but now one flap was no longer held firmly in place. Instead, it was sticking up half an inch from the surface.

"Tell me you didn't open this," I turned and asked Travis.

"I swear," Travis replied.

"Who else has been in here?"

"I don't know. Jadie and Lindsey were already home when Lorna and I got here. Then Dad got home. But I've been in and out since then, so anybody could have opened it."

I placed my hands on top of my head and looked up at the ceiling. "Crap! You know we're gonna be blamed for this."

"Wait a minute." Travis wheeled his chair back a couple of feet. "How do I know you didn't open it?"

"What? I wasn't even here."

"I mean, right now. I wasn't paying attention. You could have opened it yourself when I wasn't looking."

MOVING FEAR

I let my hands fall into my lap and sat back in the chair, bummed. Now my brother was becoming suspicious of me.

"You don't believe me either, Travis? I thought you were the only one who did."

Travis sat there for a moment, thinking.

"You're right. I'm sorry. I do believe you."

"Thanks, Bro."

"Hey, it's open now. Look inside and see what's in it."

"You don't have to tell me twice." I sat forward in the chair again, rolled closer to the box, and then reached out to take hold of the loose flap. It opened the rest of the way without resistance. Then I grasped the other fold and pulled it up as well. Under the first set was a second pair of perpendicular flaps. Moving faster now, I tugged both open and exposed an opening down into the box.

Travis rolled up closer, and the two of us leaned forward to look inside.

A loud knock at the front door caused us both to jump.

Ignoring whoever it was who was at the door, I returned to the box. The inside was just as dark as the outside, making it hard to see anything. I tentatively put my hand down into it and felt around, making sure to find each corner.

I sighed and slumped back into the chair. "It's empty," I said, unable to keep the disappointment from my voice.

"Maybe it's always been empty," Travis said.

I shook my head. "Remember when Dad moved it into the living room? He said it wasn't heavy, but he could feel something shifting around inside. No, whoever opened the box must've taken out what was inside."

"I wonder what it was, and who took it?"

"You and me both. And why hasn't anybody said anything?"

At the front door, I heard Dad greeting a visitor and recognized the second voice immediately.

"Grandma," I moaned at Travis, which made him shake his head.

I pushed all the flaps back down, restoring it to its unopened look, then rose from the chair and reluctantly followed Travis to the hallway.

Grandma Fuller was our mom's mom, and one of the reasons I was uneasy about moving to Ox-Bow. She was still a bundle of energy at seventy-four, but she was also not shy about showing her dislike for our dad. According to him, Grandma had never forgiven him for stealing her daughter away at such a young age. And it wasn't just taking her away, but moving her to places far away from Ox-Bow, which really meant anywhere out of the state of Oklahoma. She was also open about her views on how her daughter's children should be raised, which recently made me a prime topic. Still, one reason Dad picked Ox-Bow to settle in was so we could develop a better relationship with her. I wasn't holding my breath.

Grandma was the same height as me, with blonde hair that had a fair amount of gray mixed in, since she refused to color it, but her youthful face was the place where wrinkles never seemed to form. She kept busy with her tennis and volunteer work at the local clinics. Although she was a worthy foe in a game of chess, I always found it a struggle to talk to her.

"There are my boys," Grandma exclaimed as we came out of our room. She was standing next to Dad in the foyer.

She gave Travis a hearty hug before moving over to me. As we broke apart, she held onto my elbows and looked me straight in the eyes.

"How are you doing?" she asked solemnly.

"I'm fine, Grandma," I answered. "Really."

The look she gave me told me she doubted my sincerity, but I knew whatever I said would receive the same response.

"GRANDMAAAAAA!" Lindsey's voice preceded her down the stairs.

It was no secret in our family that Lindsey was Grandma's favorite, and it was something else Grandma didn't hide. Even though she was a twin, older than Jadie by ten minutes and officially making her the first grandchild, to me, it was Lindsey's personality that made her and Grandma inseparable. Lindsey was a bona fide scholar and destined for college somewhere. That quality only intensified after Mom was gone. She dealt with mom's death by burying herself in schoolwork and not facing what we were going through. Ironically, that made her more like me — without all the books and good grades, that is. She shared a lot of interests with Grandma, so it wasn't a surprise that the old woman spoiled her rotten. Lindsey, of course, played the preferential treatment to the hilt. It was almost embarrassing watching her suck up like she did.

Jadie, to her credit, couldn't care less.

I watched Grandma pull Lindsey into a long embrace, which didn't stop Lindsey from talking.

"Why haven't you come to see us before now?" Lindsey asked.

Grandma separated herself from her granddaughter and smiled.

"I was giving the family a chance to settle. I see you're still ignoring my advice, David. Didn't I make it clear you should pass on this house? Your neighbors are loony tunes."

I had to give dad kudos; his smile didn't dim one bit.

"The price was too good to pass up, Ginny, but I appreciated the input. Lorna's making spaghetti for dinner. Can we offer you a plate?"

"If that's what it takes to see my grandkids, I guess I'll have to say yes," she said, winking at Travis.

"Wonderful," Dad replied, not even trying to mask his lack of enthusiasm.

"Come see what we've done with our room, Grandma," Lindsey insisted, which I knew translated into *let me show you what you can buy me to make it better*. She dragged Grandma up the stairs by her arm.

Returning to our room, Travis and I stopped in the space between our two beds and regarded the mysterious box once more.

"What do we do now?" Travis asked.

The fact that my brother had used we wasn't lost on me. With everything Travis had been through over the last eighteen months, the one thing he never would do that everyone else was determined to do was blame me for his situation. Our bond was just as strong as it had ever been, and if my lack of ripples today was a trend rather than a fluke, maybe I could put some of my guilt aside.

"I don't really know," I answered, sitting on his bed.

"Should we tell someone?"

I thought about what Lorna had said during the ride home.

"Lorna told me on the way home that she was considering opening it. Maybe we can just say—"

"Listen," Travis interrupted me. "Do you hear that?"

I listened carefully and thought I heard a high-pitched hum, like that of an electric weed whacker, only more powerful and oscillating more frequently. The odd noise seemed to come from outside and was growing even louder.

I stepped to the window overlooking the front porch and saw nothing unusual. Then I went to the other window by my bed and peered outside. What I saw there made me smile.

Hovering right outside our room about six feet off the ground was a remote-control drone.

I had seen these types of drones before, featuring a coaxial rotor, a built-in gyroscope for precise movement, and a 4K camera. If I remembered correctly, it had approximately twenty minutes of flight time before its Ni-MH battery pack gave out.

I looked past the drone to the house behind it, scanning the windows, searching for the pilot. On the second floor near the front of the house, there was a window open, and the top half of Lewis's body was sticking out of the window, the remote control in his hands.

When our eyes met, Lewis made a motion indicating I should raise my window, which I did. With the window open, the sound of the hovering drone now filled our room. Then there was a clicking sound from beneath the drone, and a silver missile sailed through the window, past my ear, and bounced harmlessly off the TV monitor.

Travis laughed. When I retrieved the missile from the carpet, I noticed a tiny piece of paper attached to the shaft with a rubber band. Pulling off the band and unfurling the paper, I read the neatly written script.

It was the WEP security code for a Wi-Fi network.

Twelve

Lewis

Lewis's butt ached. He'd been parked in front of his 75-inch Plasma TV in the basement for going on three hours now, unwilling to move for fear of missing the much-anticipated PS5 Live friend request pop-up on the screen. He tried playing a couple of matches of Call of Duty to pass the time, but he couldn't keep his mind focused, so now he was just watching some YouTube videos to pick up some gaming tips. His bladder was fine, hunger wasn't a problem because his mom had forced him to eat a filling dinner of stuffed bell peppers with a side of rice, and his usual bottle of Yoo-hoo was sitting an arm's length away on the plastic milk-carton converted into a makeshift end table. But now the extended wait was getting to him in other ways.

Standing up for the first time since finishing his mandated dinner, he kicked the beanbag to the side so he could have more room to pace. Patience was usually one of his strengths, but this was becoming torturous. What made things worse was the fact that Brodie wasn't answering his calls or returning the messages he left, and that had never happened.

He was sixty percent sure he had seen a smile on Knox's face when the drone delivered the WEP code for his wi-fi network. At least it looked like a smile. So why hadn't he connected yet? Maybe it wasn't a smile, but a smirk. Lewis pushed that thought out of the way and forced himself to think positively. Still, three hours was plenty of time to get whatever homework he might have out of the way, so what else could he be doing? Maybe he was grounded from his PS5 altogether? Knox's mom seemed really upset about that weird-looking carton, and if she were anything like his mom, a grounding from online gaming would be the first tool out of the discipline bag.

Lewis tried to bury that thought as well. He was finding it harder and harder to think positively.

He snatched his phone from its holster to try Brodie again when a pop-up message appeared on his screen, accompanied by a blurb sound out of his stereo.

Browncoat2011 wants to be your friend.

As much as he had yearned to see that request appear on his screen, Lewis still couldn't help but feel both a rush of surprise and excitement. Before the message disappeared, he depressed the guide button on his controller, highlighted Browncoat2011's gamertag, and selected add. In the pop-up box that appeared, he typed HI and clicked send.

The seconds that passed seemed to last an eternity until another pop-up window appeared.

Browncoat2011 has invited you to a private chat.

Lewis grabbed the wireless headset from the monitor stand and fumbled nervously as he hooked it onto his ear. When it was finally in place, he accepted the chat request.

After a moment, a tinny-sounding version of Knox's voice spoke into Lewis's ear.

"Hey, Lewis."

"Hey," was all Lewis could think to say.

"Thanks for the WEP code."

"You're welcome. I... I figured I owed you something for this afternoon."

"You don't owe me anything, but I'm grateful for the wi-fi access, anyway."

"I think you'll be pleased. It's lightning fast since I upgraded it. At least I think it is, and I don't experience dropouts anymore. I didn't know you had a headset. You never chatted when we played before." He was feeling like a little kid who didn't know when to shut up.

"Travis uses it mostly. I rarely say much online. I prefer just to play."

"Me too." *Okay, maybe that was overcompensating.* Lewis pulled his bean bag back into the center of the room and sat down.

"When it warms up, maybe you'll invite me over to use your swimming pool?" Knox asked.

"Sure, except I don't know how to swim."

"Then why do you have a pool?"

"Because my mom thought I needed to learn how, and she wanted me to get more exercise. So, she had one put in."

Knox laughed. "I guess you can do that type of stuff if you can afford it."

Lewis suddenly had a pretty good idea why Brodie hadn't been returning his calls.

"You've been talking to Brodie," Lewis said.

"Yeah. You know that after-school meeting she canceled? That was her way of getting me alone so she could give me the 411 about you. I wouldn't get twisted about it, though. She's just looking out for you."

"I guess I should have figured she would do something like that. What did she tell you?"

"The whole shebang. Abandoned by your dad, your mom's meltdown, problems in foster care, my Chipper Jones card, and your compulsive stealing. Did I leave anything out?"

Lewis's grip on his controller slipped as his palms began sweating. "And I've been told I was the blunt one."

"You call it being blunt. I just call it being honest."

"Fair enough. I'm really sorry I took your baseball card."

"I got it back, so no worries."

"I guess now you think I'm pretty messed up, huh?"

"Listen, Lewis, as far as I'm concerned, it's all your dad's fault. I'm trying to turn a new leaf when it comes to being honest, so if we're going to be friends, let's not lie to one another."

Lewis smiled widely, then instinctively glanced at the stairs. "I can do that."

"You have to tell me what your secret is."

"Secret?"

"Yeah, what's Brodie's story? How did you get someone like her to stand up for you? She really is something else."

"I'm not sure. She just started hanging out with me when I came back to school, and we've been friends ever since."

"You think maybe it has something to do with your money?"

"Absolutely not," Lewis said. He hoped he wasn't lying to Knox any more than he was lying to himself. "We were friends before the money."

"But you are rich, right?"

"Most of the money is in a trust that I can't touch until I go to college or turn 21, but you gotta swear not to tell anyone about it."

"Why the big secret?"

"I don't want anyone to be my friend because of the money. Understand?"

"I guess. How much are we talking about?"

"Somewhere around fifteen million."

"Shit! Where did it come from? You win the lottery or something?"

"My dad did."

"I thought your dad ran out on you."

"He did. He ran off with another woman, who eventually dumped him. But he's always stayed around Oklahoma, and one day he hit it big with a winning lottery ticket. Unfortunately for him, he died a week later."

"Wow. Should I be sorry?"

"I'm not," Lewis lied again. "But since he never officially divorced my mother, she inherited his winnings."

"Talk about karma."

"I know, right."

There was a blast of static in Lewis's headset, followed by a "WHOA!"

"Knox?"

"You still there, Lewis?"

"Yes. What's going on?"

"Our lights just flickered… big time. I thought we were about to lose our power and our connection along with it," Knox said.

"I'm still here. That reminds me, I saw the strangest thing in your house today."

"What do you mean?"

"I was looking out my window to see if you were home yet when I noticed the inside of your house got really dark for about thirty seconds."

"My brother told me about that. Said it was freaky."

"It was. Never seen anything like it," Lewis said.

There was an extended silence.

"You have any theories about what could have caused that?" Knox asked.

Lewis thought about the possibilities that had run through his mind after seeing it happen, but he couldn't bring himself to voice any of them. Knox was a gamer, but he might not be into sci-fi and things that go bump in the night, so he thought it better to keep them to himself. This blossoming friendship was fragile enough as it was.

"Nope."

Another long pause made Lewis wonder if his lack of a theory was a reason for disappointment.

Knox broke the silence. "So, they call you *Villain* at school?"

"They're making fun of my name. I hate it."

"I think it's kinda cool. You know, when people call you names, it only hurts if you let it get to you. Want my advice? Lean into it. Once they see it's not bothering you, they'll forget about it."

"I liked the way you handled Tug this afternoon."

"What's the deal with that name, Tug? That's not his real name, is it?"

"No. His real name is Brad, but everybody calls him Tug. I've heard two theories about where the nickname came from. One is he was a big baby when he was born, and the doctors had to use forceps to pull him out. His dad supposedly gave him the name."

Knox laughed. "What's the other theory?"

"Something to do with masturbation."

Knox laughed even harder, and the two of them chuckled off and on several times before they could continue.

"Can I ask you something, Knox?"

"Sure."

"What happened to your brother? How did he wind up in a wheelchair?"

There was a long pause before the response came. "It was a freak accident. My dad was carrying a box during one of our moves and kicked the door open, not knowing my brother was on the other side, bending over to pick up something he had dropped. The door hit him on the top of the head with so much force it severed part of his spinal column."

"Ouch."

"He was totally paralyzed at first, but then he regained feeling and movement for everything except below the waist."

"Your brother said that he was hoping to get the feeling back in his legs soon."

"Yeah... well... the doctors say otherwise. He refuses to accept that, and I can't say I blame him, so we don't push the issue."

"Wow, that really sucks. I bet your dad must have felt terrible."

There was no response.

"Did you hear me, Knox? I bet your dad felt terrible."

"Actually, the whole thing was my fault."

"Huh?"

Lewis could hear a deep sigh.

"My dad just got out of the service—the Navy. We've been transferred from post to post every year or two since I can remember, and I absolutely hated it. When I was younger, I would pitch a fit every time we moved, but then as I got older, I found other ways to show them how I felt."

"Such as?"

"Once, I pretended I left something valuable at our old house and begged my parents to go back and look for it. Another time, I ran away and disappeared on the day we were supposed to leave."

"Wow. That's pretty mean."

"That's only the tip of the iceberg. I was a real prick. I can admit that now. Anyway, our last move before this one, I was especially angry. My mom had been dead for a little over a year, and my dad had just married Lorna, my stepmom, and not even a couple of months later, we were moving again."

"How did your mom die?"

"Cancer. It was really quick. She died just seven months after they diagnosed her."

"That's awful. I'm really sorry."

"Thanks. I miss her a lot."

Lewis let the silence fill the airwaves between the two of them, unsure of what to say next.

"Anyway, like I said, I was upset," Knox continued. "So, when the boxes were being loaded into the truck, I secretly sliced through a portion of the bottom tape on a few of the boxes so they would break open while being carried into our new house. And it worked. After the fourth or fifth box busted open, my dad figured out what I had done. He was PISSED. That's why he kicked in that door so hard. He was trying to carry a box that was falling apart, and he was mad at me. And the worst part was my brother was bent over in front of that door because he was picking up stuff from another box I'd cut."

"Man. That sucks. I thought I had problems," Lewis stated.

Knox chuckled. "Yeah, don't we make a pair?"

"Thanks for telling me all that. I guess Brodie spilling all my dark secrets isn't so bad."

"I haven't talked that much since the last time I saw my therapist. I feel like we should play a game or something, but to be honest, I think I'm kind of tired now."

"Maybe tomorrow?"

"Sure. Thanks again for the security code. See you at school tomorrow?"

"You bet. See you then."

Browncoat2011 has left the private chat appeared on the screen.

Lewis pulled his earpiece off but didn't get up from the beanbag.

He thought it better to let the ear-to-ear smile fade from his face before seeing his mom, or her questions would be endless.

Suddenly, the TV screen came to life again. The words Browncoat2011 has joined the private chat popped up.

Odd, Lewis thought. *Did Knox forget to say something?*

Lewis put his mic and earphones back on.

"Knox?"

A sprinkling of static was all that he could hear.

"Knox, are you there?"

Still no reply.

"Come on, man, stop messing around."

Then he heard it. Soft at first, growing stronger, then fading away again. A sort of whispered grunts and groans, but Lewis couldn't understand what was being said. He strained to make out what it was streaming into his headset. A hissing sound, maybe a type of language, but nothing he had ever heard before.

Was Knox pulling a joke? If so, it wasn't funny. He had heard of gamers hijacking someone else's tag, but had never experienced it himself before. Could this be someone else?

"Who is this?"

BZZZZT. CRACKLE.

A static burst came through the earpiece, offensive and grinding like a revved-up chainsaw. It was so intense that Lewis rose to his feet and tore the headset from his ears, his heart pounding. With trembling hands, he held the device in front of him. He could still hear the jarring sound coming from the tiny speakers, so he grabbed the cord and yanked it out of the PS5.

Lewis stood in the silence, confused. Feeble explanations about what happened ran through his mind, but nothing made sense, and that bothered him. He would have to give his system a complete once-over.

He was about to drop his headset into the beanbag when he paused. There it was again, the hissing, rasping voice. His eyes went to the end of the cord leading from the headset in his hand, where it lay disconnected on the ground in front of the stereo cabinet.

Lewis slowly raised the headset and pushed one earpiece against his right ear.

Nothing. And then a single word came through. More of an exhale of air than an actual voice.

"*Villain.*"

Lewis threw the headset across the room and watched it land on the carpet, then skid under a table.

Another message appeared on the TV screen.

Browncoat2011 has left the private chat.

Thirteen

Knox

Why am I awake? Something had interrupted my restful sleep and jolted me into this daze between slumber and consciousness, trying to figure out what put me there. I vaguely remembered a feeling of being moved or shifted, but now everything was still. There was nothing out of the ordinary. Brushing it off, I rolled onto my stomach and nestled in for a return to oblivion.

The bed then began shaking violently, almost tossing me onto the floor.

Snapping into a sitting position, now wide awake, I looked at the base of my bed. I half expected one of my sisters to be standing there with their hands on the bed frame like they used to do when I overslept—no such luck.

Was it an earthquake? Do they even get earthquakes in Oklahoma?

I thought I'd read news stories about Oklahoma experiencing some tremors, but those were tiny and barely noticeable. I looked to the other side of the room, and Travis was still sound asleep in his own bed, his wheelchair in its usual spot. Whatever that was, it hadn't affected my brother. Then I felt my eyes being drawn to the freaky box, still resting where we left it. It stood out in the room's gloom, like an eclipse's shadow. The longer I stared at it, the weirder I felt. I knew I was letting my middle-of-the-night imagination take over, but I couldn't help myself.

Knox.

Did someone just whisper my name? Surely that was just my imagination. An immense feeling of dread swept over me, making my skin tingle in a cold sweat. That's when I noticed how chilly the room had become. Freezing. The nights had been relatively cool, but there was no way the temperature outside had dropped this much. It was cold enough I could probably see my breath if I turned on the lights.

I hadn't dreamed the bed shaking, of that I was positive. I was also sure the door to the hallway had been closed when I turned off the lights for the night. We always slept with the door closed. But now it was half-open. Somebody must have shaken my bed and ducked into the hallway. That's the person who must have whispered my name. And the frigid temperature I was feeling was because someone had cranked the air conditioner down. That was the simple explanation. It was either that or our family had moved into a haunted house. But I didn't believe in ghosts.

Wrapping myself in a comforter, I climbed out of bed and headed for the bathroom. Even though the surroundings were still new, I made my way past Travis's bed and into the next room without incident. Using my hand in the darkness to feel around the sink, I turned the hot water faucet on and waited for the cool water to warm. As I waited, I glanced into the mirror above the sink and my heart stopped. There was a shadow of someone behind me. I whipped around, raising my arms and allowing the comforter to drop, only to find nothing there. There was only a towel draped on the bar mounted on the wall. *That isn't what I saw,* I briefly told myself, but I allowed myself to accept the rational explanation anyway.

I splashed some warm water on my face, gathered the comforter around me, then left the bathroom.

Whoever was up to this mischief was going to pay for waking me up at—glancing at the luminous numbers on my clock—2:12 in the friggin' morning. It must be one of my sisters, and my money was on Jadie. Between the two, she's the one who has changed the most since Mom died, becoming more mischievous. The way I saw it, Jadie was always a boy-chaser, but it became an obsession after Mom died. Before then, she'd been interested in art, specifically painting, and her watercolor portraits were fantastic. Now she viewed school only as a means to an end... which was more boys. What had once made her interesting had slipped away.

Lindsey's head was always buried in a book, so I couldn't imagine her taking the time to bother with something so trivial as a prank. Jadie was just as smart as Lindsey, but her priorities were wired differently. Could I believe she took the black box from Dad and Lorna's room and put it back in ours? Maybe. And maybe she was even behind the appearance of the box in the first place. If she was, then I had really misjudged her and had to give her credit. Not only had she put together an intricate prank worthy of my stamp of approval, but she had me catching the heat for it. Well played.

I was greeted by an eerie quiet when I crept into the hallway. We had been sleeping in the house for only a few days, not long enough to learn its subtle noises yet. Those creaks, groans, pops, and hisses that all homes made at night. But as I stood there listening, I could hear nothing. There was only a stillness in the air.

One of my sisters had to be hiding somewhere. There was no way they could have covered up the sound of their footsteps on the stairs as one of them bolted back to their room, but I looked up to the second floor anyway—nothing but murky darkness. My gaze shifted lower to the hallway leading to the kitchen, but there was nowhere to hide except the closet. The vacuum cleaner and miscellaneous other cleaning supplies would make hiding inside virtually impossible, definitely not without making some noise, so I ignored it and moved on. I slowly stepped down into the living room, my eyes adjusting to the darkness. I could make out the couch, recliner and coffee table in the middle of the room, the TV and its stand tucked away in the corner, and the table that held the decorative knick-knacks against the near wall. As I made my way around the furniture, heading for the study, I kept my eye warily on the couch. It would be the perfect spot for someone to pop up from behind and scare the crap out of me.

Maybe it was because I was moving so slowly, or the fact I was dragging a comforter behind me, but for once I didn't trip on the step heading into the study. My dad's desk and chair were positioned on the right wall, alongside a waist-high bookshelf. On the opposite wall stood a pair of individual six-foot bookcases pushed together, every shelf overflowing with hardcover books. The top two shelves on the right bookcase held the trash novels that had previously decorated the hardwood floor.

There was no one hiding in this room, either.

I froze when I heard a clinking sound from around the corner. Then there was another.

I raced through the study and stopped in the doorway, looking into the kitchen. That room was darker, and my eyes needed to readjust, but I could make out a dark shape on the far side of the serving island. I gasped, now hoping that it really was Jadie or anyone else in the family. The shape wasn't moving, nor did it react to my presence. The dark region of my imagination, the one that only came out after binge-watching late-night horror movies, was screaming at me to turn and run. Whoever was there in the dark wasn't acting like a teenage girl, ducking for cover after being discovered. Instead, it was somebody, or something, just watching me. The hairs on the back of my neck stood at attention.

"Chace?" a female voice said, which caused me to flinch. The shadow moved to the left, her arm stretching out towards the light switch, flooding the room with light. Through squinting eyes, I could see Lorna, dressed only in an oversized Snoopy t-shirt, standing next to the light switch.

"What are you doing up?" she asked.

I was so startled that I didn't even bother to correct her about my name. Surely her being in the kitchen right after what happened with my bed wasn't a coincidence. Should I confront her and force her to tell the truth, or let it slide and play it safe?

I went with, "I was thirsty?"

She moved back over to the serving island where her own glass of milk was sitting. "What are you doing in your father's study?"

It was too early in the morning to think this fast on my feet. "I thought I heard something. I guess it must have been you."

"Are you cold?"

I looked at the comforter around my shoulders and realized I was no longer cold, and the temperature in the house seemed reasonable.

"I was, yes."

"I hope you're not coming down with something. It would be a shame to miss school just as you're getting started." She picked up her milk and took a sip.

"Why are you up?" I asked.

"Oh, I get up a lot. I have bouts of insomnia from time to time, and a cold glass of milk sometimes helps."

I managed an awkward smile, unsure of what I should do next.

"Well, I guess I'll be getting back to bed," I said, turning to head down the hallway.

"What about your drink?"

I half-smiled again, walked over to the cabinet between Lorna and the light switch and took out a small glass, filled it halfway using the sink faucet, took a couple of sips, and left the glass in the sink.

"Goodnight," I said and hurried down the hall back to my room.

Closing the door behind me, I took the comforter and unfurled it over my bed before climbing back in.

"Knox?"

This time, I almost jumped out of my skin. I spun around to face my brother's bed.

"What did you do that for?" he asked.

"Huh? What are you talking about?"

"Why did you shake my bed?"

Fourteen

Knox

Travis and I both rose fifteen minutes early because I wanted to have our sleeping bags stowed before anybody checked on us. When I finished rolling mine up, I started on my brother's. Answering questions about why we had been sleeping on the floor was something I wanted to avoid because I simply didn't have a good reason for them or myself.

I put the bags in the closet, and when I came back out, Travis rolled out of the bathroom. The two of us looked at each other, neither sure of what to say.

"Ready for breakfast?" I finally asked, purposely trying to sidestep the elephant in the room.

"Are you going to tell Dad and Lorna about the beds shaking?"

The elephant had just stepped on my head. "Let's say that we do. What do you think they'll say?"

Travis thought that over for a moment. "They probably won't believe you, but I'll be there to back you up."

"And then they'll just accuse me of shaking your bed. I've been over this in my head, and I can't see a way where I don't come out being blamed. I think the smart thing is to keep it between ourselves for now."

"But my bed shook. What do you think it was?"

I glanced at the black box before I answered. "I don't know yet, but we'll figure it out. Okay?"

"Yeah," Travis replied. I wondered how he felt about burying his head in the sand next to mine.

Picking up my backpack and slinging it over my shoulder, I followed my brother's wheelchair out the door.

In the kitchen, Lorna was already churning eggs in a glass bowl. I picked a spot at the dining room table instead of the serving island so I could sit with Travis, dropping my backpack beside my chair. I mumbled a good morning as I made my way to the counter.

"Eggs?" Lorna asked.

"No, thanks," I answered as I reached into the cupboard for a bowl. "I'll just have some cereal."

"I'll just have cereal as well," Travis said.

"Suit yourself." She poured the contents of the bowl into the frying pan that was already heating on the stove. The sound of sizzling eggs filled the kitchen.

Minutes later, Lindsey came strolling into the room wearing her designer jeans and one of her very colorful tops.

"Don't take all the milk," she said, depositing a purse the same size as my backpack on top of the serving island while simultaneously typing a text on her phone.

"Crap," Travis blurted out as he backed away from the table. "I forgot to feed Bowzer."

"Want me to do it?" I offered.

Travis was already gliding down the hall. "I got it."

"Is—" Lorna looked up and studied Lindsey before continuing. "—Jadie right behind you?" Lorna still hadn't mastered the art of telling my sisters apart without using Lindsey's mood ring necklace as a clue, and I wasn't about to help.

"I think she's still in the bathroom."

From upstairs, the three of us heard Dad yell, "Honey, have you seen my watch?"

Without hesitation, Lorna yelled her reply. "I saw it on the desk in your study last night."

I listened to the rumble of Dad's footsteps coming down the stairs as I poured milk over my Honey Nut Cheerios. I was about to stuff a spoonful in my mouth when his voice boomed loudly.

"LORNA!"

The mix of anger and surprise in Dad's cry made Lindsey turn away from her phone and look towards the doorway.

I got up from the table and headed for the study, Lindsey and Lorna right behind me.

What we found made all of us stop dead in our tracks. Someone had stacked all the books from my dad's bookshelves in the middle of the room, from the floor to the top of the vaulted ceiling, in one massive tower. It was like something out of Harry Potter. Putting aside the who and why for a moment, I couldn't imagine the how. Paperbacks and hardcovers seemed to be intermixed randomly. It would have been next to impossible to put together the column of books without it toppling over. But yet there it stood... a ten-foot literary mountain.

Dad just stood there, staring at the impossible structure.

Lorna stepped around me into the room. After a few seconds, her eyes met Dad's, and then they both turned to look at me.

Jadie came bounding down the stairs at that moment. "What's going on?" she asked as she entered the room. "Whoa."

"I did not do this," I answered the question I knew was on everybody's mind.

"You were in here last night," Lorna countered at once.

I felt trapped again. I didn't know what I could say to make them believe me. Heck, I was starting not to believe myself.

"You were down here also," I blurted out, regretting it as soon as I said it.

Lorna's eyes darkened, and she stiffened. "You're accusing me of doing this?"

"No. I just know it wasn't me. I didn't touch these books."

"That's enough," Dad barked. "Everybody, finish getting ready for school. Knox, Lindsey, and Jadie, when you get home from school this afternoon, I want you all to put the books back where they belong."

Jadie was in the middle of taking a picture of the tower with her phone. "Why do I have to help?" she whined, dropping her arms to her sides and tilting her head to one side. "I had nothing to do with this."

Travis wheeled into the living room, and his mouth fell open.

"Jadie, just do as I say." Dad's tone made it clear there would be no further discussion on the matter.

"Yes, sir."

"Um... Dad," Travis said, his eyes still on the books.

"What is it, Travis?" Dad snapped.

"Uh... Bowzer is missing."

Dad whirled around to face Travis so fast I thought he might fall over. When he spoke, his voice was noticeably louder.

"What did I tell you about taking him out of his cage?"

The concerned look on my brother's face told me something wasn't right.

"I didn't. I locked Bowzer in his cage when I went to bed last night, but when I checked on him just now, he was gone. He's not in our room anywhere."

My mind immediately went back to last night's bed-shaking incident and seeing Lorna in the kitchen. Maybe she could have shaken our beds and turned down the A/C, but no way would she have picked up Bowzer.

115

"We can't leave him running loose in the house all day. Everybody fan out and find him," Dad commanded.

"I'm not getting anywhere near that rat," Jadie announced, wrapping her arms around herself.

"Jadie, I don't want to hear it," Dad barked, his voice louder than I'd heard for a long time. It shocked Jadie so much that she became perfectly still. Dad must have realized the effect his shout had because he paused a moment to take a deep breath, and when he continued, his voice had returned to normal. "I'm not asking you to pick it up. Just find him, and either Knox or I will come get him."

"Okay," Jadie replied, her voice barely more than a whisper. She did an about-face and headed out of the room.

I walked past the book stack, giving it a wide berth, then past Dad and up to Travis.

"You checked everywhere in the room?"

"I couldn't see under your bed."

"Let's check it out," I said, and led him back to our room. I dropped on all fours and lifted the bedspread. Nothing, except one of my socks. Just to be sure, I looked towards Travis's bed, which had little room underneath because of the mechanics required to shift its position, but Bowzer wasn't there either.

"Zip," I told my brother as I got back on my feet. His wheelchair had come to rest at the base of his own bed.

"Knox, Bowzer's cage was locked. I'm sure of it. Somebody had to open it and let him out on purpose."

"I know."

My brother rarely lied, and when he did, it was because he was protecting somebody else, usually me. The quiver in my stomach from the middle of the night had turned into queasiness when I'd seen the stacks of books in Dad's study, and it was now a full-blown ache.

"What's going on?" Travis asked.

I don't know where the thought came from, but it just popped into my mind. Then it was all I could think of—the *box*. Everything started happening after it appeared. *It wouldn't surprise me if…*

"Did you look in the box?" I asked Travis.

My brother looked to the corner where it stood. "The flaps are closed. Bowzer couldn't get in there."

That made sense; nevertheless, the thought persisted. I had to know for sure. I stepped over to it, pulled back the first set of flaps, then the inner set.

There at the bottom of the box lay Bowzer's lifeless body.

Fifteen

Knox

Lorna pulled our SUV into the first available slot in the high school parking lot, nowhere near the entrance, and slammed the gearshift into park. I watched as she helped Travis into his chair and then spun and walked away at a brisk pace. She didn't bother to wish either of us a good day.

"Why is she mad at us?" Travis asked, watching Lorna head into the school.

"I don't know. Maybe because I'm the prime suspect and you're the unwitting accomplice."

Turning his chair so he faced me, I could see the hurt on Travis's face.

"Thank you for burying Bowzer for me."

"You don't have to thank me for that. I liked him, too."

"Do you believe Dad? That Bowzer must have been sick, and he crawled inside the box to die?"

I dug my hands deep into my pockets and shook my head. "I don't know, Travis. I just don't know."

"It doesn't explain who let him out of his cage."

"I know. But we can't think about that now... we have to get to class," I said, trying my best to convince my brother of something almost impossible to accomplish. I started walking backward towards the sophomore wing of classrooms. "Come on."

Travis pushed on his wheels and followed me.

The irony of the situation wasn't lost on me. School, or rather the drama and social calisthenics that went with it, was usually what caused the chaos in teenagers' lives and home was our refuge. With everything going on at our house, none of which was my doing this time, school had become my asylum.

The morning of my second day of classes was pretty much a repeat of the first. I spotted Travis a couple of times with his entourage, happy and animated. He had obviously embraced his short-term memory and shaken off this morning's events. I also once saw Jadie with a group of boys in pursuit. But I didn't see Lindsey anywhere, which wasn't unusual. When she wasn't in class, my smarty pants sister would spend time in the library. We all had the same lunch hour, but, in typical sibling fashion, we went our separate ways and pretended the others didn't exist.

I kept my head down, answered questions when called upon, and resisted the temptation to be drawn into casual conversations. If school was going to be my haven until life at home straightened itself out, then I couldn't afford to do anything that would muck that up.

The one exception—or should I call it two—was Lewis and Brodie.

I had just sat down at one of the corner tables in the cafeteria, about to dig into my plate of spaghetti and what was supposedly meatballs, when Lewis slipped into the seat beside me and Brodie into the one opposite.

"Hi," Lewis said. His broad smile displayed a set of perfectly aligned and snow-white teeth.

"Hey," I answered, looking first at Lewis, then at Brodie. Amazingly, I could already feel my mood lighten.

"We switched lunch periods," Lewis announced. "It was my idea."

I noticed that Brodie's smile seemed robotic, which made me wonder if Lewis had already informed her that I had spilled the beans about her 'private' conversation with me.

"You can do that?" I asked, watching Lewis unpack this massive Tupperware container filled with food.

"We both had study hall before lunch, so it was no biggie," Brodie explained. She paid no attention to the elaborate meal Lewis was laying out for himself.

"Aren't you eating?" I asked her.

"Oh, I never eat lunch. If I get hungry, I munch on some of Lewis's vegetables."

Lewis showed me a sealed plastic container holding carrots and cauliflower, then put it back down.

"Can I ask you something, Knox?" Lewis asked.

"Sure."

"After we ended the chat last night, did anyone else get on your system?"

I shook my head. "No. Travis was already asleep, and I powered down and zonked out myself. Why?"

Lewis answered without taking his attention from seasoning his food. "No reason. Just curious."

"Those are some serious bloodshot eyes. Did you not sleep well last night?" Brodie asked.

Lewis glanced at me with a mouth full of something, and I was unexpectedly embarrassed. Did I even remember to comb my hair before we left home that morning? How good a job did I do brushing my teeth? What was I wearing? I couldn't remember the last time I actually cared about how I looked to someone else.

"Uh... no, I didn't sleep well. Still getting used to the new house, I guess," I answered.

"Does it have anything to do with that creepy box?" Lewis asked before taking a sip of bottled water.

"What box?" Brodie asked.

Before I could answer, Lewis continued on. "Ever find out what caused your house to go all dark yesterday?" he asked, ignoring Brodie's question altogether.

With everything that happened this morning, I had honestly forgotten all about the dimming lights from yesterday. Something else to add to the creepy list.

I debated my answer before speaking. "Nope."

Brodie offered Lewis a stern look, obviously not accustomed to being cut out of a conversation. "So, Mr. World Traveler, where have you lived before coming to Ox-Bow?" she asked, her sparkling blue eyes eroding away my current worries.

"Maryland, North Carolina, South Carolina, Louisiana, Virginia, Georgia, Illinois, Ohio, Washington, California, Texas, Oregon, and now here." I rattled off the list as if I were reading them from the phone book. The question was a familiar one, and I was well-versed in our travel history.

"Wow, you really got around. Which was your favorite?"

"My favorite place has always been wherever I'm at right then, so I guess that makes it Ox-Bow." I kept my eyes focused on my food. I didn't intend to act so blasé. It was just that this was a topic I really didn't enjoy talking about.

Brodie looked at me carefully before responding. "Bitter, much?"

Her remark caught me by surprise and when I looked up, a tilted head and half-smile that melted away every piece of tension in my body greeted me. No matter how tough I was determined to act, I couldn't stop a smile from breaking out across my face.

"Why Ox-Bow?" she asked while she reached over and pinched one of Lewis's cauliflower florets and popped it into her mouth.

"Excuse me?"

"Why did your family move here to Ox-Bow? It's not exactly on the beaten path."

"My dad just retired from the Navy. I guess he picked Ox-Bow because it was situated close to Ft. Hurst and a college where he could finish his degree. Plus, he wanted us to be close to our grandmother."

"Ever find out where that box came from?" Lewis asked suddenly. "It was really different."

"What's so strange about this box Lewis is curious about?" Brodie asked, probably deciding to take the *if you can't beat 'em, join 'em* tactic.

"That's kind of a mystery," I answered as I pinched open my carton of chocolate milk. "It kind of just appeared out of nowhere. It's not one of ours, nor was it left in the house by the previous owners. So, no one really knows where it came from."

"What does it look like?" she asked.

"It definitely wasn't a box used for moving," Lewis answered instead. "About the same size as a moving box, a little bigger. All black, and not that glossy black either, but more of a flat, charcoal black. It wasn't taped shut, but probably glued or something. But the strangest thing about it was the markings that were etched into the surface."

"It looked like some sort of hieroglyphics to me," I added.

"Exactly. Hieroglyphics."

"And this was in your house?" Brodie asked.

"Still is, although it's empty now."

I could see Lewis getting more excited, dropping his half-eaten chicken leg into its container. "What was in it?"

"I don't know. Somebody opened it yesterday. I found the flap sticking up when I got home from school and there was nothing inside."

"You don't know who opened it?" Lewis continued probing.

I shook my head. "Everyone denied it. I could tell my dad was pissed, but he didn't make a big thing out of it."

"Why was your mom—"

"Stepmom," I corrected in a tone that told him he needed to remember that distinction.

"Stepmom, so angry at you that day you found it?"

"She thinks... heck, everybody thinks that this is another one of my moving pranks."

Brodie shifted back in her seat, which to my self-conscious mind was a subtle move to put distance between us. "Lewis told me a bit about your past troubles. I'm not sure you could blame your parents for thinking you were up to something," Brodie said.

And there it was, the thing about having a social life I missed the least—being judged. Or was I just being defensive? Is that why Brodie seemed so distant when she and Lewis sat down? Lewis told her about our conversation the other night, and maybe she didn't like everything she heard. She knew next to nothing about me, so could I blame her for taking sides with my parents?

I fought the urge to get up and walk off, leaving my food and everything just sitting there, responding to the negative voice in my head. But I didn't. Instead, something held me in my seat. That something was what I found when I looked into Brodie's eyes again, or rather, what I didn't find. No criticism, no blame, no moral superiority. Just pure inquisitiveness.

The old me would have stalked off. Actually, I wouldn't have been at this table with the two of them in the first place. This was unfamiliar territory, and it mattered. What Brodie thought of me mattered. For the short time I'd known her, I could tell she wasn't afraid to tell it like she sees it, and I shouldn't either. And Lewis didn't know how to hold anything back. Whatever was on his mind was out of his mouth, unfiltered and unrepentant. That's probably why I decided to say what I said next.

"You haven't heard the weirdest part yet."

Brodie's expression didn't change, but Lewis sat forward in his seat and pushed his glasses further up on his gigantic nose.

I glanced at nearby tables to make sure nobody was eavesdropping, fully aware of how goofily dramatic it made things appear. "Ever since the box showed up, strange things have been happening."

"Strange how?" Lewis asked. I think he may have even licked his lips.

"Last night—" I hesitated. Was I really going to say this out loud? Would doing so somehow make it more real... and therefore more terrifying... or just incredibly silly sounding? "—something shook my brother's bed and mine."

"Something shook your bed?" Brodie repeated, skepticism dripping off every word.

"So hard that it woke us up. But there was no one there. And the room got really, really cold. When I got up to see who might have done it, I found my stepmom in the kitchen, just standing there."

"Your stepmom shook your bed?" Brodie asked, her brow furrowed. Lewis continued to just listen intently.

"No... maybe... I don't know, but that's not all. This morning, we found this tower of books in my dad's study. Somebody had taken all the books off the shelf and stacked them from the floor to the ceiling. It was almost ten feet tall. Definitely bizarre."

Brodie didn't have a comment this time, but I could tell there was serious brainwave activity behind those eyes.

"Is that it?" Lewis asked.

I shook my head, then looked directly at Brodie. "My brother's ferret, Bowzer, disappeared this morning. Somebody took him out of a locked cage. We searched everywhere but couldn't find him at first."

"But you found him, didn't you?" Brodie asked solemnly.

"Yeah. We found him inside the black box. He was dead."

As much as I needed to know what Brodie was feeling right then, her face was unreadable.

It was Lewis who broke the brief silence.

"This is awesome," he said before chomping on a carrot.

Sixteen

Lewis

As Lewis slid into his chair beside Brodie for Mrs. Allen's Language Arts class, he felt different.

Just one lunch sitting at the same table with Knox, and now the kids who "accidentally" bumped into him in the halls, or called him *Villain*, fell silent and were leaving him alone. It was probably his imagination, or maybe just a lull in an ongoing onslaught called public education, but he couldn't help but hope. Could gossip that someone actually stood up for him really spread that fast? Maybe things might turn out as Brodie had predicted.

He and Knox might become friends, maybe even good friends. It was too soon to tell. Lewis was smart enough to know he was providing Knox something he probably needed right now, something more powerful than shared likes or common interests. Lewis believed him.

The things going on in Knox's house were strange and stretched believability, but Lewis didn't care. Knox had stood up for him when he didn't have to, and Lewis was going to do the same for him now. He was going to get to the bottom of whatever was going on next door, and that was that.

But he wasn't sure how Brodie would react. Her reaction when Knox was telling them about the box, the shaking beds, the tower of books, was hard to gauge. There was definitely heavy skepticism involved, but maybe she'd give Knox the benefit of the doubt for Lewis's sake. Whichever way she was going to swing, the jury was still out. He'd known Brodie long enough to realize that when she faced an uncertain situation, her modus operandi was to go silent and process her thoughts internally.

She hadn't said a word since lunch.

Mrs. Allen marched into the room with an armful of papers, placed the stack on the corner of her desk and stood before the class with her hands on her hips. That sent everyone scurrying to their seats and quieting them.

"Well, ladies and gentlemen, I promised yesterday that you'd have Tuesdays and Thursdays to work on your projects, so let's quietly form your groups and get to work."

Lewis and Brodie stood up immediately, expecting Knox to join them once again as they moved to the front to sit with Tug, but Knox remained seated. He motioned to the empty seats around him and smiled.

Lewis returned the smile, looked at Brodie, who was smiling as well. The two of them walked to the back of the room and took chairs on opposite sides of Knox. They all looked at Tug sitting by himself at the front of the class, staring defiantly back at them.

The battle of wills lasted a couple more minutes before Mrs. Allen looked up from grading papers and used her voice to shatter the deadlock. "Mr. Dempsey, I believe your team is awaiting your presence in the back of the room."

The entire classroom grew still, and Lewis could feel everyone waiting to see what would happen next. Tug still did not move, his attention focused on the top of his desk.

"Mr. Dempsey," Mrs. Allen's voice boomed again, a couple of decibels higher this time.

Tug shot Mrs. Allen a withering look but began to move. Rising in slow motion, he snatched the notebook from his desk and headed for the rear of the room. When he reached the others, he jerked one of the empty chairs around and over-dramatically dropped into it.

As soon as Tug was in his seat, the room returned to a hum of murmured discussions.

"Glad you could join us," Lewis said, eliciting a suppressed chuckle from Brodie.

"Shut your hole, *Villain*," Tug growled.

"I'd keep yours shut, Tug," Knox countered quickly.

Tug turned to Knox, leaning across his desktop. "You know something, new boy, you sure talk hard for somebody who ain't all that. What makes you so tough?"

Lewis watched Knox level his eyes on Tug. *This should be good,* he thought.

"You ever been to the beach?" Knox said.

Tug looked confused. "Sure, who hasn't?"

"I love the beach. The sun, surf, girls, volleyball, the sound of the waves hitting the shore, the smell of the ocean air, almost everything about it. But you know the one thing about the beach I can't stand… absolutely despise it… the sand. As soon as you set foot in it, it's all over you. In your cracks, in your pants, every nook and cranny, and no matter what you do, you can't get free of it. Regardless of how many dips in the ocean or freezing showers you take, you still can't shake the feeling that sand is still on you. For hours and hours afterward, you can still feel it. It stays with you."

Knox was leaning forward now, just a few feet away from Tug's face.

"I hate to fight, but when I'm forced to… I'm like sand. I may not be as big or strong as the person I'm fighting, but I'm all over them. They can't get rid of me. Whatever they do, no matter what they throw at me or how much they hurt me, I stick with them and keep coming back." Knox leaned back in his chair and crossed his legs. "So, most of the kids I come across who feel a need to throw down with me end up doing one of two things. Care to guess what those are?"

Tug appeared to be mesmerized. "What?"

"They learn to love the sand… or stay away from the beach."

Knox glanced at Lewis, giving him the briefest wink.

"As much as I would just love to continue swimming in this sea of testosterone," Brodie said. "We have a project to complete and have zilch so far. So, all of you need to get over yourselves and pitch in."

Tug was still looking directly at Knox, but his expression had softened. Something else had replaced the anger and resentment, something less antagonistic, but Lewis could not decipher what it was.

"Where do you think we should start?" Lewis asked.

Brodie opened her notebook and removed the handout Mrs. Allen had distributed on Monday.

"We need to choose the type of show we want to create, and then work on the script."

"What are the choices again?"

"Comedy, Drama, Mystery, and Westerns are a few of the choices. Any of those sound interesting?"

Lewis didn't have a good feeling about any of them, and apparently, neither did anybody else.

Brodie shook the paper in front of them. "Well, we have to pick something, guys."

Lewis wished Brodie would just choose and tell them all what they needed to do.

"Come on, if somebody doesn't suggest something, I'm going to choose a musical and make you all sing."

The silence that followed made Lewis wonder what kind of singing voice Knox might have.

"Horror," Tug suddenly said. Everyone turned to stare at him. He sat there with his legs stretched out in front of him and crossed, scrutinizing the tips of his fingernails. "My grandpa used to tell me stories about a thing called Friday

Fright Theater. He listened to it on the radio when he was a kid." When Tug looked up from his cuticles, he seemed embarrassed by the attention his suggestion had received. "They broadcast horror stories."

We all sat there in stunned silence.

"I like it," Knox finally commented.

"I do, too," added Lewis immediately.

Brodie looked at Tug like she was trying to figure out a puzzle in her head. "Okay. Then it's settled. Friday Fright Theater. Good job, Tug."

Brodie's praise turned Tug's embarrassment into something resembling a prideful smile, which Lewis thought looked awkward and ill-fitting on the bully's face.

"Now, we need a story."

Lewis looked at Knox. "Have you written any horror stories?"

Knox seemed surprised by Lewis's question. "Um... I've never let anyone read my writing."

Brodie picked up on Lewis's idea. "But could you write one for our project?"

Lewis saw her blue eyes doing a number on Knox and knew the answer before Knox even spoke.

"I—"

Lewis watched her go in for the kill.

"Pleeeeaaasssssseeee?" Brodie pleaded.

Knox rubbed the back of his neck. "Okay, but you guys have to help me come up with an idea for the story."

"Great! Lewis, I'm putting you in charge of all the technical aspects of recording, including any music or sound effects we might need."

"I can do that."

"Tug, is your grandfather still alive?"

"Yeah."

"Do you think you could talk to him and find out any more details that you can about what it was like to listen to Friday Fright Night?"

"I guess."

"We all have something to do except you, Brodie," Knox said, a cocky smile on his face. "Just how do you plan to contribute?"

Lewis grimaced, knowing full well the extent of the lecture Knox was about to receive. He had heard it countless times.

Brodie's back stiffened, she crossed her arms across her chest, lowered her chin, and looked up at Knox.

"Listen, funny-boy, if it wasn't for me, all of you would still be sitting here like a trio of awkward mimes. I don't have 4.0 GPA because I sit around and wait for good things to fall into my lap. I take charge."

"Well… I know there's one thing you can't take?" Knox answered back, his smile gone now.

"And what's that?"

"A joke."

"Ohhhhhh… burn," Tug howled, which drew a look from Mrs. Allen at the front of the class.

Lewis's eyebrows went up as he watched Brodie and Knox stare at one another. After a few seconds, the hint of a smile appeared on the corner of Brodie's mouth.

"I hope you write horror better than you write comedy," she said.

Seventeen

Knox

After school, I broke away from the crowd and headed for the side door leading out to the staff parking lot. Stepping out into the late afternoon sun, I spotted Travis already sitting behind Lorna's car, an open book in his lap, oblivious to anything or anyone passing him by. I started strolling in that direction when activity on the field to my left caught my attention.

The open ground that bordered the parking lot was approximately the size and shape of a football field and looked as if it were used as a PE activity space. One side butted up against the school, another bumped up against a section of thick woods, and a public road hemmed off the side farthest from me. A four-foot chain-link fence encircled the entire area, with gates positioned at three walkways leading out from the school.

Set up in front of a section of the fence separating the field from the woods were four large, three-legged archery targets, evenly spaced apart. Positioned twenty yards in front of each target was a teenager with a bow, about to let loose their arrows. Standing behind each archer were more participants waiting for their turn.

Leaning up against the fence, watching the activity on the field, was Lewis.

I scanned the school entrance and parking lot for any signs of Lorna. When I didn't see her, I changed direction towards the fence.

"Hey," I called out.

Lewis turned, and smiled when he saw me.

"Hey."

"Whatcha doing?"

Lewis returned his attention to the field. "Watching Brodie practice."

"She's out there?" I took up a position along the fence next to Lewis.

"Yeah. She's in the group closest to us, waiting to go next."

She wasn't hard to spot. Even though she was only one of three girls on the field, there was something special about her standing there in her faded jeans and loosely fit gray t-shirt, with a bow in one hand and an elongated leather pouch full of arrows in the other. Unlike everyone else, Brodie kept her focus on the shooter in front of her instead of engaging in idle chatter. A gentle breeze blew a strand of disheveled hair across her hypnotic blue eyes, but she gave no sign it bothered her.

I couldn't take my eyes off her.

"Is she any good?" I asked, even though my instincts told me the answer already.

"Second-highest score on the team."

The group on the firing line released their arrows. I watched as the projectiles impacted the targets, and after everyone had shot, a whistle sounded, signaling that it was safe for the shooters to retrieve their arrows. When that group returned, the next stepped up, but the only archer I was interested in was Brodie. A male coach I hadn't noticed before was standing on the far side of the shooting range with a whistle in his mouth and his arm raised, no doubt waiting to give the ready signal. When the coach's arm dropped, Brodie nocked her arrow in her bow.

Keeping her bow pointed to the ground, she looked downrange at the target, used her right hand to tug her left sleeve higher on her arm, gradually raised her bow to point at the mark, drew back the string with three fingers on her right hand until it was resting against the cleft of her chin, her draw elbow the same height as her ear, then became very still.

Her release was so smooth it was almost unnoticeable. I tried to follow the arrow's flight, but it reached its destination about the same time my head turned.

The arrow stuck in the red area just to the left of the yellow center circle.

Showing no emotion, Brodie repeated the process. This time, the head of the arrow buried itself directly in the center of the bullseye, the shaft quivering behind it.

"YEAH!" I yelled, drawing looks from Lewis and everyone else on the practice field.

"You're not supposed to cheer," Lewis instructed me, half-laughing. "It messes up the others who haven't shot yet."

"Oops, sorry," I said. Then I repeated it louder to everyone on the field looking at me.

The archers returned to practicing, all except Brodie. She was smiling at the two of us. Her smile was worth the embarrassment. I shrugged my shoulders and smiled back.

A voice from behind startled me. "What are you doing?"

Lewis and I both swiveled around to see Lorna standing there, her arms folded across her chest. She didn't look pleased.

"Do you remember our next-door neighbor, Lewis?"

"Hi, Mrs. Gidden," Lewis said.

Lorna's disposition softened. "Hi, Lewis. How's your mom?"

"Doing great, thank you."

"We were just watching the archery team practice," I explained, not sure why I was feeling defensive.

Lorna looked past the two of us to the activity on the field behind. "Anyone in particular?"

Lewis half-turned and pointed to Brodie, who was just raising her bow to prepare for her last shot. "Right there, in the gray t-shirt. Brodie is my friend."

The three of us watched as Brodie drew back the string to her chin. But as she released the arrow, she seemed to lose balance and stumble. The arrow sailed to the right, totally missing the target and continuing its flight until it disappeared into the woods beyond the fence.

"Looks like she could use the practice," Lorna said flatly. "Knox, we need to go."

I didn't want to take my eyes off Brodie, who was just standing there staring at her empty bow, looking confused.

Turning around and putting my back against the fence, I said, "Can't I stay here and watch some more? I can get a ride home with Lewis."

Lorna's arms crossed against her chest again, signaling the return of her unpleasant temperament. "No, you cannot. Remember, you have something important to do with your sisters."

The creepy book tower. With that reminder, the feeling of dread returned.

"Oh yeah, I forgot." I looked over my shoulder and saw Brodie retrieving her arrows from the target. One of her male teammates was scaling the fence to search for her errant shot.

Suddenly, I had an idea. Pushing myself away from the fence, I took a few steps towards the parking lot, then turned around, purposely putting myself between Lewis and Lorna.

"Lewis, don't forget you and Brodie are coming over tonight to work on our project." My right eye winked several times as I spoke.

Thankfully, Lewis didn't miss a beat. "What time did we say again?"

"Eight o'clock."

"We'll be there."

My parting smile communicated my gratitude before I spun around to join Lorna. Suddenly, a scream echoed from the field behind us, drawing my attention. Out on the range, another female archer had joined Brodie and that girl now stood with her hands covering her face. What she refused to look at was their heavyset teammate struggling to return over the fence, the lost arrow held high in the air, something impaled on its tip. A mass of gray and red was all I could make out.

"Brodie went all Hunger Games on its ass," the chunky teammate called out, wheezing from the exertion of climbing the fence.

"It's a rabbit," Lewis remarked, sorrow evident in his voice.

The expression on Brodie's face was a combination of disbelief and sadness. It looked like she was doing everything she could not to cry.

I turned to say something to Lorna, but she was walking away. Lindsey and Jadie had joined Travis by the car. They were all staring at the field. Jadie's hand was over her mouth, and Lindsey seemed unusually intent on watching the morbid events.

Lorna continued strolling back to the car, ignoring the commotion on the field entirely.

MOVING FEAR

Eighteen

Knox

It took my sisters and me almost an hour, working in hushed silence, to take down the eerie book tower and return them to their proper spots on the shelves. My fingers tingled as I touched every paperback and hardback, but I knew that was just my imagination on overdrive.

After telling Lewis and Brodie about everything going on in our house, it made me realize I could no longer deny that something unexplainable was going on, and it seemed to have something to do with the box. This tower almost certainly had to be the work of a poltergeist or ghost. Could our new house be haunted? And what part did the box play in this? Did something that used to be inside it do this?

The dismantling was slow work because Lorna insisted we treat the books delicately, which meant we couldn't allow them to fall over, so I had to use a step ladder to take down the top layers carefully. When Lindsey picked up the last handful of books and placed them on the shelf, I noticed she still had one in her hand.

I recognized it immediately. It was my journal.

The scornful look Lindsey gave me when she handed me the book was withering. Then she immediately marched out of the room and up the stairs to her bedroom. Jadie wasn't far behind, leaving me alone in the room, staring at the book in my hands.

I couldn't remember the last time I had written in it, but I was sure I had left it in my backpack.

I'm sure the cold shoulder from my sisters was punishment for them being unjustly included in the unpleasant task, especially after finding my journal at the bottom of the pile. I couldn't say that I blamed them. They were experiencing just a small portion of what I'd been going through since Dad had announced the family was going to move again.

"What are you thinking about?" Dad asked from the door leading into the kitchen.

"Nothing," I answered, moving the journal so it was slightly behind my back while trying not to be noticeable. "We just finished putting the books back."

Dad walked into the room. "I'm glad you're still here because I need to talk to you. Take a seat."

I sat down in Dad's desk chair and slid my journal behind me, dreading yet another lecture.

My dad looked into the living room. "Travis, can you hang out in your bedroom for a couple of minutes while I talk to your brother?"

Travis glanced over his shoulder. "Sure, Dad."

Dad and I watched as Travis wheeled himself up the ramp into the hallway and out of sight.

Dad walked over and grabbed the extra chair next to the desk, spun it around, and sat down. "I think it's about time you and I had a heart-to-heart about a couple of things. In fact, it's long overdue. I want you to know that's my fault. I should have sat you down a long time ago. It's just that everything has been so crazy, and I couldn't—"

Dad stopped talking and just stared at the floor.

"It's okay," was all I could think of to say.

Dad looked uncomfortable but determined.

"I thought that sending you to see that therapist would help, and you could sort through your issues together. With what's going on around here lately, maybe I should have..."

"Dad, I have nothing to do with the books or the box. You have to believe me."

"I want to Knox... I really do. It's just so hard. You really believe that one of your sisters would do something like this?"

I could feel the anger inside me building slowly. "And you think I could? After what happened, you really think I'd still do something like this?"

"I don't know what to think anymore. You haven't warmed up to Lorna like your brother and sisters have."

"Yeah... well," I said, looking away.

"And I think that has a lot to do with you blaming her."

I lied by saying, "I don't blame Lorna."

"Knox, we're talking man to man here... not father and son. So, I need you to be honest with me... and yourself. Otherwise, all of this will be nothing but wasted words."

"I have been telling the truth. Okay, so maybe I do blame Lorna a little."

"For pestering me to move away from California after we were married, the last home where your mom was still with us and we were a family."

I couldn't help myself. The tears came despite all my efforts.

"Knox, the truth is, it was me who wanted to move away from California. Not Lorna. I was never man enough to set the record straight, so I'm embarrassed to say that I let Lorna take the heat... and she let you think it was her idea. She didn't want the relationship between you and me to sour.

"The fact of the matter is that I had to get away from California. Everywhere I turned, everything about that place reminded me of your mother, and that wasn't fair to Lorna or our future together. So, as much as I knew you hated moving, as much as you were clinging onto memories of your mother, I put in for that transfer."

I didn't know what to say. I was reeling from what I had just heard. Though my eyes were still moist, my mouth was bone dry.

"And that means what happened to your brother, the accident, was ultimately my fault. My selfish need to get away from your mother's memory brought out your anger at moving. And the anger I felt when I kicked that door into your brother was directed inward at myself, as much as your prank. I mishandled it badly, and I want to apologize to you for that."

"What I did was stupid."

Dad sighed. "You were a kid, Chace. I was the adult, and I was the one who failed us."

It didn't go unnoticed that Dad hadn't used my middle name. I waited to see if he would say anything else before I asked the obvious question.

"Didn't you love Mom anymore?"

The pain that registered on my father's face went a long way toward answering my question.

"Oh, Knox. I loved your mother very much. I still love her. Those last couple of months were hard on all of us, especially your mother. Not because of the cancer, but because she could see what her cancer was doing to all of us. At the end, I believe she was relieved when she finally found peace, because she knew we could then move on with our lives.

"I didn't think I could move on at first, and the only reason I got through it at all was you, Travis, Lindsey, and Jadie. But over time, an emptiness inside me replaced the pain. You probably feel that I didn't mourn your mother long enough, but for me, it felt like forever. And when Lorna came along, she helped me become more than just a lonely widower and a single parent, and I dare you to say that I've not been a better person, a better father, since she's been in my life.

"Lorna has never tried to replace your mother to you kids, and just because I love her with all my heart doesn't mean I loved your mother any less. Your mom would actually be pleased that I've found someone who makes me happy and cares deeply for the four of you.

"But living in California would never allow Lorna and me the chance to create our own memories without the ever-looming shadows of your mom. Sure, I could have waited a couple more years until it was time to retire, but I didn't want to wait. Can you understand that?"

I wiped the tears from my eyes.

"Then why did we move here to Ox-Bow, to mom's hometown? Aren't there memories here too?"

My Dad shook his head. "Not really. Your mom and I didn't know each other all that long before we moved away from Ox-Bow. Because of the rocky relationship with her parents, we've only been back to visit a handful of times, so it's not the same. Definitely not the same as California, which was nothing but terrible memories. And despite what your grandmother thinks of me, we want her to be a large part of your life, all four of you. Since I used to be stationed close by, I'm familiar with the area. Lorna took some convincing, but Ox-bow meets all our needs."

I wasn't sure of how I should feel. My emotions were all over the place. But one thing I was sure of was that I was tired of being mad. The pent-up resentment about a life of constant moves, the bitterness of losing my mother, and the wrath directed at the woman I thought was trying to push our family away from my mother. I no longer had room for any of it. I wanted to be free from its influence.

"I still miss her a lot," was all I could choke out.

"I know, bud. And whether you believe it or not, I do too. A lot."

That's when the curtain came down. The same ones kids like me used to hide our insecurities, making us appear grown-up in front of our fathers, emotionless and self-reliant. With it down, I was helpless. I rose and fell into my father's arms, wrapping my own tightly around his waist. A constant stream of tears ran down my cheeks.

I don't know how long we stood there together. At one point, one of my dad's hands began stroking the back of my head, which made the tears flow even harder.

For whatever reason, the memory of Lorna walking away from the school practice that afternoon popped into my head.

"I'll try to get along with Lorna better."

"That's all I'm asking. Since we're being totally open here, are there any questions I can answer for you?"

Have you noticed Lorna acting strangely? Do you still think I erected that tower of books I just spent an hour cleaning up? Those were a couple of questions that came to mind.

Instead, I simply said, "No."

Nineteen

Lewis

Lewis stood in the darkness on the sidewalk between Knox's house and his, staring at the watch on his wrist. The glowing numerals read 7:58. Knox had said eight o'clock, but Lewis didn't want to show up early and appear too eager, though he couldn't take pacing around the house much longer either. That and his mother's hovering. She was acting more like her son was heading off to his first prom, not going next door to do homework.

Part of his nervousness was the fact that Brodie wasn't coming. He was unsure if what happened at the archery range shook her, or whether it was the creepiness of investigating Knox's puzzling box. Whatever the reason, she politely turned down the invitation without giving an explanation. It shouldn't really matter, but Lewis couldn't help worrying that the only reason Knox had invited them both was to spend more time with Brodie, and now that she wouldn't be there, he would have little use for Lewis. He wondered to himself why it was so unbelievable that someone would want to be his friend, other than to get close to Brodie or his money. Unfortunately, the answer was simple... it had never happened before.

The digital readout changed to 7:59. It was time to go.

Lewis had only taken a few steps when he thought he saw movement in the darkness on the side of Knox's house. He stopped and stared, wishing he had brought a flashlight with him, but when nothing materialized, he shook his head and continued on.

Lewis mounted Knox's front steps and reached to press the doorbell button before pausing. *Do guys ring the doorbell or knock on the door?* He played it safe, pulled open the glass storm door, and knocked.

Only a few seconds passed before the door opened to reveal Travis in his wheelchair.

"Hey, Lewis," Travis greeted him, smiling.

"Hi. I'm here to work on a school project with your brother."

"Sure. He's in the bathroom right now, but come on in." He wheeled himself backward to make more room.

"I was sorry to hear about your ferret," Lewis said as he stepped into the foyer.

"Thanks. We didn't even know he was sick."

"That's too bad. So... how are you liking Ox-Bow and school?"

"What I've seen of it looks fine. The school is great. Hey, those cookies your mom baked weren't half-bad."

"Oh... good. I was worried. I thought you might have fed some to the ferret."

Travis and Lewis were both laughing when Knox came walking out of the bedroom. He had changed clothes since Lewis last saw him at school, now wearing a plain white t-shirt and jeans with holes in both knees. Lewis still had on the same khaki pants and polo he wore every day. Today's polo color was light green. The combination, with differing color options, had become his de facto uniform of sorts.

"Hey Lewis, where's Brodie?"

"She said she couldn't come. I think she was doing something with her dad tonight."

"Oh... okay... well, come on back."

Lewis couldn't be sure, but he thought he recognized a glimpse of disappointment on Knox's face. Lewis closed the front door behind him and watched Travis roll down the ramp into the living room. Glancing into the room, he could see Knox's stepmom sitting at one end of the couch and one of his sisters... he wasn't sure which... at the other end.

Following Knox through the door into his bedroom, Lewis paused at the foot of the bed. His eyes fell upon the empty cage on top of the dresser. He stared at it for a moment before his attention shifted to the black box, still resting in the same spot he had seen it the first time he was there. Knox walked over and sat on the corner of Travis's bed, watching as Lewis approached the box.

"Dad wanted us to throw it out after we found Bowzer in it, but I kept it so you could look at it again."

"The first place anyone saw it was right here?" Lewis asked, squatting down to take a closer look.

"You're actually the first one who saw it. My dad and stepmom took it upstairs to their room, and the next morning it was right back in that spot. We left it there ever since, and yesterday is when I noticed someone had opened it."

Lewis lifted the loose flap and peered within.

"And you're positive there was something inside?"

"My dad said it wasn't heavy when he picked it up and moved it into the living room, but he definitely felt something shifting around inside."

Lewis closed the flaps, then kneeled and peered across the top of the box

"I've read that ferrets are very inquisitive creatures, so it's not inconceivable that yours found a way inside."

Lewis stood up and reached into his pocket, pulling back something that looked like a pocket calculator. From a corner, he took hold of a small circular ring attached to a black string and pulled it out of the device, placing it across the face of the box.

"What's that?" Knox asked.

"It's a digital tape measure. Width is 87 centimeters."

"You can't use inches like the rest of the world?"

Lewis looked up from his task. "The metric system is the universally accepted system of measurement for the world and was officially sanctioned for use in the United States since 1866, but we remain the only country that hasn't adopted it."

Placing the device on the ground and the end of the string at the top, he took another reading. "Height, 88 centimeters."

"Just how much did you read about ferrets?"

Lewis put the end of the string on the top of the box nearest the wall. "I did some research, is all. Depth, 87 centimeters."

"What do you make of the markings?"

Lewis put away the digital tape measure and pulled his cell phone from the holster on his hip.

"I don't know, but I'm going to take some pictures and see what I can find out. Can I pull it away from the desk so I can get a better picture?"

"Sure. I know it sounds crazy, but Travis thought some of the symbols moved around."

Lewis scrutinized the box closely. "How do you mean?"

"They were in one place in the morning, and in a different spot that evening, without the box being moved."

Lewis set his phone on the desk and grasped the sides of the box, pulling it further out into the room. Then he reclaimed his phone, selected his camera app, lined up what seemed to be a good shot, and then touched the shutter button.

He immediately checked his photo storage to make sure he got the picture he wanted, but the most recent image in the folder was a solid black square.

"Huh. That's weird," he commented.

"What's wrong?" Knox asked.

Lewis held up his phone to show Knox the screen, letting him see the wasted picture.

"Is your camera okay?" Knox wondered.

Lewis quickly snapped a picture of Knox sitting on the bed, then showed him the successful high-quality picture.

"Try it again."

Lewis switched positions, lining up a picture from a different angle. After a few moments, he held up another black screen for Knox to see.

"You see... you see," Knox said excitedly, using both hands to point at the box several times. "I told you, there's something friggin' going on with this box."

Stay calm, Lewis told himself. His mouth was suddenly like cotton. He swallowed twice to produce saliva, with no result. He returned his phone to its holster and started looking at Knox's desk. "Do you have a piece of paper I can use?"

Knox rose from the bed and reached past Lewis to pull a piece of lined paper from one of the cubbyholes. Lewis picked up a pencil from the desk and studied the box more intently, then began drawing on the paper.

"What are you doing?"

"There are some symbols that appear to repeat more often than others, so since I can't take a picture, I'm sketching them," Lewis answered without interrupting what he was doing.

He had just finished his third symbol when the doorbell rang. Midway through his fourth drawing, Travis called Knox's name from the foyer.

Lewis and Knox exchanged a look before they both headed towards the hallway.

Brodie stood right inside the doorway, chatting with Travis. She had changed clothes into something more fashionable, which Lewis noted as unusual. He also noticed that her hair was no longer held back in her customary ponytail, but hung freely on her shoulders, combed and shiny.

"Hey," Knox greeted her first. "I thought you had something to do with your dad?"

Brodie shot a glance at Lewis. "I got out of it. I'm only a couple of blocks away, so I wouldn't miss this for the world."

"Awesome," Knox replied. He pointed towards his room. "We're back here."

"You're not going to introduce me to your parents?" Brodie asked coyly. "I'm sure Lewis got introduced."

"Yeah, Knox," Travis chimed in.

Lewis watched Knox put on a pretend smile. "Actually, he didn't. But let's do that now," Knox said.

Travis preceded them into the living room, and Knox stood at the top step with Brodie at his right and Lewis on the other side.

"Hey everybody, this is Brodie from school, and you remember Lewis from next door—except I don't think you met him, Jadie."

Jadie barely lifted a hand off her leg and offered a weak smile.

"Brodie, that's my stepmom, Lorna," Knox continued. "My sister Jadie, my dad is back there in his study with his headphones on, and you already know Travis. I have another sister who is upstairs studying."

"Nice to meet everyone," Brodie said to the room, and everyone smiled back at her. "I hope you all enjoy it here in Ox-Bow."

"It's nice to meet you, Brodie," Lorna spoke for everyone. When she said nothing else, Lewis noticed Knox furrowing his eyebrows, appearing confused.

"Well, we got work to do," Knox said, quickly spinning and heading back to his room.

Back in the bedroom, Knox straddled the desk chair and watched Brodie take in the room's decor before plopping down on Knox's bed.

"Why'd you make that face when your stepmom greeted us?" Lewis asked.

"It's just that she's usually more talkative than that. A real chatterbox."

"So, where's this mysterious box?" Brodie asked the two of them.

Lewis turned to point at the far side of the desk, then froze.

The black box was gone.

MOVING FEAR

Twenty

Knox

"No friggin way!" I blurted, rising from my chair just as Lewis stepped back from where the box used to sit.

"What?" Brodie asked, confusion on her face.

"The box was right there, sitting next to the desk when we came out to answer the door," Lewis answered.

"And nobody could have taken it. You saw my entire family out there when you came in," I added.

"Except your other sister," Lewis pointed out.

I turned on him quickly, which made him take a step backward. "You think she snuck down the stairs behind us, grabbed the box, then snuck back upstairs, all while we were standing right there?"

"I'm just saying."

"Wait a minute, you guys are serious? The box disappeared? Into thin air?" Brodie said.

"That's exactly what I'm saying," I said, still looking at Lewis. "And you were a witness. You see... I'm not making this shit up."

"I never thought you were." Lewis looked at his forearm. "I've got goosebumps."

"This isn't funny, guys. Don't joke around," Brody said, wrapping her arms around herself.

"I'm as serious as a heart attack. It vanished, the same way that it appeared."

Lewis rushed over to the desk and snatched up a piece of paper. "Phew. I was worried my drawing had disappeared too."

Brodie jumped up from the bed and looked at it suspiciously. She must have remembered my story about the shaking bed.

"What do we do?" I asked, desperately needing a sense of direction. I was more shaken than ever now. We had definitely entered *Weirdsville,* and I didn't know how to deal. This was something I'd never experienced before. I could feel panic beginning to creep up on me.

"What do you do about a haunted house? You move out, is what," Brodie remarked.

"This can't be a haunted house," Lewis spoke up. "The Franklins lived in this house for as long as I can remember, and they never had problems."

"What happened to the Franklins?" I asked.

"It was Mr. and Mrs. Franklin, along with her mother. The mother was an invalid, and when she died, the Franklins moved into a condo on Mulberry."

"Did the mother die in the house?" Brodie asked.

Lewis shook his head. "No, in the hospital, that's why I don't think whatever is going on here is a haunted house."

"Maybe we should look around the house to see if the box just moved," I suggested. It was something to do, and that was something I needed right now. "Remember, it moved from my parents' room back here, so maybe it went in the other direction this time."

"And how should we explain searching your house to your parents?" Lewis said.

"I have a better idea," Brodie interjected. "Why don't we just tell your parents what's going on?"

"Because they think this is one of my pranks."

"But now you have Lewis as a witness."

Lewis nodded.

"Either I tricked Lewis into thinking the box disappeared, or it actually pulled a Houdini and disappeared. If you were my parents, which would you believe?"

Brodie looked back and forth between the two of us, then slumped back down on the bed. "The first one."

"I know what we can do. Knox, if your stepmom asks, we're just getting something to drink," Lewis said. "Brodie and I can go to the kitchen, and you duck upstairs to take a quick look around."

I nodded my head. "That could work. Okay, Brodie?"

"Actually, I was going to suggest we get out of this house and go next door to Lewis's, and finish discussing it over there."

"Do this first, okay?" I asked, putting a hand on her shoulder.

A deep sigh signaled her agreement.

"Let's do it then. Follow me."

I led them out the door and a partial way down the hallway, pausing at the base of the stairs.

"Kitchen's straight ahead on your left. Help yourself and keep your eyes peeled. I'll be right back."

When the two of them nodded their understanding, I surged up the stairs, taking three at a time. On the second floor, I looked into Dad and Lorna's room first, and when I didn't see the box, I stepped quickly over to my sister's room. The door was partially open, so I nudged it open a bit more so my head could fit through, peering inside.

Lindsey was sitting at the desk with her headphones on and her back to the door. As slowly and quietly as I could, I slipped the rest of my body through the door and tiptoed over to the closet. Luckily, the door was ajar and the light was on, so I could see pretty well. The box wasn't there.

I made my way out of my sisters' room undetected, then checked the storage closet and bathroom just to be thorough. Nothing. I headed back down the stairs.

At the bottom of the stairs, I was turning to head for the kitchen when I heard Lorna's voice from the living room. "Knox, what are you doing?"

Thinking quickly, I answered, "Lewis got a paper cut and I don't have any Band-Aids in my bathroom."

"You find what you needed?"

"Yeah, we're good."

Walking into the kitchen, I found Brodie and Lewis sipping on bottled water.

"Anything?" Lewis whispered.

I shook my head and held out my hand for a drink, fully expecting Brodie to screw up her face and demand I get my own. Instead, she handed me hers without hesitation. I smiled and gulped down a swig.

"I'm going to stick my head in the other room and see if it's in there," I said, handing the drink back to Brodie.

I stepped through the door leading into the study, where Dad was at his desk writing. Glancing around the room, I didn't see the box. I was about to turn around and rejoin the others when Lorna called out from the living room.

"David, there's something wrong with the satellite TV."

I looked into the living room at the TV against the far wall. On the screen was a scene depicting some kind of violent attack on a group of young women. It must have been a horror flick because the attackers looked creature-like, like orcs from the Lord of the Rings movie, while the women were dressed in modern clothes.

"What?" Dad responded after he removed his headphones.

"We were watching American Idol, and the channel changed all by itself."

"Then change it back."

"It won't let us. No matter what we do, it keeps switching back. Watch."

I watched Jadie work the remote control and the numbers 115 appeared in the left-hand corner of the screen. The display blinked once, then returned to the same scene. The screams coming from the TV were now deafening. Jadie repeated the task with the remote, and the exact three numbers appeared on the screen with the same result.

The TV seemed to be stuck on that one channel, and the violence unfolding before us was turning gruesome and bloody.

Dad got up from his chair and walked over to take the remote control from Jadie.

"What channel did you want?"

"115"

The numbers 1 - 1 - 5 appeared in the corner, and seconds later, the image of a woman with her intestines being savagely ripped from her midsection popped up. Almost immediately afterward, the house lights flickered.

"Ewwwww," Jadie whimpered.

I felt Lewis and Brodie come up beside me, transfixed by what was going on with the television.

"David, turn it off," Lorna pleaded urgently.

I watched Dad press the top button on the remote, with no result.

"Lewis, I want to go home," Brodie said quietly, her hands jammed underneath her armpits.

Dad walked around the couch and approached the satellite box on the stand below the TV.

Then the power went out.

"Crap," Travis said in the pitch black.

I felt Brodie's hand find mine, squeezing incredibly tight. Not knowing quite what to do, I used my other hand to sandwich hers.

"Does anybody know where a flashlight is?" I heard Dad saying in the dark.

"I put one in the drawer next to the refrigerator in the kitchen," Lorna said.

"Everybody stay where you are. I'll get the flashlight and—"

An ear-splitting scream came from Jadie.

"What was that?" Jadie cried out.

"What was what?" Lorna yelled almost as loudly.

"Something ran across my lap, and it felt hairy. That is not even close to being funny."

I could feel Brodie's hand trembling in mine.

"Knox?" Dad said.

"It wasn't me, Dad. I'm standing here next to Brodie."

"It wasn't him, Mr. Gidden," Brodie said softly.

"What's that smell?" Travis said.

That's when I noticed what Travis was referring to… a pungent, spoiled meat kind of smell. It was so strong I had to bury my nose into the crook of my free arm.

"Where's that coming from?" Lorna choked out.

"What's going on down there?" came Lindsey's voice from the top of the stairs.

"Just lost the power, Lins. Stay put," Dad responded.

The silence that followed only magnified the creepiness in the dark room. Then the quiet was shattered by a reverberating creaking sound that seemed to emanate from every direction. It was as if the entire house was shifting on its foundation.

"Are we having an earthquake?" Jadie cried.

Then just as suddenly as the noise had started, it was gone, and with it the disgusting smell.

"David, maybe you should check the breaker. Is the box in the basement?" Lorna said.

"I can see lights in the house across the street, so it must be the breaker," Travis called out.

"I'm heading in that direction," Dad answered, the sound of his voice now farther away.

Suddenly, I felt Brodie jump. "Get off me!" she shrieked, throwing her arms around my neck.

"Brodie!" Lewis called. "What's wrong?"

Then the lights clicked back on.

While the whirs and beeps of the electronic devices returning to life filled the room, I blinked, fighting to see in the brightness. Everyone had remained in the same spot they were in when the lights went out, except for Dad, who was now standing near the door leading into the kitchen.

Brodie still had her arms wrapped around my neck and face buried in my chest, shaking like a leaf.

"Are you okay?" I asked.

"I want to go home," she answered without raising her head.

I looked over at Lewis, who appeared both shaken and concerned.

"Where does Brodie live?"

"Just three blocks over. I can take her."

"We'll both walk her home."

Brodie didn't wait to be told. She disengaged from me and darted straight for the foyer with her head down. Lewis and I followed close behind her. As we were moving toward the front door, I heard everyone in the living room talking nervously. I could make out Dad saying something about checking on Lindsey.

"Lorna, we're going to walk Brodie home," I said over the din of voices.

"Is she alright?"

Brodie and Lewis were already out the front door, but I paused before following them.

"Yeah, I think she just got spooked," I said. Then I was out the door.

The three of us walked in the middle of the street, Lewis attempting to get Brodie to open up about what happened, and she was just shaking her head. When we arrived at Brodie's house, a simple brick ranch with a carport instead of a garage, I thought she was going to walk straight into the house without saying a word. Then she paused just as she opened the front door and turned to face us. Framed by the porch light, I could see that her face was pale and her eyes puffy.

"Something grabbed my arm," she said flatly.

I looked at Lewis.

"It wasn't Lewis," she said.

I felt the goosebumps popping up all over my body.

"How do you know?" I asked, even though I really didn't want to know.

"Because it was cold. Frigid. I felt it through my shirt. There was something else in the room with us."

She half-turned to go inside, then changed her mind and faced us again.

"And I felt the same thing at the archery range this afternoon. When I missed that last shot, something icy cold touched me. It caused me to flinch."

Her bottom lip quivered slightly.

"I don't know what you're dealing with, or what you've got Lewis mixed up in, but it was there at the school also. This is much more than a haunted house."

Twenty-One

Wilfred

Wilfred directed the early-model Dodge pickup, with red paint peeling badly from a large area of the hood, in front of the Ox-Bow Power & Light company. The pickup slid effortlessly into a parallel parking space being vacated by a blue minivan. Wilfred turned off the ignition and checked his image in the rearview mirror, tucking his bleached white hair up under his baseball cap and making sure his shirt was straight, with the top button fastened tightly and the collar pulled up high. He grabbed the three-ring binder off the seat beside him and opened the door to climb out.

He looked out over the tranquility of the city square with the obligatory historical courthouse situated in the middle. They had obviously restored the old building to its original condition, with its first and third story constructed of cut stone sandwiching white painted brick on the second floor. A large clock tower, including a replica of the Liberty Bell, sat atop of the impressive building, overlooking the professionally maintained grounds, a fully packed parking lot, and a quadrangle of local businesses.

He had researched Ox-Bow on the internet before he took to the road. It was a city with a population of just over twenty-five thousand, which would make his job much more manageable. Small enough for everybody to know everybody else's business, big enough for a stranger to blend in. It was located forty-five miles north of Tulsa and very close to the Kansas border. The primary employers in the area were a few mid-sized oil companies, although unemployment was fairly high. The city also had its fair share of arts and crafts shows, music festivals, and classic car shows.

Wilfred pushed the door of the truck shut, not bothering to lock it, tugged on his collar and sleeves one last time, then headed towards the Power & Light entrance.

Walking through the glass doors, he inspected the two service windows in front of him and the women behind them. They were helping customers, so he stayed back against the entrance wall and watched the way they interacted. Both women were approximately the same age, late forties or early fifties, but the woman on the right had more lines on her face, darker rings under her eyes, and took fewer pains to hide her age with makeup. The woman on the left was wearing a newer dress with earrings that matched, and her hair was perfectly kept. She also made frequent eye contact with the woman she was helping.

Wilfred stepped into line behind the customer on the left.

While he waited, he read the nametag on the Power & Light employee's chest, Beverly Baker. He also made a mental note of the family pictures suspended on the side of a filing cabinet by magnets shaped like tiny daisies.

The customer at the other window finished her business and departed. The employee with dark rings under her eyes said, "Next."

Wilfred didn't move.

The woman looked up, directly at him, and repeated, "Next."

"I'm waiting on Beverly," Wilfred answered, smiling, which elicited a shoulder shrug from the woman.

The entrance door opened, and another customer came in. The Black woman stood there confused for a moment, not understanding why there were two people standing in one line and none in the other.

"Next," tired eyes announced. The new customer glanced at Wilfred. When he didn't move, she took a spot in front of the service desk.

When the woman in front of Beverly concluded her business, Wilfred stepped forward and turned the brightness of his smile up several notches.

"Good morning, Beverly. How are the grandkids?" he said in his most chipper voice.

Beverly's own smile dimmed slightly as she struggled to remember where she knew him from.

"They're just fine. Thank you for asking. I'm sorry, I can't recall your name."

"Tom, Tom Kellogg. From church. Me and Betsy sit in the back row every Sunday."

"Oh sure, Tom," Beverly replied unconvincingly. "How is Betsy?"

"Fretting over her rose bushes. If we don't get some serious rain soon, I'm afraid she'll just have a cow."

Beverly smiled again, this time more genuinely. "How can I help you, Tom?"

Wilfred brought up his notebook and showed it to her.

"I don't know if you remember or not, but I work with Alicia at the Newcomers group, and she sent me over to get the list of this month's additional service requests."

Beverly's brow furrowed. "We still have another week to the end of the month. Isn't it soon to be taking up the list?"

In his mind, Wilfred blew out a sigh of relief. The name he jotted down of the person who answered the phone when he called the Newcomers group proved to be a useful one.

"Alicia is organizing a special mailing going out this week, and we need the most up-to-date list possible. I hope it's not an imposition."

"Not at all. In fact, all she had to do was call, and I could have emailed her the list."

"I had to come to the courthouse anyway, so I told her I would just drop in."

"Not a problem. I'll send it to her right now."

"Can I trouble you to print a copy for me as well?"

"What for?"

"I have to take the updated list directly to the printers for the mailing, so if I can get a copy from you, then I don't have to go get it from Alicia."

"Oh, I see. Just a minute then."

Wilfred smiled his thanks to the woman, nervously tugging his shirt collar up higher on his neck. He watched as she worked on her PC for a minute and then stepped towards a large printer on a shelf against the near wall.

Beverly returned and handed him a piece of white paper.

"There you go," she said, smiling.

"Thank you so much, Beverly."

"Not a problem," she said. Then, after a pause, "Tom, are you feeling okay?"

"Couldn't be better. Why do you ask?"

"It's just that the whole time we were talking, I couldn't help but notice your tongue is really discolored. Almost black."

Wilfred's hand went to his mouth, then he smiled. "I had a blueberry snow cone before I came here. It's just the food coloring from the syrup. Nothing to worry about. Well, we'll see you on Sunday."

Wilfred left quickly, walking directly to his truck and climbing inside. He instantly unbuttoned the top button on his collar, removed his baseball cap, letting his long white hair spill out, then finally looked at the paper handed to him. On it were twenty names, addresses, and dates representing power turn-on requests for the month. His attention dropped to the bottom of the list for the connections within the past week, of which there were eight. Of those, three were obviously apartments, and two had an asterisk beside them, which usually represented reconnects after service interruptions due to non-payment, so that left three to check out.

Piece of cake.

MOVING FEAR

Twenty-Two

Knox

"Where's Lewis?" I asked Brodie as she approached the cafeteria table where I was sitting. I really liked her casual, no fuss style of dressing. She was wearing black jeans, black Converse, and a lightweight striped sweater over an olive-green t-shirt. It really suited her. The handbag she toted, which she must have traded in her backpack for, appeared handmade, and its bright colors contrasted with her conservative wardrobe.

She ignored my question and looked down at the book sitting in front of me. "You're not eating?" she asked.

I shrugged my shoulders. "Not really hungry. After last night, I wasn't sure if you'd talk to me again."

Brodie grinned. "Let's go sit outside. I need to be in the sunshine."

I returned the history book to my backpack and walked beside Brodie as she led me to an oval seating area outside the cafeteria. Concrete benches bracketed the open walking space, and the school flagpole stood proudly in its center. Open benches were available on either side, but since the ones on the left were in the shade, Brodie chose one in the sun, facing the way we had just come. It was chilly, but felt good as long as you were in the warm mid-day rays.

I sat down opposite her and watched as she closed her eyes and turned her face towards the sun. She had flawless skin, rounded cheeks, and thin lips. I wondered if she knew how beautiful she really was.

"So, where's Lewis?" I asked again.

"He didn't come to school today," she answered without moving.

"Is he sick?"

Brodie opened her eyes and looked directly into mine.

"It depends. If you consider staying up all night researching what's going on at your house a sickness, then yes, he's sick."

"I didn't ask him to do that."

"You didn't have to. I told you, Lewis will jump off a cliff to please you. He's been desperate for a genuine friendship, any kind of relationship with another guy, for a very long time. And now you have him wrapped up in this paranormal stuff. I told you I didn't want you doing anything to hurt him."

This took me by surprise. Why did I always seem to be a lightning rod for blame? And now Brodie was joining in on the guilt parade.

"Brodie, please believe me when I tell you I have no intention of hurting Lewis or you. I really like him, and despite what you think, I'm not using him as some kind of puppet. I wouldn't do that. And as far as this paranormal shit goes, this is happening to me, to my family. It wasn't a choice. I only told you and Lewis because I really needed people whose first reaction wouldn't be to blame me. I didn't know where that would lead."

Brodie's eyes softened as she listened to my explanation, turning downward when I mentioned blame.

"What are you going to do?" she asked, looking at me again.

I shook my head. "No clue."

"Well, maybe Lewis will turn up something that can help. He's brilliant with computers and the internet. But just so you know, I'm not going back into that house again. This stuff really scares me."

I grinned. "I don't blame you, but I'm a little surprised. Lewis tells me you don't back down from anyone."

Now it was her turn to grin. "I'm not afraid of any 300-pound ignoramus whose only accomplishment in life is pushing other people around. That I can deal with. I know what makes those kinds of people tick. But the supernatural, unseen forces, I go all wet noodles inside just thinking about it."

"I hear ya. Does Lewis's mom let him stay home from school when he wants?"

Brodie's sly smile made my heart race. "His mom, Jules, does anything Lewis wants. Her entire life, ever since she got him back from the state, has been about making up for what she did to him. Lewis is her entire world, and everything revolves around him. What surprises me is how little Lewis takes advantage of it. After they inherited all that money, they could have moved into any mansion in Ox-Bow, but Lewis wanted to live right there in that small house he grew up in."

Out of the corner of my eye, I half-noticed someone on the far side of the quad wearing a dark hoodie who seemed to be interested in our conversation. When I looked in their direction, they twisted their head and walked away.

"Lewis never offered to buy something for you, something you really want?"

Brodie frowned. "No, why would he? He's not that kind of friend."

I looked deep into her eyes. "What kind of friend are you?"

I must have struck a nerve because she averted her eyes, and a blushing red blossomed on her cheeks.

"You'd have to ask Lewis that question."

"I don't have to, but there is a question I'd like to ask. How is it you don't have a boyfriend? I mean, a girl like you usually has a swarm of guys around her, but all I ever see you with is Lewis. What gives?"

Her eyes locked onto mine, almost defiant. "I don't need a boyfriend, and besides, who needs the distraction. I have enough on my plate between schoolwork and watching after Lewis."

But I wasn't buying it. I had my own theory.

"You know what I think? I think you use Lewis like your own personal boy repellent. You consider all the guys in this school vampires, and Lewis is your garlic."

Brodie's mouth flew open, and her eyes grew wide.

"That is not true," she barked back at me, rising at the same time.

"Then why else can you explain being attached at the hip to him?"

Brodie stared at the doors leading into the cafeteria, contemplating something.

Turning to look at me again, her eyes were moist with tears.

"When Lewis's father abandoned him, the woman he ran off with... was my mother."

Twenty-Three

Knox

I could hear someone inside the house bounding down the stairs, and then the front door opened to reveal Lewis, breathing heavy.

"Hey, you got my text," Lewis got out between gulps of air.

"Yeah, I got it," I said as I stepped inside. "But I'm in hot water with Brodie because of everything you're doing, so you need to cool it before she gets really pissed."

"That would be smart," Brodie's voice came from the back of the house.

I looked down the long hallway and watched Brodie appear from the kitchen with bottled water in her hand.

"I... I didn't think you'd be here," I said.

Brodie walked towards us with a neutral expression. "I came here for Lewis and you. That's what kind of friend I am."

The two of us exchanged a silent moment until Lewis broke it up.

"We need to get started. There is a lot to share with you both. I would have invited your brother, Travis, but we're not set up for his wheelchair yet. I asked my mom to have the adjustments made. The carpenters should be here tomorrow."

This took me by surprise. I was slowly realizing just what kind of friend Lewis was going to be, and what kind of mother he had.

"Where is your mom?" I asked.

"She's at church. We have at least two hours before she gets back. Let's head down to the basement."

Following Lewis and Brodie back down the hallway towards the kitchen, it amazed me at how similar the layout of the house was to my own.

"Your house really is laid out like ours, but it looks a lot different. I guess that's what happens when you actually decorate. I think Dad and Lorna are still getting used to that."

"I think when they constructed this neighborhood, the same builder built many of the houses, and he used the same floor plans. The only difference between yours and ours is that everything is reversed. Mom's bedroom is on the right when you come in, and your room is on the left."

Lewis turned the corner into the kitchen, pulled open the door leading to the basement, and then I followed him and Brodie down the stairs. At the bottom, Brodie went directly to the red beanbag in the center of the room and plopped down into it, leaving me standing to admire the surroundings.

The entire back wall was an audiophile and gamer's wet dream. A giant 75" 4K HDTV digital television on a solid black TV stand dominated the impressive setup, with massive four-foot-tall speakers on each side of it. To the right was a rack audio system with all sorts of equipment — amplifiers, pre-amplifiers, CD players, Blu-Ray players, and a few I didn't even recognize. On the left was a similar racking system holding an original Xbox 360, two Xbox Ones, a PS5, a Wii, and a shelf for controllers and recharging batteries.

There was probably lots of other neat stuff to see in the rest of Lewis's basement, but I couldn't take my eyes off the back wall.

"Oh... my... god."

"This is Lewis's boy-cave," Brodie commented before taking another swig of her water.

Lewis appeared from the back of the room, carrying two other bean bags, which he tossed next to Brodie.

"Isn't your own basement finished?" Lewis asked.

"No. It's on Dad's to-do list, but I doubt it'll end up looking anything like this. If it gets done at all."

Lewis sat down in one of the beanbags, then I followed in the other one, still unable to pry my eyes off the back wall.

My trance was broken by what Lewis said next.

"Are you ready to hear this?"

Brodie and I turned our full attention to Lewis. I might have even gulped.

Lewis pulled something out of his pocket and showed it to both of us. I remembered it as the measuring device that resembled a pocket calculator Lewis used to measure the black box.

"This device told me just how serious things were. If you remember, the measurements of the box were width, 87 centimeters, height, 88 centimeters, and depth, 87 centimeters."

"And that's important because—" Brodie prompted him.

"When you multiply those three measurements together for the volume, it calculates to .666 cubic meters."

I knew what the numbers represented, but I was waiting for Lewis to bust out laughing and tell us he was joking.

"You're talking 666, like in demonic stuff, right?" I asked when Lewis said nothing else.

"I'm afraid so."

I don't know what I expected to hear, but it definitely wasn't that. I could almost feel the mood in the basement sinking. "There is going to be some good news eventually, right?"

"I'm afraid not," Lewis answered bluntly. "It's actually going to get much worse."

"Oh, geez."

Suddenly, I wasn't sure I wanted to know anything else. Everything in my life right now, all that I was dealing with, was enough. Too much, actually. So, I didn't need anything else piling on.

"Maybe we shouldn't—"

"I did a series of internet searches using different combinations of the term black box, the symbols on it, along with the other odd things you told us about as reference criteria. What I discovered was surprising. There were numerous mentions that I believe pertain directly to your situation. After that, I went to the library to confirm my research and dig deeper, and I think I now have a good idea what's happening to you and your family."

After an elongated pause, Brodie broke the silence. "Come on, Lewis, stop being so dramatic and tell us already."

Lewis frowned at Brodie before continuing.

"The most recent incident I could find involved a mother in Ft Smith, Arkansas. Six months ago, she bludgeoned her husband to death with a pipe wrench and then turned around and drowned her three children. The oldest was seven years old, the youngest was only eleven months."

"I remember seeing that on the news," Brodie said. "It was so awful. The mother tried to drown herself also, but her sister got to her before she was successful."

"That's right. But what you probably didn't know was that after they took her into custody and interviewed her, she said the last thing she could remember before her sister pulled her out of that tub was opening a strange black box and a vague memory of finding an old book inside. Nothing else until she awoke drenched in bathwater next to her dead children. They found no trace of a black box or an old book."

Now I was sure I didn't want to hear anything else, but Lewis was determined.

"Before that, in 2009, a family in Houston died in a house fire, husband and wife with their four children. They ruled it a murder/suicide carried out by the husband, but what was strange was, shortly before it happened, the neighbors reported that the mother had been highly agitated about some sort of mysterious black box and asked questions about the house being haunted. There was nothing like a black box ever found.

"In 2008, a woman in Manchester, England, poisoned her entire family, along with a visitor. They were all found dead, sitting around the living room, sharing tea and cookies, with the couple's son and daughter lying amongst the Lincoln Logs they were building. In their home, they found a drawing that looked very similar to this."

Lewis held up the sketches he had made from the symbols on the box and pointed to the first one. It resembled the stick-figure symbol used to represent the female sex, with a single dot for an eye in the middle of the face, a half-moon swirl on top of the head like a crown, and a pair of loops for feet.

"This symbol, which I drew from Knox's box, is an ancient symbol for demon worship."

"I think I'm going to be sick," Brodie said quietly. "Can't we talk about something else?"

I felt the same, but couldn't muster the energy to agree with her. This couldn't be happening to me. Was this some sort of karma payback, punishment for all my past deeds? Wasn't I penalized enough already?

"There were even some deaths close by in Oklahoma City. In 1979, a woman stabbed her husband and son to death while they were sleeping and then slit her own throat. Days before, the husband had mentioned to someone that his wife had been obsessed with an odd box."

"I don't want to hear anymore, Lewis," Brodie said, her voice weak.

"Wait, you need to hear the *coup de grâce*. In each of these stories, the slain family had recently moved into their new homes. I've found veiled references to this box and the deaths of entire families from across the globe as far back as the 1800s."

"Stop," Brodie cried out, jumping to her feet. "Just Stop. Listen to yourselves. Are you actually saying what I think you're saying?"

"I gotta side with Brodie here. This isn't Buffy the Vampire Slayer. Demons? Really? Come on, Lewis."

"I know how all this sounds, but from everything I read and learned, I've formed a theory. There's this concept of multiple dimensions, quantum physics, and a multiverse, which is everywhere you turn these days. Comic books, movies, television, books—both fictional and nonfiction. It's everywhere. What if something we historically labeled as a demon is actually an inhabitant of one of these other dimensions? If you strip away the religious element, it doesn't sound all that crazy. So, what if the box, or maybe the book that is in the box, is a type of portal to a dimension inhabited by some sort of demon, for the lack of a better word? It targets families that have recently moved. I don't know why. But when the box is opened, the demon takes possession of that person and uses them to murder the family and then commit suicide. I think this possession took place when I saw your house go dark on Monday."

"I can't believe you," Brodie said, looking down at Lewis in complete disbelief. "You actually said it. Possession? Really?"

"It was that night when I noticed it had been opened," I agreed, almost monotone.

"Lewis, you're trying to tell us that a demon has possessed someone in Knox's family?"

Until now, I'd watched Lewis maintain a sour but serious look on his face. But now, with Brodie's question, he appeared confused and a little embarrassed. "Uhhh... well, it might actually be something from another dimension, but yeah, I guess that is what I'm saying."

"An actual fire-and-brimstone demon?" Brodie asked, her voice a couple of octaves higher now.

"Or something similar."

Brodie continued to stare at Lewis for almost a minute. Finally, she plopped back down in her bean bag and looked over at me and said, "Knox, get your family to move out of that house right now. I mean today. Then we call a priest, or go to our church and get Father Benton. Surely there's someone who can help us?"

"It may not matter," Lewis said solemnly.

"What? Why not?" Brodie answered.

Lewis lowered his head and fidgeted with the paper in his hands. "Moving out of the house won't do any good because a member of Knox's family is already possessed."

"There's something else you're not telling us, isn't there, Lewis?" I asked.

"Ummmm... the visitor who was also killed at the home in Manchester—"

"What about him?"

"He was a priest."

Brodie buried her face in her hands, and I lay back and stared at the ceiling. I was feeling lightheaded. This was one blow after another.

Brodie lifted her head and asked, "So, what do we do, Lewis?"

My admiration... and affection for Brodie were growing by leaps and bounds. This was the girl Lewis had told me about, the one who wouldn't back down. She absolutely refused to stay negative for very long or give up without a fight, and I was falling for her... hard.

"Well, we try to find out who's possessed. There wasn't a book in the box, so we have to assume whoever's been possessed hid it somewhere, so we should find it."

I sat back up. "I have a pretty good idea who it is. My stepmom, Lorna."

"Do you know how cliché that sounds? The evil stepmom?"

"Yeah, maybe, I don't know. There's just something off about her lately."

"So, we keep an eye on her. In the meantime, we find the book."

"What good will the book do us if Lorna is already possessed?" Brodie asked.

"I'm not sure, but it must be important somehow. If the book serves as some sort of portal the demon uses to move between worlds, then maybe we can use it as leverage?"

"What makes you think this book, whatever it is, is still in the house? The box disappeared. Why not the book?" I asked.

"I don't know for a fact. It's just a hunch. Besides, it's all we have right now."

I rose from my seat. "At least it's some kind of plan. Dad and Lorna are going to a school function tomorrow night, so I'll search the house from top to bottom then."

Lewis got up from his bag at the same time. "I can help."

I glanced at Brodie, whose disapproving look told me how I should answer. "I got this, Lewis. You wouldn't know where to look, anyway."

The three of us made our way up the staircase as we talked.

"But you'll need someone to be your lookout. Won't your brother and sisters be suspicious if they find you looking through everything?"

"I'll make something up."

"Come on, let me help. I can... what's the phrase... have your back. Please?"

In the kitchen, I stopped and looked at Lewis and then Brodie, whose stern look was faltering.

"Okay, I'll call you when Dad and Lorna leave."

"Yes!" Lewis said under his breath as he led us to the front door.

"I'm not sure I want you going back over there, Knox?" Brodie said.

I didn't dare show her how much I agreed with her. "Someone's gotta watch out for Travis," I said instead.

Brodie thought about that, then nodded her head.

We both said our goodbyes to Lewis and descended the porch steps to the sidewalk.

"Want me to walk you home?" I offered.

Brodie stuck her hands in her pockets. "That's okay. Without my garlic, I'm not sure I can trust you," she said with a smile, playfully bumping his hip with her own and then turning and strolling away.

A demon had possessed somebody in my family, and there I was standing on the sidewalk with a goofy smile on my face.

As I walked towards the house, my attention was drawn to a red Dodge pickup parked across the street with a man in the driver's seat looking down at something. *That's a shame*, I thought as I climbed the steps of the front porch. *The peeling paint on the hood really ruined what otherwise was a decent-looking truck.*

MOVING FEAR

Twenty-Four

Lewis

Lewis rolled over in his bed, trying not to look at the glowing digits of his clock-radio, but he couldn't help himself. Fourteen minutes past midnight, just a mere two minutes from the last time he checked. Sleep wasn't anywhere to be found, and he'd have to try something different because tossing and turning wasn't working.

He sat up and swung his legs over the edge of the bed, contemplating what he could do. There were several books he could read, or he could turn the TV back on and watch reruns of Monk, but neither option interested him. This was unusual for him. He had trained himself to be a dependable sleeper, in bed by ten with a bit of light music playing in the background, and then out like a light by ten-fifteen. Tonight, his routine was wrecked, and he knew why.

He stood up and walked to the window, bending the slat in the shade to look down at Knox's house. All the windows were dark, and everyone, no doubt, was sound asleep. Or were they? He wondered if whatever possessed someone in Knox's family slept. Then he realized why he was so restless; who could sleep when there were real live demons out there?

He briefly considered turning his Mac back on and doing some more research, but he knew it would prove useless. He was confident about the facts he relayed this afternoon, spending all day searching every place he could think of on the internet and at the library that might have a clue. Everything had been double and triple-checked. But he wanted to do more. Knox had agreed to let him help with the book search tomorrow, though that was probably just to appease him.

He finally decided that a couple of games on his PS5 would clear his mind, as it usually did, so he opened the bedroom door and made his way quietly down the stairs. He was cautious on the landing near the entrance to his mother's bedroom, even though she was most likely passed out with her nightly sleeping pill. Nothing short of a sonic boom would wake her from her slumber.

Opening the door to the basement and flipping on the light switch, he was about to descend when something caused him to pause. He felt a presence behind him, as if the air itself was breathing. The feeling you get when somebody stands right behind you but never touches you. Lewis swung around and surveyed the darkness. Nothing was there. He chastised himself for acting like a five-year-old, then turned and continued down the stairs.

He couldn't help but flinch with every creak of the staircase on his way down. Why was he creeped out all of a sudden? He had been down these stairs hundreds of times, night and day, and he had never felt like this. The room he was descending into was well lit, as it always was, so why did the shadows seem so much deeper tonight?

In the basement, he grabbed his controller and the universal remote, then dropped into his customary beanbag centered in front of the big screen. Using the remote, he turned on the TV, switched it to the HDMI input, then used his controller to power on his PS5.

As the game system whirred to life, Lewis cursed under his breath. He meant to grab a drink before settling in. Rolling off the beanbag, he crawled on his hands and knees to the small refrigerator in the corner. Opening the door, he found it empty. Cursing again, he got to his feet and silently climbed back up the stairs into the kitchen. He grabbed a bottle of water from the large refrigerator, turned around, and then froze.

The basement lights were off.

Confusion swept through his brain, leaving him feeling momentarily disoriented. Did he turn them off as a force of habit when he came up? He honestly couldn't remember. Walking closer, he could see the glow of the TV from the top of the stairs. *You must have turned them off*, he told himself. He flipped the switch again and headed downstairs.

Back in his beanbag, his drink on the plastic milk carton he used as an end table, Lewis signed into the account he used when not playing online and activated the Call of Duty disc already in the tray. A couple of rounds of killing zombies should do the trick.

The game logo had just faded from his screen when a metal clanking startled him. If he didn't know any better, he'd say it sounded like the sound the back gate made when it slammed shut, but his mom kept that gate locked because of the pool, and who would be up and around at this time of night anyway... besides him, of course.

Seconds later, there was another sound, again from the back of the house, but this time it sounded like a splash. The pool was twenty feet from the house, but underground acoustics meant they could hear any activity in the pool, albeit muffled, in the basement. What Lewis heard now was definitely splashing.

Lewis rose out of the beanbag, then halted. A muted cry for help had joined the splashing sound.

Letting the controller drop to the ground, Lewis dashed up the stairs to the back door. He tugged on the doorknob, but it didn't budge. Locked. His fingers fumbled with the deadbolt and sliding chain guard. The gurgled cries for help grew louder. As the chain dropped free, he hit the switch that activated both the flood and pool lights. Then he was out the door.

Racing across the back patio, he could see somebody in the center of the pool. Whoever it was, they were struggling mightily, thrashing their arms against the water to stay afloat. And they weren't doing a very good job of it. The person's head was above the surface of the water just long enough for them to exhale and inhale, then it disappeared again.

Ignoring the steps, Lewis jumped down onto the wooden-planked walkway to the stone pool deck. As he drew closer, he could make out that the person in trouble was a kid smaller than him, wearing a white t-shirt, and only using his arms to keep his head above water.

The realization hit him like a load of bricks. "TRAVIS!" he called out.

Even though Lewis couldn't swim, he still had to fight the urge to jump in. He remembered something from a book his mother had given him just after they installed the pool, a passage about people in trouble and what you should do to help them. He quickly scanned the area around the pool. *Where is it? Where is it?* He had only been out here one time since his mother christened the pool, and he couldn't remember where she stored everything. His friend's little brother was going to drown right in front of him because he couldn't remember where the damn accessories were.

Then, there it was, hanging from the privacy fence that ran alongside the pool. Lewis was there in no time and slid the aluminum life hook off its holder. Turning towards the pool, he extended the double crook tip until it was in front of Travis's flailing arms. Lewis pushed it closer as Travis stretched to reach it.

"Hang on, Travis. I got you."

When Travis finally made contact, he frantically latched on with both arms. The tug almost pulled Lewis into the pool. He struggled to keep control, choosing to wait a minute to pull the boy to the side until he had calmed down.

Travis was relaxing when Lewis had a thought. He twisted his body as far as he could to look behind him. *Whoever had thrown Travis into the pool could still be there.*

Suddenly, the back gate flew open, causing Lewis to jump, and Knox came rushing in. His friend was barefoot, wearing a Nike T-shirt and black running shorts. Knox dove into the pool and helped steady Travis as Lewis steadily pulled him to the side.

After they had lifted Travis from the pool, he lay beside Knox on the pool deck, coughing heavily. Lewis sat down next to them.

His mother's voice came from the back door. "Lewis, what are you doing out here?" Lewis looked to see her standing there in a yellow robe and shielding her eyes from the bright lights.

"Swimming," he answered.

"Who's that with you?"

"Knox, from next door."

"Okay. I'm happy you're finally taking an interest in the pool, but it's kind of late. I'm afraid your friend will need to go home."

"Okay, Mom."

With that, the backdoor closed, and they were left alone.

"What the hell, Travis?" Knox blurted out. "How did you get into Lewis's pool?"

Travis coughed one more time and propped himself up on his elbows. "I don't know. I was asleep in bed, and I think I kinda remember somebody picking me up, but I couldn't fully wake up. It was like a dream. Then I was in the pool... drowning. Lewis saved me."

"I heard the splashing and found Travis already in the pool. I didn't see who threw him in."

"How did you know I was here?" Travis asked Knox.

"I couldn't sleep, so I went out to the living room to watch TV. I guess I must have drifted off, but then something woke me up. When I came back to our room, I saw your bed was empty, but your wheelchair was still beside it. Then I saw these pool lights come on from our window, and I knew something strange had to be going down over here."

Travis looked at Lewis, then back at his brother. Lewis thought he might cry at any moment. "Does this have anything to do with our shaking beds and the books?"

Knox looked at Lewis before answering. "I think so, Travis. I've got some things to tell you, but first, we need to get you back home."

"You need some help?" Lewis offered.

"Nah... I got him," Knox said as he got to his feet and easily lifted his brother into his arms.

"See you at school tomorrow?" Lewis asked as the two brothers turned to leave.

"Sure thing," Knox answered, then stopped to face him. "Thank you, Lewis."

"Let's not do it again soon."

Knox smiled, and Lewis watched him leave with his brother through the back gate.

Twenty-Five

Knox

I woke up the next morning... if you could call it waking up, because I had slept very little... to the sound of my cell phone chirping. I picked it up, thinking it would be Lewis. Besides my family, he was the only person who ever called or texted.

"Hello?"

"Lewis doesn't know about my mom and his dad," Brodie said, skipping any formal greeting. "So, I would really appreciate it if you'd please keep that to yourself."

I turned onto my other side, facing away from Travis.

"Where is your mom now?"

"She lives somewhere in Texas. I'm not exactly sure where. It's just my dad and me now, and I like it that way."

"So, for some reason you feel responsible for what your mom did, and that's why you watch out for Lewis?"

"Listen, it's a long story, and maybe I'll tell it to you someday, but for right now, I just wanted to make sure you keep it between us."

"Sure, but you know—"

"Promise me."

"I promise."

Brodie hung up before I could say anything else.

I laid there and allowed my mind to drift. Normal was taking on a new definition. I used to tell myself that life got real when mom died and turned surreal after Travis's accident, but that almost seemed trivial now. My worries about ripples of guilt seemed so insignificant compared to what I was currently facing. My family was under attack, from within, and today's normal meant there were demons, the supernatural, and a girl I really liked who was asking me to keep secrets.

All that, and I had a project due in two weeks.

After the events of the last three days, the assignment in Language Arts Class with Lewis and Brodie seemed irrelevant. In fact, so was school altogether. A demon tried to kill my brother last night and had designs to murder my entire family, so the least of my concerns was whether my GPA was 3.0 or 0.0.

Travis took the news about the black box and what was going on in our house better than I expected. He was more upset knowing someone in the family had murdered Bowzer than he was about being thrown into a pool. We stayed up the most of the night, speaking in whispers, coming up with different theories about who it might be. We both concluded that Lorna was our prime suspect. The first clue was her complete change of attitude toward the box. Then I saw her in the kitchen the night our beds went all magic fingers on us, and she was acting very odd when Brodie had the accident during archery practice. Of course, we still had plenty of doubt, but it was a start. The thing is, what could we do about it?

As hard as it was to do, we both decided getting expelled from school wasn't a good idea. Apart from the obvious reason, it might tip off the demon that we suspected what was going on, so we needed to soldier on like nothing was happening. We both would continue to go to classes and turn in our assignments like everyone else. Besides, Lorna worked at the high school, and that meant when I wasn't in class, I could keep an eye on her. We got ready for school that morning, just like any other.

Everyone in our family was under my intense scrutiny now, and I could tell Travis was doing the same. We were looking for any clue, a sign that a demon was hiding behind a smiling face. It was surprising how many little things seemed so nefarious when you looked at them with a different frame of mind. False smiles, grimaces, frowns, eyes that seemed to linger just a little too long, all gave off signals that could be interpreted in different ways. And this morning, everyone was transmitting like crazy.

On the drive to school, I sat and stared out the window at the arctic blue sky marked only by the billowy jet stream of a passing airliner. *How could things like this be happening on a beautiful day?*

Before today, I never had a reason to care where the nurse's office was at any of my schools. I was never ill or suffered an injury that called for a visit, and even though Lorna always invited my brother and me to wait in her office after school, we both felt it was better to hang out outside. Today, the first thing I did when we got to school, instead of hanging out in the commons area waiting for the bell to ring, was follow my stepmom and find out where she worked.

It turned out that the nurse's station was located right next door to the main office, with a door between them and another door accessible from the hallway. From the brief glimpse I took when I strolled by, I could see a bland, compact room with a small desk in the middle and a cot in the back—nothing like the doctor's examination room I'd imagined.

During the day, between classes, I walked by her office whenever I was on that side of the building. I often found her sitting at her desk, doing paperwork. *Who knew a school nurse's job could be so dull?* But one time I did see Lindsey in there talking with her. Curious. Did either of my sisters regularly visit our stepmom during school? I didn't know that, and I wondered what else I didn't know about my family members.

At lunch with Lewis and Brodie, no one said much. Lewis and I agreed via text messages beforehand that we wouldn't tell Brodie about what happened in the pool with Travis. It felt wrong not telling her, but doing so could lead her to having a total freak out, which we couldn't afford right now. Lewis made me promise, at least a half a dozen times while we ate, that I would call him when my dad and Lorna were out of the house so we could search the house for the book.

In Language Arts class, no one waited for Mrs. Allen's instructions to form into groups because Thursday was project day. Brodie, Lewis, and I arrived together and joined with everyone else in moving chairs. We placed ours in a circle at the back of the room. Tug showed up a couple of minutes later and decided not to make an issue of where he sat, but he still had to make a scene by noisily dragging a chair over to complete our ring. Today he was sporting an unbuttoned and untucked Chicago Cubs baseball jersey with a matching cap turned backward on his head.

"Mr. Dempsey, if you would please remove the hat," Mrs. Allen requested, making it sound more like a command. Tug whipped the hat from his head as if he forgot it was there and threw it underneath his chair.

After the bell sounded and Mrs. Allen gave the directive to get started, Brodie took control once again.

"Has anybody thought of a story we can use for Friday Fright Theater?"

I knew better than to look up from my desk because Brodie's disappointed eyes would be waiting for me. Lewis and Tug matched my silence, so I wasn't the only one lacking ideas. For a moment, I worried Lewis would make a suggestion about writing a story revolving around a possessed box. I hated to admit it might be the only way we could ensure that story could have a happy ending.

"Fine. Then let's brainstorm something and see what we can come up with. Let's start by determining a setting. Somewhere creepy to create a mood."

I had a thought. "I was up late last night because I couldn't sleep, and there was this old movie on. It was the original zombie movie, Night of the Living Dead."

"We are not doing zombies," Brodie told everyone, emphasizing her point by tapping her pen on the desk.

"No, I didn't mean zombies," I explained. "At the beginning of the movie, there's this scene in an old cemetery when the first zombie shows up. It was daytime, but it was still really creepy. How's that for a setting?"

"That's a good start. I like it."

"Man, I hate cemeteries," Tug spoke up, pushing his long hair behind his ears. "I've only been to one funeral. It was when my grandmother died, but that place gave me the creeps. Something about walking around all those dead people."

"What about you, Lewis?" Brodie asked. "What do you think about cemeteries?"

When Lewis didn't answer right away, I turned my head to look at him.

"Rain," Lewis finally answered softly, a faraway look on his face.

"Rain?" Tug repeated.

"I think I was ten or eleven. I had only been back living with my mom for less than a year, and we were still getting used to each other again. It was a Saturday morning, early. The sun wasn't up yet, but I remember hearing the rain coming down really hard. Mom pulled me out of bed and told me I had to hurry and put on my clothes, which was hard because she didn't turn on the lights, and I couldn't see what I was doing. I didn't even get my second shoe on before she grabbed me and put me in the seat beside her in the car.

"We drove for a long, long time… neither of us saying a word and no radio. Just the sound of the road, the rain, and the wiper blades flipping back and forth. I thought about asking her where we were going, but I could tell she didn't really want to talk. When we finally pulled over, it was in front of this small cemetery next to this old white church out in the middle of nowhere. It was midday by then, but it was still dark because of the rain and clouds.

"Mom told me she would be right back. Then she climbed out of the car, and I watched as she walked over to the cemetery. She began reading the headstones one by one. Finally, she found the one she was looking for in the corner of the very front row, and she just stood there in front of it. It had to be close to an hour. I watched her get soaked by the pouring rain while she stared at that stupid gravestone."

Until then, Lewis appeared as if he was telling his story in a trance, but then he blinked his eyes once and looked at Brodie.

"I found out later that it was my dad's grave we went to. He had been dead for about six months, but we didn't go to the funeral. When my mom finally came back to the car, she was soaking wet and shivering, but she still wasn't saying anything. We sat there for another thirty minutes, my mother unable to take her eyes off the gravesite until she finally turned to me. I remember her eyes. They were so sad. Eventually, she noticed my missing shoe, and that's when something in her changed. She started the engine, put it in drive, and stomped on the gas pedal. The car jumped a small curb, barely missed a tree, then plowed right over the top of my dad's headstone. She never slowed down or looked back, just steered the car back to the road, and we headed home."

Nobody said anything. I think everyone was like me… both stunned and feeling sorry for Lewis at the same time.

"I've never told anyone about that. Neither my mom nor I has ever said anything."

"I'm so sorry, Lewis," Brodie said softly.

"You want to know what the ironic part is?" Lewis continued, looking at all of us now. "My dad was killed by a hit-and-run driver."

Tug snorted, his hand flying to his mouth, struggling to contain his laughter. The look of horror on Brodie's face at Tug's apparent unfeeling response softened when we heard Lewis giggle.

Then I couldn't help but laugh myself. Maybe I was releasing the tension brought on from the last twenty-four hours, or perhaps it was just the fact that Lewis's father, a despicable man, got what he deserved... twice. Whatever it was, I laughed like I hadn't for a very long time. Soon, all of us were laughing so hard we had to gasp for air while holding onto our sides. The kids from other groups all looked in our direction.

Brodie stopped laughing long enough to squeak out, "I told you Lewis's mom was a terrible driver," which elicited another wave of laughter.

When I realized Mrs. Allen was standing beside us, I tried to stifle my laughter.

"Please tell me that your group's topic is something comical."

Brodie composed herself first. "Actually, it's horror," she answered, which brought another round of laughter from the four of us.

Mrs. Allen continued standing there, watching us all laugh, amusement in her eyes. It wasn't long before her hovering over us became the reason for the hilarity itself, and the laughter increased in volume. Finally, the teacher shook her head and wandered over to another group.

It took a couple of minutes, but eventually, the laughing subsided into chuckles, and then was gone altogether.

When it did, Lewis turned to look at Tug. "I'm sorry your grandmother died."

The long-haired jock looked at Lewis for a moment before replying, "It was a long time ago."

MOVING FEAR

There was a softness in Tug's eyes I hadn't seen before.

Twenty-Six

Knox

"What took you so long to call me?" Lewis said when he strolled in.

I closed the front door behind him, using my eyes to gesture towards the living room where my brother and Jadie were watching television. I led Lewis into the bedroom.

"I had to wait until Lindsey left," I said. "She had to go somewhere but wouldn't say where, so I waited until she was gone. Travis knows what's going on, so he'll help keep Jadie occupied."

Lewis sat down in the desk chair. "Where do you want to start?"

"Upstairs. I'm thinking this demon, or whatever it is, would need to keep a watchful eye on the book at night, so it'd be close. I want to start in my sisters' room first to rule them out, then my dad and Lorna's room. Oh... there's also a storage closet up there, and that's actually the easiest because it's secluded at the end of the hall down from the girls' room, so I guess we'll start there."

"Okay, lead the way."

I walked out of the room with Lewis close behind me, making sure we kept to the left side of the hall that was hidden from view from the living room. We were at the base of the stairs when Jadie called out to me.

"Knox, we're not supposed to have friends over when Dad and Lorna aren't here."

I looked back at Lewis when I answered. "He won't be here for long. We're just going to brainstorm a couple of ideas for our project, but we're getting a drink first."

When there was no response, the two of us tiptoed up to the second floor.

The storage closet was all the way at the end of the hallway. I paused at the top step, making sure nobody was moving down below, then continued down the hallway. I pulled open the closet door and yanked the string hanging from the ceiling. The room filled with harsh light from the bare incandescent bulb, illuminating the six-foot-wide and ten-foot-deep room and casting a bright glare on a jumble of cardboard boxes and plastic bins.

"Keep an eye on the top of the stairs and signal if Jadie comes up," I said to Lewis before entering.

Working quickly, I opened each box and bin to look inside. I emptied a couple to make sure there wasn't anything buried beneath the layers. I had just about finished when I came upon a box with a single name written across the side. CRYSTAL. It was the box holding many of my mother's possessions, most of which would someday become Lindsey's or Jadie's. I put it aside and saved it for last.

After going through all the other cartons and finding nothing, I returned to my mom's. I hesitated before opening it. Whatever possessed Lorna would have to be genuinely monstrous to have hidden the book in this box. An ache in my heart grew as I thought about the memories attached to the contents inside. I took a deep breath, then tore open the top and looked inside.

There was nothing unusual. Just a collection of pictures, treasured knick-knacks, jewelry and other miscellaneous items. I hurriedly put the lid back in place.

Putting everything back in the shape I found it, I pulled the light string and closed the door.

"Nada," I informed Lewis, who was biting his nails. We moved back down the hall towards the bedrooms.

As we were about to open my sister's bedroom door, Lewis sneezed. The two of us turned into statues, Lewis with both of his hands covering his nose and mouth. We listened for sounds from downstairs that might suggest Jadie had heard Lewis's slip, but all I could hear were muffled sounds from the television. I gave Lewis a you-got-to-be-kidding-me look, which he answered with a sheepish grin. I turned the knob on my sister's bedroom door, and we both slipped inside.

My sisters' room was surprisingly messy, worse than mine. As the oldest, they usually got rooms to themselves, but obviously sharing a room now wasn't as easy for them. Their double beds, each with a wicker basket at the base with clothing piled on top, were against the left-hand wall. There was a simple bedside table and lamp between the beds, but the desk on the opposite wall, close to the window, seemed organized.

"Check under the beds. I'll get the closet," I instructed Lewis as I opened the closet door.

The closet didn't take very long, with no large boxes inside, just clothes and shoes. I didn't find anything.

"Nothing under the beds," Lewis said when I emerged.

"There's a storage compartment under the window seat," I pointed out to him. "It lifts up."

The comfort seat built into the bay window at the end of the room held even more clothes and a tennis racket. Lewis walked over to the window, delicately moved a handful of clothes, which included at least one bra, then lifted the seat. He looked back at me and shook his head, then let the seat drop and replaced the clothes.

"Dad and Lorna's room next," I said, but then stopped short.

Someone had hastily yanked the comforters up over the pillows without straightening the sheets underneath, a half-hearted attempt to make both beds presentable. It was something else that drew my attention.

In the middle of each bed, underneath the lavender comforters, I could see a small raised bump.

I wasn't sure why that interested me so much. Seeing how my sisters kept their room, they'd probably covered up some of their clothes in a hurry. But in the same spot, and the same size, on both beds?

I stepped over to the nearest bed and tossed back the comforter. I immediately wished I hadn't.

Lying in a small heap on the sheets was Bowzer's dirt-covered body—or at least half of it.

Lewis must have seen the look on my face because he came to my side, looking at the bed. Both his hands flew to his mouth.

"That's probably the other half," I whispered, tilting my head towards the other bed.

"I think I might throw up," Lewis gagged.

"Don't you dare, not in here. Take some deep breaths or something."

After a few seconds, Lewis lowered his hands low enough to say, "Somebody dug him up and cut him in half?"

"More like ripped in half," I observed. I poked him with my elbow and pointed to something at his feet. "Hand me that plastic bag."

Lewis bent down and grabbed the wrinkled Glad bag on the floor between the beds, and handed it to me. I opened it up, tentatively picked up Bowzer's mangled body with my thumb and index finger, and dropped it in the bag.

"Get the other half," I whispered.

Lewis shook his head and stepped back.

I shot him a frown and went over to the other bed, pulled back the comforter, and picked up the bottom half of the ferret. After I deposited it in the bag as well, I gave it a twirl to close the top. I swept away the loose dirt still remaining on both sets of sheets and replaced the comforters.

"Let's go."

Closing the door behind us on the way out, we stepped down the hall, past the stairs to the last door on the right. I led us into my parents' room, flipped on a pair of switches that controlled the overhead fan and its attached light fixture, then closed the door after Lewis was inside.

This was the first time I had been in this room since moving day, and it was just as crowded as I thought it might be. Their king-size four-poster bed dominated the room, with one post less than an inch from the rotating blades above. There was barely enough space to make your way alongside the bed to the three-drawer dressing tables on either side. At the front of the room sat a five-drawer bureau next to the closet door. An antique make-up table sitting on the other side of the closet left very little room for navigation.

"You check the dresser and the make-up table. This time I'll take under the bed," I instructed.

The bed was up off the floor two feet, and various Rubbermaid storage boxes and pieces of luggage had been shoved underneath. I placed the plastic bag with Bowzer's remains on the floor just inside the door, dropped to my knees, and pulled out the closest box. It was full of Lorna's off-season sweaters. The next box held a collection of woman's shoes. I slid a small travel bag out of the way to get to the next box, pausing to check on Lewis's progress.

"Hey, be careful how you handle that," I said when noticing how rough he was with the clothes.

I turned back to the box, but I had second thoughts and focused on the travel bag I'd moved aside instead. It was Lorna's bag and one of those small enough to carry on the airplane when she flew. I pulled it back in front of me and unzipped it. When I did, the bag fell open and I knew we had found what we were looking for.

"Lewis."

My friend looked up from what he was doing, then moved to my side.

The book was black, just like the box it came from, so black that it seemed to absorb all the surrounding colors. It was almost as if there was a black hole to infinity resting inside the travel bag. The same markings on the box also coated the book. On its surface were five circles, four in each corner and one in the middle, with the stick figure that Lewis had sketched featured prominently in its center. Its binding was composed of a thick leather material, which my imagination told me was similar in consistency to aged human skin.

"Did it just turn freezing in here?" Lewis asked, looking over my shoulder.

It had, I thought. I also found it hard to breathe.

Lewis dropped to his knees beside me.

"Open it," Lewis said.

I hesitated. "You think I should? What if I get possessed?"

The last time I saw a look similar to the one Lewis was giving me, I think my dad was trying to convince me there were no monsters under my bed.

"You think this is a multi-occupancy demon portal? Here, let me do it," Lewis said.

"No, I got it."

I reached down and picked up the book. It felt heavier than it appeared, and when I lifted it, a wave of intense nausea swept over me. It took several deep breaths to fight back the urge to vomit, but after I did, I opened the cover of the book.

Inside the opening page was a faded and mottled piece of old parchment. On it were four columns of handwritten script, composed of various symbols and languages I had never seen before. Flipping through the book, it seemed to contain nothing but these uneven parchment pages, all with tattered edges and torn-away pieces. The pages felt fragile to the touch, almost to the point they might crumble into tiny pieces.

Lewis adjusted his glasses as he looked closer.

"Turn to the last page," he instructed me.

I did as I was told, taking care as I did so. The last page contained only two columns of writing, and I could read most of it.

"These are names," I said to Lewis.

"I know. Look at the last group of four."

I focused on the names. "What about them?"

"Remember the family in Arkansas last year, the mother who killed her husband and drowned her children? Those are their names."

"Are you sure?"

"Clear as day. That's their names. And I think some of those names in the different handwriting might also be some of the other names I read about."

"Jesus."

"Hey, at least your name isn't in there yet."

It was at that moment that a loud creaking noise came from right outside the room. Then another. Someone was coming up the stairs.

Lewis froze in shock. I placed my forefinger against my mouth, then slowly put the book back into the travel bag. I shuffled on all fours over to the door and peered under the lip into the hallway. Through the quarter-inch gap, I could make out a pair of feet. They were obviously Jadie's from the purple and green striped socks, and they had just topped the stairs and were turning down the hall towards the girls' bedroom.

I lay on my side and held my hand up towards Lewis, signaling for him to remain still. He nodded his agreement. I returned to my spying position, and I didn't have to wait long until Jadie's feet returned.

But they didn't go downstairs.

Instead, they paused at the head of the stairs, then continued up the hall towards my parents' bedroom... and us. Her feet stopped outside the door. The hairs on the back of my neck rose. I tried to think of an explanation for being in our parent's room if she opened the door, but I was coming up empty.

The feet remained there for what seemed like an eternity, unmoving. Abruptly, they swiveled around and walked away, back down the stairs and out of sight.

I let out the breath I had been holding and rolled onto my back.

I sat up and smiled at Lewis. "That was close."

Lewis didn't reply. He sat back on his heels and wiped his forehead.

"Now that we found it, what should we do with it?" I asked.

"I think we should get it out of your house. I can take it to my house, then tomorrow take it to school and put it in my locker. That should keep it safe."

"Good idea," I said. I zipped up Lorna's travel bag and returned everything underneath the bed the way I found it, then picked up the book and rose to my feet.

"Let's go."

We slipped silently out of the bedroom, grabbing the plastic bag as we did. Creeping down the stairs, I held the book against the right side of my body, blocking any view from the living room as we passed by, straight out the front door onto the porch.

I paused while I watched Lewis pull the door shut. "I'm not so sure taking this to your house is a good idea, Lewis."

"What else are we going to do with it?"

"I have another idea. Maybe we should just take it down to the park and burn it."

"I wouldn't do that, boys," came a voice from the shadows.

I instinctively took a step backward and almost dropped the book. Lewis took refuge behind me.

A man with long white hair stepped out of the darkness.

"You need to put that back right now," the stranger said, "or else you're all going to die."

MOVING FEAR

Twenty-Seven

Knox

"I mean it," said the man with the flowing white hair. "You need to put that back right now."

I clutched the book tighter to my chest. "Who are you?"

I estimated the man was in his mid-forties, but fit. The long-sleeve flannel work shirt he wore buttoned all the way to the top of the neck couldn't hide his impressive build. Even though he was standing at the bottom of the steps, I could tell he was a good four inches taller than I was. His hair fanned out across his shoulders, and by the oily look of it, it needed a shampoo. The faded blue jeans with dark stains around both pockets and scuffed-up brown work boots rounded out his grizzled blue-collar look, which was solidified by his gray stubble.

"Name's Wilfred. You need to return that to where you found it, or else we're all going to regret it."

Lewis cleared his voice and asked over my shoulder, "Put what back?"

The man we just learned was named Wilfred frowned. "Let's not play games, boys. Put THE BOOK back."

"How do you know about the book?"

The stranger climbed a step, and Lewis and I moved backward in unison.

"We don't have time for twenty questions right now, boys. I'll answer everything for you after you put the book back," Wilfred said, emphasizing the last words.

I turned to look at Lewis, who answered my unasked question with a shake of his head. I considered this for a moment, then handed him the plastic bag with Bowzer's remains.

"We have to," I said before opening the door and stepping back into the house.

My brother gave me a confused look as I re-entered the foyer, but I continued up the stairs and returned the book to where we found it. I heard my brother call me on my way back to the front door.

"Knox, who are you talking to out there?"

"Just somebody taking a poll," I answered, then was out the door.

Lewis and the stranger were still where I left them, although Lewis had put a little more distance between them.

"Okay, now time to answer some questions," I said.

The white-haired man put his hands on his hips. "What's in the plastic bag?"

I took the bag back from Lewis. "You need to answer our questions first."

The man shrugged his shoulders, turned, and took a couple of steps until he realized that Lewis and I weren't following him.

"Not here. My truck is just down the street," the man said, then continued.

We stood there for a moment, then I started to follow. Lewis didn't move.

"Where are you going?" Lewis called after me.

I stopped at the bottom of the steps and looked back at him. "He has answers, Lewis. We have to follow him."

"But we don't know him at all. He could have a machete or something worse in that truck."

I had to suppress a smile. "We don't have many options. We are flying blind here, and this guy seems to know what's going on."

Lewis rocked back and forth, both of his hands running through his curly hair. "I don't know."

I glanced at the white-haired stranger who was still casually making his way down the sidewalk, then back to Lewis. "Please, Lewis. I need you." And I meant it.

Lewis's movement stopped, and his back stiffened. Suddenly, he pulled something out of his pocket and handed it to me, then stepped off the porch and walked away quickly.

"Before I forget. And just so you know, I don't think this is a very good idea," Lewis said as he passed by.

I looked at the pocket watch Lewis had handed me.

"You stole my dad's watch?"

I jammed the watch into my pocket, and then jogged to catch up with Lewis. We followed the man to a red pickup —the same one I had noticed the other day, with peeled paint on the hood —parked under a streetlight two houses down from mine. He opened the driver's side door, pulled out a duffel bag, and tossed it into the bed of the truck, then climbed in behind the wheel. I walked around to the other side and opened the door so that Lewis could enter first. Lewis hesitated, shaking his head vigorously, so I scrambled inside. Lewis finally followed me in, closing the door behind him.

The inside of the truck was dimly lit from the streetlight, but I could see that it was a mess. There was a bundle of road maps shoved up against the windshield on the dashboard, various fast-food wrappers scattered across the floorboard, and empty Red Man chewing tobacco packages strewn across the seat. The cup holder on the driver's door contained a mason jar half full of dark sludge. The smell inside the cab was worse than the boy's locker room at school.

"What did you say your name was again?" I asked.

"Wilfred. Wilfred Pennington. I'm here to help."

Lewis pulled a package of Slim Jims out from under him and tossed it on the floor.

"Help with what, exactly?" Lewis asked.

Wilfred turned in his seat, resting the crook of his arm on the steering wheel.

"You recently moved into your home, right? Then a black box appeared out of nowhere. You've seen some pretty strange things since then, and now the box has disappeared. How am I doing so far?"

Neither Lewis nor I said a thing. I didn't know about Lewis, but I was both in shock and excited at the same time.

"I saw you with the book on the porch and heard you talking about burning it, so I assumed you've figured out part of what's going on, and you're trying to do something about it."

"Part of what's going on?" I repeated.

"A demon has possessed someone in your family," Wilfred answered matter-of-factly.

"I was right." Lewis blurted out, slapping his hand on the car seat.

"We think it's my stepmom," I said, unable to prevent the words from spilling out of my mouth. "We're pretty sure she's the one possessed. What can we do about it?"

Wilfred seemed to think about this for a moment and then shook his head. "Sorry to break it to you, young man, but it's not in your stepmom."

I was stunned. "What? Why not? How can you be so sure?"

The man turned his head and seemed to scan the street. "Because last night I was watching your house when I saw a girl, not much older than you, carry the boy who uses the wheelchair to the house next door. From what I could see, I'm guessing she threw the boy in the pool? To me, that's something the demon would do."

I straightened in my seat and turned to face the white-haired man. For the first time, I noticed there was something odd about the man's tongue. I brushed that thought aside as a trick of the light.

"She's my sister, and my brother's an invalid! Why didn't you stop her?"

"Listen, I didn't know what was happening. By the time I figured out something fishy was going on, you seemed to have everything under control."

"Where are you from, and how did you find us? And why is it you know all this?"

Wilfred shook his head. "Huh-uh, the real question is—how do you? The way this usually happens is, the children are pretty much clueless until it's too late. Why is it that the two of you know so much?"

"First off, we're not children. Second, the box first showed up in my room. Lewis lives next door, and he's a friend, so he helped me figure everything out by searching the internet and going to the library. That's how we knew about the book."

"The box appeared in your room?"

"That's what I said."

Wilfred brought a hand to his face and stroked the stubble on his chin. "That's odd. It's always appeared in the parents' room before."

"You never answered my question—how do you know all this? How long has this been going on?"

The man looked to his side-view mirror, then returned his attention to us. "This has been happening as far back as recorded history, and probably before. I know about it because—I'm supposed to."

"What's that mean?" I asked.

"Ever since my eighteenth birthday, I've been having visions that are connected to the box and book. Every time the book possesses a new soul, I get a vision. I'm supposed to do whatever I can to help."

"How often do these possessions happen?"

Wilfred shook his head. "There's been three in one year, then gone five years before another one. There is no pattern."

"What are they like? Your visions?" Lewis asked.

"I can tell you this—they're not pleasant. For a short period, during the time the demon is fighting for control of the person it's possessing, I can see out of the victim's eyes. I see what they see. That's my only clue to locate where they might be, so I try to remember everything I can, no matter how small the detail. My challenge, if you can call it that, is to locate the family in danger and get them to safety before it's too late."

"That can't be a lot to go on."

"Like I said, sometimes it's just the small things. Hints from the mail lying around the room with an address on it, the weather outside, what's playing on the television, school logos, anything that will help me find them."

"And how many times have you been successful?"

"You're only the third family I've found in time. But you have to understand — many of my visions are from possessed family members on the far side of the world, so there is really no hope for them."

"The entire world?" Lewis sounded shocked.

"Why do you sound so surprised? The globe is this demon's playground, and no one is safe. I've structured my life to remain as mobile as possible, so I can give chase when I need to, but unfortunately, my efforts aren't usually successful."

"When did you realize what your visions meant?" Lewis asked.

"Oh, I knew right away. My father told me about them."

"Your father?"

"Yes. Before me, he had the visions, and his father before him. It runs in our family."

"You're a family of demon hunters?"

Wilfred smiled. "Something like that. Everything I know has been passed down to me through the generations."

"What do the names in the book mean?" Lewis interjected.

Wilfred shifted his weight, his attention heightened. "You looked inside the book?"

"You haven't?"

"The first time I've seen the book was tonight, on your porch. Tell me, what did it contain?"

"Nothing but names. Page after page of names."

The man considered this, nodding his head slowly.

"Can you tell us what we're up against? What does this demon want? My sister might act a little weird, but nothing like Linda Blair."

"Who?"

"The girl from the Exorcist. I guess you don't watch many movies?"

"This isn't Hollywood, kid. It's something far, far worse. Real demons, the oldest tortured angels, are ancient, savvy, and devious. They love to lie and play tricks. Although their goal is to decimate your family, think of it more like a cat with a mouse. It enjoys playing with its food before killing it. It will instill fear in your home, feeding off it like a bear after honey, and when it gets bored, kill everyone and move on. That's what it does. That's all it does. At the very end, that's when you might see your Linda Blair."

"Does the demon have a name?"

Wilfred sniffed, then pinched his nose. "One of the symbols on the box translates into the Hebrew word seraph, which means 'to burn'. There's a demon called Seraphim that originated in ancient Judaism, so I've taken to referring to it by that name."

"Hold on. I know that name from church. Seraphim isn't a demon. It's supposedly one of the six-winged angels standing in the presence of God," Lewis said.

Wilfred grinned. "Right you are. But like I said, demons like to play tricks, kid."

"But why families who have just moved? Why us?"

"Our family had a theory. Do you realize how stressful moving is? It's right up there with a death in the family and divorce. Families in transition are off-kilter, more likely to accept the introduction of a strange object like the box, and more likely to open it out of curiosity. It's as good of a theory as I've heard."

"So, how do we get this thing out of my sister and kill it, or vanquish it, or do whatever you do to demons?"

Wilfred closed his eyes for a moment, and when opened them again, they were softer. "Son, maybe you misunderstood me. The best we can hope for is to get you and the rest of your family away from its clutches. That's all I've ever been able to do. I'm afraid your sister is lost."

"What?"

"Seraphim will only return to the book after it finishes with your family and the possessed person is dead. If you destroy the book before the demon has finished, it will trap Seraphim in the host without a portal back to where it came from, forever. So, if it thinks you've found the book or if it feels threatened in any way, it will forgo the games and slaughter your family like a pissed-off grizzly shreddin' some rabbits. It's why I couldn't let the two of you take the book out of the house."

My body went numb. This stranger had just given my sister a death sentence, and it felt like someone was sucking every ounce of feeling out of me. The numb feeling turned into a feverish heat, followed by a tingling all over my body. I had heard of the seven stages of grief, and I think my body was attempting to experience them all at once.

"What you're telling us is that all you can do to help is damage control? There's no way to beat this thing?"

"I'm sympathetic, son. I really am. But you don't understand what I'm up against. If you destroy the book while Seraphim is still possessing its victim, the demon will remain trapped inside that person. It will then certainly kill everyone in the family and then vanish. However, when the host dies, there is a narrow sliver of time after the demon returns to the book before the portal disappears again, and that's when it has to be destroyed. But that would also mean I'd have to stand by and watch that person die. There's just no way to save the person it inhabits."

"What about the box?"

"The box is of no concern. Until recently, I thought the box was the key, but now I'm certain it's just a way to deliver the book and for Seraphim to choose its host. It's the book we need to focus on."

"What would happen if we destroyed the book before the demon could return, and then the host died? What would happen to *Seraphim*, then?" I asked.

"Demons cannot exist in their true form in our world. That is why they must use hosts, but to answer your question... I don't know."

"What about the church? Can't they help? What about an exorcism?"

Wilfred shook his head. "It won't work. Demons have been here for eons, but they're not all the same. Most are simply a nuisance. Others are more determined. The church... organized religion... knows about them and has for a very long time. Exorcisms have been successful in some rare cases. But Seraphim is too powerful, and the church knows it, so they've buried their heads in the sand and do nothing. They won't come anywhere near this."

"So, what you're telling me is we're on our own?"

"What I'm trying to get across to you is that the only people who can even try to deal with this demon... are us. There is no cavalry coming to the rescue. And even if there were, your house would be considered the Alamo."

MOVING FEAR

Twenty-Eight

Knox

"Wilfred, the demon hunter? Really?" Brodie said, not bothering to mask the sarcasm in her tone. "Please tell me you're joking."

Girls at the adjacent lunchroom table looked over at us. I flashed a brief smile and then shot Brodie a *'keep it down'* face. I anticipated this type of response from her, which was why I instructed Lewis not to fill her in on the details until the three of us were together. Lewis was already skeptical, and even though I wasn't sure how I felt about Wilfred's story, it was still better to have at least one partial believer present when Brodie was told.

"Jeez Brodie, a little control, please," I said, scanning the other tables for more eavesdroppers.

Brodie brushed off my warning, refusing to lower her voice. "Oh, I'm in total control. Do you know how silly all that sounds?"

Lewis came to my defense. "To be fair, the man doesn't look like a Wilfred. He's kind of intimidating, actually."

"And he knows about the box, the book, and everything else that's been going on. I really believe he's here to help," I blurted out, trying to pile on the momentum.

"He also witnessed Knox's sister toss Travis into my pool," Lewis tacked on.

The skeptical expression on Brodie's face turned into confusion.

"Wait—what? When did that happen? One of your sisters threw your crippled brother into Lewis's pool?"

I shot Lewis a withering look for letting the cat out of the bag, but he couldn't see it because he'd already covered his face with his hands.

"It happened Wednesday night, but Lewis was there to save him."

Brodie looked back and forth between the two of us, her mouth opening and closing as if she wanted to say something, but no words came out.

"I'm sorry we didn't tell you, but we knew you'd be concerned," I added.

Her face suddenly changed as she seemed to realize something, then she rose from her chair and started scanning the room. "Which sister?"

"Don't do that," I hissed. "Sit down. You need to chill so she doesn't suspect we know."

Brodie sat back in her chair, then reached out and put her hands on top of mine. "I've been petrified since that night at your house, but now I'm really concerned. You need to get your family out of there. Now!"

I found it difficult to concentrate on anything but Brodie's hands on mine. "It's not that simple."

"Why not?"

"First, we'd have to figure out which of my sisters is possessed, then we'd need to convince everyone else. My dad is not going to just walk away, he'll want to fight for her. Besides, Wilfred says if the family were to move out, Seraphim would suspect it's been discovered and kill as many of us as it can. When it's finished, it'll return to the book and move on to the next family. That's why I had to put the book back where I found it. Whatever we do, we must do it covertly."

"I still don't understand why we can't just hold the book hostage," Lewis said.

"What do you mean?" Brodie said.

"Lewis thinks that since Seraphim has to return to the book to go back to wherever it came from, we should take the book and hold it hostage. We threaten to burn the book if it kills one of my family."

"What's wrong with that idea?"

"Wilfred says Seraphim is too powerful and not the negotiating type. As soon as it suspects we know the truth, it will slaughter us and take the book. There won't be time to burn anything."

"So, what's *Wilfred's* plan?" Brodie asked, still using mild disdain when pronouncing his name.

I exchanged a look with Lewis before answering.

"Wilfred is keeping a close eye on the twins. In fact, I expect he's out there somewhere in the parking lot right now. But Lewis and I think that his actual plan is to figure out which one it is… and kill her himself."

"But I thought he was here to help," Brodie said.

"In his mind, that is helping. He seems desperate to kill this demon. By killing the possessed person, Seraphim would have to return to the book. That way, only one person dies and everyone else is saved. Wilfred believes Lindsey or Jadie, whichever one it is, is already lost, so he'd be doing us a favor."

"He said this to you?"

Lewis looked at me. "No, not in so many words. But he dropped a couple not-so-subtle hints."

"But don't worry, Lewis thought up our own plan," I said. "And I think it might actually work."

"What might that be?" Brodie asked. Lewis looked confused.

I reached out and grabbed the banana Lewis had brought as part of his lunch. "Can't tell you yet. I have to check one thing after school first."

"School lets out early today," Lewis said. "There's a pep rally this afternoon."

"What for?"

"The basketball team has a conference tournament game tonight," Lewis explained.

"Can we skip it?" I asked, peeling the banana. "We've got more important things to do."

Brodie shook her head. "They're pretty strict about making everyone attend. The teachers and office assistants patrol the exits to catch any ditchers."

"Okay. The other schools I've been at make it optional, but that's fine, then right after," I said with a mouthful of fruit.

That's when things got strange.

Lewis was saying something back to me, but for some reason, I couldn't hear him. It was like someone had hit his mute button. Then I looked at Brodie, and she was talking also, but there was no sound coming out of her mouth either. That's when I noticed that the usually noisy cafeteria had gone completely silent, yet everyone was still carrying on as if nothing was wrong.

The back of my neck began tingling, and my throat felt constricted. What was going on?

"Can you guys hear me?" I asked, hearing myself speak. But I lost interest in the answer when I noticed the light in the cafeteria dimming. It grew darker and darker, seemingly closing in on our table, but neither Brodie nor Lewis acted like anything out of the ordinary was happening.

"GUYS—" I shouted, rising from my chair.

Then everything went black.

I was isolated in the darkness. No Lewis. No Brodie. No one. Just a dark void. I was completely alone.

I could feel panic rising in me. Heat prickled my body and my breathing felt shallow. But I was determined to stay calm. Whatever this was, surely it would pass soon enough. Right? I reached out to steady myself using the back of my chair, but it was no longer there. I explored the area in front of me for the table, but it wasn't there either.

I thought about moving around and probing, but somehow staying put felt safer.

Then I sensed movement all around me. Still no sound, still pitch black, but I knew that something was out there in the dark. I swept my arms from side to side, trying to make contact with whatever was out there, but nothing.

I blinked, and suddenly a woman was standing ten feet from me. There still wasn't any light, but an unearthly glow illuminated the new arrival. Her complexion was ashen, her eyes were dead, and her arms hung loosely at her side, with one enveloped in a cast. But it was the ragged slice across her neck and the crimson covering her chest that drew most of my attention. That and the bloody steak knife dangling from one of her hands.

Suddenly, a large man and a small child were standing next to the woman. Both of them were draped in blood-soaked clothes.

I was petrified, staring at the chilling apparition, so much so that my ears began to ring.

Then I believe two more adults and a child appeared next to the throat-slit family. I had to guess because all three of them had been burned beyond recognition.

Then another dead family appeared, this time the woman and three children's heads had all been severely beaten. Half of the man's head was altogether missing, and a shotgun was lying at his feet.

I let out a gasp as the entire cafeteria was suddenly filled with dead bodies, displaying all manner of wounds, mutilations, and fatal injuries.

The silence was shattered when all the unearthly bodies let go a torrent of blood-curdling screams, forcing me to put my hands over my ears.

I closed my eyes and screamed, "STOP!"

Then the silence returned.

When I opened my eyes, I was back in the cafeteria, and it seemed like the entire student body was staring at me.

I glanced at Lewis and Brodie. They were both looking at me like I had just ... well, like I had just screamed at the top of my lungs in a crowded lunchroom.

I grabbed my backpack and bolted out of the room.

Twenty-Nine

Knox

Following the stream of kids into the gym, I was still shaken from what had happened during lunch. Both Brodie and Lewis approached me afterwards and wanted to know what happened, but I refused to say anything more than that I got freaked out by a spider. Of course, they didn't buy it, but I didn't have a good explanation. I didn't want to scare them because I was scared enough for all of us.

I soon discovered that Brodie hadn't downplayed the school's insistence on taking part in the prep rally. Using the intercom to call the students to the assembly by class, one by one, it felt more like a procession of desperate criminals being led out for exercise period, with a contingent of guards watching our every move, waiting for one of us to make a run for it.

As far as high school gyms go, BMH—which I had come to learn was deemed Bowel Movement High—was a step above. A row of retractable bleachers lined both the north and south walls, though only the northside bleachers were extended for seating, and seven banners celebrating previous district championships hung from the rafters above the locker room entrances. The school colors, black and gold, were everywhere, including the impressive image of the ram covering the center of the basketball court. There were four additional rims, two on each side of the court, that had been retracted into the ceiling to provide better viewing.

I found Lewis and Brodie sitting on the top row of the wooden bleachers, so I sprinted up the stairs to join them. I settled in next to Brodie, Lewis on the other side of her, then turned my attention to the organized migration. As more and more kids filled the stands, I looked around until I spotted Travis off to my left. He and his wheelchair were next to the base of the bleachers, and he was carrying on a conversation with a red-haired girl sitting next to him. When the seniors filed in, I watched as Lindsey and Jadie entered separately, each with their own respective friends around them, taking seats somewhere to my right. Lorna was there as well, standing in an alcove on the other side of the arena, chatting with a group of teachers while monitoring the proceedings.

When it appeared that the last of the stragglers had been herded into the gym, I watched as the school's Principal strolled out into the middle of the court, microphone in hand.

"Good afternoon, ladies and gentlemen. If ya'll please settle down, we'll go ahead and get this thing started."

My attention wandered as our principal made his remarks. I tried to locate where my sisters had landed, but I didn't have the best vantage point. I thought I could see the back of Jadie's head, but Lindsey was blocked from me.

The next thing I knew, music began blaring from the overhead speakers, and the varsity cheerleaders spilled onto the floor from the locker room, immediately breaking into a choreographed dance routine.

I turned to Brodie. "Are you a basketball fan?"

"Not really. I like baseball more."

"Interesting. What about you, Lewis? What sport do you like most?"

"Cricket," he said with a straight face.

I opened my mouth to respond when an outburst of laughter drew my attention. Scanning the gym for something comical that might cause that sort of response, I noticed that the cheerleaders were now standing in a line facing the crowd, performing a cheer, but the girl at the end was having some sort of problem with her outfit. As I watched, her pleated mini-skirt blew up around her waist, leaving her Spanx exposed. The girl quickly pushed the skirt down, only to have it fly back up again as if propelled by a blast of wind, eliciting another burst of laughter from the crowd. When it happened a third time, the two cheerleaders nearest to her stopped their routine and went to help. Whatever had caused the outfit malfunction must have stopped, but the cheerleader was too distraught to continue. The teammates who came to her rescue escorted her towards the locker room just as the varsity basketball players emerged.

"That was terrible," Brodie remarked. "Whoever did that should be suspended."

The basketball team had taken to the floor and broken into a traditional two-line drill. One player from the right would make a layup, and a player from the other line would rebound the ball and feed it to the next player in line. Two players had successfully made layups when the third dribbled up, laid the ball high off the glass backboard, and an unseen force suddenly rejected it. The ball slammed up against the wall and bounced back onto the court.

The players on the court stopped where they were and stared at the rolling ball, then at each other. A player closest to the sphere picked it up, twirled it in his hands, then performed a jump shot with it. The ball's trajectory looked like it was about to drop through the swishing net, but it shot off dramatically in the opposite direction, startling me and eliciting shocked responses from everyone watching. The ball sailed through the air in a high arc and bounced beneath the goal at the far end of the court.

A ripple of nervous chatter began amongst the onlookers, and I could tell from the way the coaches and players were acting that they had no idea what had happened. This wasn't a practical joke, or if it was, it was an awfully good one.

One of the tallest players on the team, a kid I had often seen walking in the hallways, because at that height he was hard to miss, grabbed a ball from the rack holding the extra balls and broke for the hoop. I'm not sure what his intention was—maybe he wanted to snap everyone out of the daze caused by the spectacle of the self-rejecting balls—but he launched himself off the ground near the foul line, the ball gripped in his hand held above his head, a monster-dunk in progress. It quickly became apparent that something was terribly wrong as the player seemed to lose control of his body, pinwheeling his arms as he continued flying past the backboard. He collided with incredible force above the padding on the brick wall behind the court, a sickening crunch marking his impact. The player hung there momentarily, seemingly stuck to the wall, before tumbling to the ground.

Turmoil erupted immediately.

I watched in shock as coaches and players rushed to their fallen teammate. Lorna sprinted onto the court and quickly took charge of assessing his injuries. Most of the students had risen to their feet, many with their hands clasped over their mouths. The teachers were doing their best to calm the crowd and maintain some semblance of order, but some were unsure what to do.

"Knox, what's going on?" Brodie asked with a raised voice. The chorus of agitated conversations around us was making it hard to be heard.

"I don't know," was all I could say.

"Do you feel that?" Lewis shouted, looking down at his feet.

I did feel something. The bleachers were vibrating. I initially attributed it to everyone jumping up when the boy hit the wall, but it kept happening and seemed to be getting stronger.

"Why are the bleachers shaking?" Brodie asked.

The trembling intensified, bouncing and rocking so much that we lost our balance and sat down heavily. Scared cries filled the gym as kids in the first couple of rows spilled out onto the court and looked back incredulously. My thoughts went back to the night when my brother's and my beds had shaken. Back then, I wondered if Ox-Bow was predisposed to earthquakes. But if this were an earthquake, why would only the bleachers be shaking?

A loud pop above us caused me to look up, and I saw that a bulb in one of the overhead light fixtures had blown, releasing a shower of sparks upon us. Suddenly, bulbs from all over the gym began exploding one by one, plunging the room into near darkness.

It was complete chaos now. Teachers were screaming in a vain attempt to restore order. Cell phone flashlights were trying to add to the little light streaming in through the doors leading into the cafeteria, the same doors now clogged with kids trying to escape the havoc in the gymnasium.

"Get Brodie out of here," I yelled at Lewis. "I have to find Travis."

Neither of them bothered to argue as I headed off in the other direction.

I felt like a salmon swimming upstream in the dark, bobbing my way in and out of the flow of my panicky classmates moving in the opposite direction. Travis had been sitting at the base of the bleachers close to the locker room entrances, and hopefully, he was still there. But when I reached that spot, he was nowhere to be found.

My heart pounded as my eyes darted from place to place for his wheelchair. He was nowhere to be found. I could make out a pair of swinging doors on the other side of the gym leading out to a hallway. The hallway ran perpendicular to the gym, in one direction towards the back of the school, where the coaches' offices and equipment room were located, and in the other direction to the weight room and another set of double doors leading out into the cafeteria. Fewer kids were making the smart choice to exit that way, so I assumed Travis would do the same and headed in that direction.

As I ran past the spot where the tall basketball player had collapsed, I noticed the boy was sitting up, a dazed expression on his face. What I didn't see was Lorna. She had disappeared.

I burst through the swinging doors and looked up the hall, hoping that I had guessed right. There were a couple of kids making their way towards the exit, but ahead of them, I could see Travis's wheelchair being guided by my step-mom. I let out a sigh of relief until I saw something that shook me. Wilfred, his massive frame and unmistakably long white hair, was standing at the end of the hall holding the door open. But it was his appearance that surprised me most. He was dressed as a priest—white-collar and everything.

I started walking fast to catch up to my brother when a figure a few yards ahead of me caught my attention. The person was wearing a dark hoodie, the hood pulled up, with one hand buried in a backpack. Whoever it was wasn't hurrying like everyone else, but rather moving cautiously, almost like they were a hunter stalking prey.

Suddenly, the hooded figure stopped, let the backpack drop to the ground, and raised both arms to aim up the hall. My eyes went wide when I saw an old-style western six-shooter in the person's hands.

I unconsciously reacted. Rushing forward, I raised my right arm and brought it crashing down across the forearms of the stranger with all my might. The gun discharged into the floor with a thunderous roar that echoed in the hallway, eliciting screams from nearby kids. When the weapon clattered to the ground, I grabbed a fistful of the hoodie and pulled, drawing back my fist at the same time. When the figure swung around, I came face to face with a young woman with short-trimmed jet-black hair, obvious surprise in her tear-filled blue eyes.

I was stunned, letting my raised arm fall to my side. The woman shook loose from my grip, grabbed her backpack, and sprinted away. I reached after her but collided with one of the panicked kids scrambling out of the woman's way. We fell to the floor in a tangle of arms and legs. By the time I was able to look up, the woman was disappearing down the hall towards the exit next to the equipment room. Damn!

I turned around to search for Wilfred. He had also vanished.

MOVING FEAR

Thirty

Knox

"And you don't know who this woman was?"

I couldn't help but give the detective a tired look. After they forced me to wait in the principal's office for almost an hour, I was now being asked to answer the same questions over and over. I understood how it worked from watching television—repetition was simply a way to try to trip me up—to see if I was telling a lie. But really, how hard is it to mess up 'NO'?

The detective didn't look like any of the characters I'd seen in the movies or on TV. He was at least six-and-a-half feet tall and thin as a beanpole. He reminded me of an anemic basketball player wearing a discount-store suit. His thin mustache was doing its best to make him look more authoritative, but it ended up being just as distracting as the globs of hair gel he used.

"No. I had never seen the girl before," I answered for what felt like the tenth time.

The detective had an annoying habit of sucking air through his teeth before he asked each question. "So, what were you doing in that hallway?" At least this question was original.

"I was worried about my brother getting out of the gym okay. He's disabled."

"We know. We've taken his statement already, along with your stepmom's," the detective said. Another intake of air through his teeth preceded his return to well-treaded territory. "And you also don't know who this priest is that the woman was aiming at?"

I was still reeling from seeing Wilfred dressed as a priest. In fact, the whole thing left me jittery. After things had calmed down and I realized what I'd done, my legs went limp, and it was probably a good thing I was sitting down. I could still feel the sweat trickling down my back, but I dared not let on.

"I'm not sure who she was aiming at, but no, I don't know him."

The detective looked at me carefully, took a deep breath, and slid his notepad into his coat pocket. "That was a brave thing you did, son, but next time, leave the heroics to the police."

I didn't think it was appropriate to point out the fact that there were no police around to rely on just then, so I just smiled at the detective instead.

"Can I go now?"

"I suppose so. We have you and your stepmom's contact information if we need to follow up."

I left before he could ask another question.

Walking into the outer office, I was about to take the door on the left into the nurses' station, where Lorna and Travis said they would wait for me, but through the glass window in the main hallway, I spotted Lewis and Brodie. So instead, I continued past the counter, out the main door into the hall.

"What's going on?" Lewis asked.

I looked up and down the empty hallways. School had let out early because of the craziness in the gym and the shooting, which was now almost two hours ago.

"I think someone tried to kill Wilfred," I said softly, despite it just being us. "And get this—Wilfred was dressed as a priest."

"A priest? That makes little sense. He didn't say anything about being a priest," Lewis said.

"Who tried to kill him? One of your sisters?" Brodie asked.

I shook my head. "No, someone else. A girl, not too much older than us."

"This just keeps getting better and better," Lewis blurted out gleefully.

"Lewis, that's not funny," Brodie said, shooting him a stern look. "I'm still shaking. What went on in that gym? Was it the demon? Seraphim?"

I nodded, afraid that Brodie was going to abandon us now.

"Knox, that thing is powerful," she pointed out.

"I know… and it has one of my sisters, Brodie."

I couldn't tell by the way she was looking at me what she was thinking. She glanced at Lewis, then placed her hands on her hips.

"Okay, so what do we do now?"

I couldn't stop myself from smiling. "Are your parents on the way here to pick you up?" I asked.

"I've already called my dad and told him I was okay. I have my car here, and Lewis told his mom I would drop him home."

"Good. We need to make a detour first. I'll tell you all about it on the way if I can get away from Lorna. Can you drive all of us somewhere?" I asked.

"Where?"

"It has to do with Lewis's plan. Can you?"

A confused look appeared on Lewis's face again.

"Sure," Brodie said.

"Get your car and pull it around to the front entrance. I'll meet you there," I said before walking to the nurses' station. Pushing open the door, I found Travis positioned next to the small bed in the back, reading a book, and Lorna sitting behind her desk, working on paperwork. Both looked up when I entered the room.

"Are you finished?" Lorna asked, gathering up the papers in front of her.

"They want me to go down to the station and look at some pictures to see if I can identify the girl. It shouldn't take more than an hour. They said they'd drop me back home when I'm done."

Lorna stopped what she was doing. "Don't they need me to come with you?"

I stuck my hands in my pockets. "Nah. The detective said it was a long shot, but he wanted to try it anyway. But they're not headed back to the police station for a couple more minutes, so you and Travis can head home now if you want."

Lorna didn't look convinced. "I... I'm not sure. Maybe I should go with you, anyway."

I had to be careful not to appear too anxious. "Lorna, I don't need you to hold my hand. I can do this by myself."

Travis was busy putting his book back into his backpack when he added his opinion. "I'm hungry, Lorna. I didn't get lunch. Let's go home. The girls are already there."

"Have they found out who that priest was yet?" Lorna asked, ignoring Travis completely.

"No, or at least they didn't say anything to me. Do you know what he was doing here?"

Lorna shook her head. "No. I was helping Travis get out of the gym towards the cafeteria when the priest just appeared at the door."

"I'm sure they'll find him. Can't be that many white-haired priests in Ox-Bow."

Lorna stared at me long enough to make me uncomfortable, then abruptly shrugged her shoulders and resumed straightening up her papers. "Okay, I'll take Travis home, but don't goof off there. Look at your pictures and get them to bring you straight home. Dinner will be waiting for you."

I hung around and watched the two of them prepare to leave just to make sure there wasn't an accidental meeting with the detective, then walked them both to the teacher parking lot and watched as they pulled away.

As soon as the car was out of sight, I turned and ran back into the school. I sprinted down the long corridor to the main entrance, where Brodie's Honda was parked in the drive at the bottom of the stairs. Lewis was already in the backseat with his face plastered up against the window, so I climbed in the passenger door and instructed Brodie to drive.

"Put your seatbelt on," she said before violently jerking the Honda , making a sharp left-hand turn, and hurling me against the passenger door. As soon as the momentum allowed, I reached over my right shoulder and pulled down the seat belt to click it into place.

"This must be your first time riding with Brodie," I heard Lewis say from the back.

"Where are we going?" Brodie asked as she guided her car onto the main thoroughfare.

"Out on highway thirty-six, a couple of miles. My grandmother's house."

"Your grandmother? She has something to do with Lewis's plan?"

I looked over my shoulder. "Did you tell Brodie?"

Lewis was sitting in the middle of the backseat, his arms out to his sides, his hands planted firmly on the seat beside him.

"I'm not sure what you're talking about. I don't remember discussing a plan."

"Well, it's not really a plan yet. More like an idea. Some of the things you said after we left Wilfred last night got me thinking."

"What things?" Brodie asked, glancing over at me, which at the speed we were traveling, made my heart race that much more.

"Wilfred told us that everyone who's been possessed has died, but Lewis pointed out that he came across a story of a woman in Arkansas who killed her entire family."

"So?"

"Tell her, Lewis."

"The woman survived. She's in a mental institution in Ft Smith, Arkansas, but she's alive."

Brodie twisted her head around to look into the back seat. "That means there's hope, doesn't it?"

"You need to turn left here," I pointed out.

Our car was in the far right of a four-lane interchange, and the turn I mentioned was approaching quickly. When Brodie's attention returned to the road, she effortlessly executed a jagged left-hand turn without slowing down or bothering to move into the turn lane, ignoring the blaring horns of the cars she cut off.

I decided to keep my mouth shut about future directions.

"Yes and no," Lewis answered Brodie's previous question, ignoring the drama on the road. "The woman survived, but the thing is, she did actually die."

"I don't understand."

"She drowned herself in their bathtub by weighing herself down with her husband's workout weights, but a family member who was training as an EMT found her in time and resuscitated her. So, technically, she did die."

"And that got me thinking," I added, my right hand now clutching the support grip over the door. "We could do the same thing to Lindsey or Jadie. We kill her and then bring her back to life."

"I get it. Like a hard re-boot on a computer," Lewis said.

"And we are going to your grandmother's house because?" Brodie asked.

"Because she's a doctor, or rather, she used to be. If anyone would know how to bring someone back from the dead, it would be her."

"And you think she'd be willing to help us?"

"Well, I'm not her favorite grandchild, but our options are limited."

We sat in silence for few moments. I think we all needed a moment to process the day.

"Should we be worried about this girl who tried to kill Wilfred?" Lewis asked. "What's her deal?"

My mind flashed to the deafening sound of a gun going off, and the tortured look on the girl's face.

"I wish I knew."

MOVING FEAR

Thirty-One

Knox

My grandma's country home was on a five-acre tract of land on the outskirts of the Ox-Bow city limits. Brodie pulled up the driveway that ran a couple of hundred yards off the street and to the detached garage slightly behind and to the left of the main house.

Brodie parked her Honda next to a sidewalk constructed from old railroad ties and white pea gravel leading to the porch steps. She swung open her door, and I touched her shoulder before she could step out.

"I need to warn you guys. My grandma can be blunt. She means nothing by it. It's just her way. Just be direct with her and you'll be fine."

Brodie and Lewis exchanged a look, then the three of us climbed out of the car and I led the way up the steps to the front door. The house was simplistic, with a roofline running parallel to the road, a covered wraparound porch, and newly painted red shutters. The front door opened before I could ring the bell.

My grandma, sporting her favorite gardening garb of a soiled University of Oklahoma sweatshirt, faded jeans and mud boots held the door wide open, but it was the menacing scowl on her face that made me hesitate, rethinking the worthiness of our plan.

"Aren't you supposed to be in school, Chace?" Grandma Fuller barked, freezing the three of us in our tracks.

"I told you I go by Knox now, Grandma," I squeaked out. *Can't let her smell fear*, I thought to myself. If I knew my grandma at all, she only responded to strength. The problem was that I needed to figure out where I could get some.

She took notice of my companions, but her eyes quickly returned to me.

"You didn't answer my question."

"School let out early after the pep rally," I improvised. Not a complete lie, but I didn't want to get sidetracked talking about the craziness that went down at school.

She seemed to consider my response, then said, "Why don't you introduce me to your friends?"

"This is Lewis and Brodie. They go to school with me."

Grandma Fuller stepped out of the door and into the sun, her arms crossing in front of her chest.

"Lewis Bonvillain? I'd recognize that nose anywhere. Isn't your mother Jules Bonvillain? We go to the same church, don't we?"

"Yes, ma'am, I believe so," Lewis replied his voice shaking.

"You believe she's your mother, or that we go to the same church?"

"I… uh… the church thing," Lewis stammered.

"She's a strange one, your mother."

"Grandma, that's not nice," I interjected. Things were starting rougher than I hoped.

"It's alright," Lewis responded quickly. "Yes, ma'am. She is, but aren't we all, at least a little?"

My grandma glared at Lewis for what seemed like an eternity, but then, ever so slightly, a side of her mouth turned upwards.

"I guess that's true," she said. Next, she turned her attention to Brodie, who looked like she was bracing herself for my grandma's third degree. My grandmother didn't disappoint.

"You, I don't know. What kind of name is Brodie, anyway? Why would your parents saddle you with a guy's name, such a pretty thing as you?"

Brodie looked at me, but all I could do was offer a weak smile.

"I don't think that's any of your business, but since you asked so nicely, I'll tell you. I'm an only child, but my mother had a previous stillborn child. It was a boy, and Brodie was the name they had picked out for him. When I came along a year later, my parents decided that in honor of him, we would share the name, and I frankly LOVE that I do."

My grandma's expression didn't change a bit.

"Well, that answers that, doesn't it? I guess you can call me Ginny. I'm not named after any unborn babies or unhealthy attachments to a dead family pet, just plain Ginny."

Brodie grinned. "Pleased to meet you, Ginny."

"I just finished working in my garden and I'm parched. Why don't the three of you join me for a glass of tea?"

The inside of the home was just as warm as the outside, with plenty of light from the tall windows and a wide-open floor plan, hardwood floors balanced by thick area rugs, a massive wood fireplace, and old-style furniture that looked inviting.

"I just made a fresh pitcher. You all make yourselves comfortable."

The three of us made our way to an oversized couch in the middle of the room with throw pillows at each corner and multiple blankets hung across its back. I sat in the middle between Brodie and Lewis. Brodie scooted right up against me, her hip and shoulder rubbing against mine, which instantly turned those parts of my body into the center of the universe. It was an odd sensation, one that I couldn't get enough of.

As soon as we settled in, I felt a nudge of an elbow from Lewis. "There's no television," he whispered. I didn't see the need to tell him that was why I knew Grandma wouldn't ask us about what happened at the school that morning, nothing to carry news coverage.

"Very observant young man," a voice from the kitchen called out. "I have little use for the petulance of the world, and I derive all of my entertainment from books, which I choose carefully."

I chuckled. "But there's a TV in the back bedroom she brings out whenever we come to visit."

"Under protest, of course," Grandma said as she rounded the corner with a tray full of drinks. She had taken off her hat, but everything else was the same, including the dried dirt on her clothes.

We each took a glass and enjoyed a long sip. Grandma laid the empty tray on the coffee table and had a seat in the chair to the right of the couch.

"So, what kind of trouble have you gotten yourself into this time, Chace?" Grandma asked before taking a sip of her own drink.

I opened my mouth to correct her about my name, but decided otherwise. "Why do you always think I'm in trouble?"

"Are you telling me you're not?"

"Yes... I mean... no," I stammered. Once again, I felt myself struggling to find the right words without sounding like a complete idiot, which is how she always made me feel. "We just have a few medical questions we'd like to ask you about a project we're working on, that's all."

Grandma took another sip of her tea, then set the glass on the table.

"Then, miracles exist. What questions do you have for me?"

"Well, we're writing a fictional story, but we want to make it as realistic as possible. We could have probably Googled this stuff, but I figured who would know better than a doctor."

"I understand. Good for you."

"The gist of the story revolves around someone who needs to die and come back to life, and we wanted to ask you if there is a drug that can stop a person's heart temporarily?"

"Darling, more than two million people a year have open-heart surgery to unblock or bypass clogged arteries, or repair damaged valves, and you can't do that without stopping the heart. Way back when, they usually stopped the heart for about an hour while the patient went under the knife because it is impossible to operate on a moving target. Adenosine, which opens some of the channels that transport potassium ions in and out of the cell, and lidocaine, which blocks sodium ion channels, are the most common drugs used to achieve this result. There are plenty of other drugs that can effectively stop the heart, but the trick is getting it started again and managing the damage to the body while it's stopped. The patient needs the function of the heart and lungs to provide the much-needed blood flow to the body, particularly to the brain. Doing this is achieved via artificial methods."

"We're talking about stopping the heart for a brief time. A few minutes at most. How long can the body go with none of these so-called artificial methods?" I asked.

"That is a tough question to answer because every person's physiology is so different. But I can tell you that brain cells are susceptible to oxygen deprivation. Some brain cells actually start dying less than five minutes after their oxygen supply disappears. As a result, brain hypoxia can rapidly cause death or severe brain damage. Just what sort of story is this again?"

"Can a layman, I mean someone not associated with the medical profession, get their hands on these types of drugs?" Brodie asked, side-stepping my grandmother's question.

"Oh, I'm sure they could if they had enough money. But if they were going to do that, they might as well just shoot the poor person in the head. Although someone might get the proper drugs, it takes a professional to administer them correctly. That's the difference between fiction and real life."

Brodie turned to look at me. I was crushed. My grandma had exposed my plan as a childish dream, and I felt the hope of rescuing my sister slipping through my fingers. Sitting there in front of my grandmother made me think of the one person I would always turn to with my problems, no matter how big or small. My mom. And it was then that I realized just how different she and her mother were. Where my grandma always saw things in black and white —yes or no — my mom didn't. Even though she couldn't fix everything, she still made me see the silver lining in every situation, and right now, that was something I was sorely in need of. Maybe this wasn't my mom sitting here, but she raised the person who would become her. These were desperate times, and it was time to lay all our cards on the table. I only hoped that the part of my mom that seemed to find a positive path through difficult circumstances was somewhere within my grandma as well.

"Can I ask you a different question, Grandma?"

"I knew it," my grandma said, a scowl overtaking her face. "You are in some kind of trouble, aren't you?"

I paused before letting the words spill out of my mouth, knowing that once I said them, there was no going back.

"Do you believe in God?"

All the emotion on my grandmother's face disappeared. She slowly studied all our faces.

Before she could respond, I cut right to the chase. "Or, more specifically, do you believe in demons?"

"Are we still talking about this story you're writing? What game are you playing at, Chace?"

"It's not a game, Mrs. Fuller," Brodie answered instead. "It's an honest question."

Grandma regarded Brodie, then retrieved her glass from the table before directing her remarks to me.

"Then, for the sake of your guests, I'll humor you. I guess you can call me a lapsed agnostic."

"What does that mean?" I asked.

Grandma rotated her glass in her hands, but she still had not taken a drink from it. "I'm someone who neither believes nor disbelieves in the existence of a deity... or God. There was a time when I desperately needed to believe, but these days, I just don't care."

"But all those times we visited you and Grandpa, we'd go to church. You still go to church now."

"Oh, your grandpa had faith. He had enough for both of us. But I'll let you in on a little secret. If you own any kind of business, especially in these parts, you have to go to church. If you don't, your business won't do very well. That goes double for people in my profession. After your grandfather passed, well, I keep going more for the social activities now."

"Does that mean that you don't think demons are real?"

My grandma looked down at the drink in her hands and sat there silently for what was becoming an increasingly uncomfortable amount of time. Then she suddenly returned the glass to the table, wiped her hands on her slacks, and looked directly into my eyes.

"What are you playing at, Chace?"

"I'm not playing Grandma. This is very real."

She rubbed her hands back and forth across the tops of her thighs, looking slowly at the three of us. When she stopped, she seemed to have made up her mind.

"Your mother and I used to have many a conversation about you and your ***stories***. "Conversation" would be the sanitized word for what we did, but the plain truth was that we argued. Real knock-down drag-outs. It seemed like you were telling these stories before you could even walk. Real doozies. She'd tell me that deep down, she knew they might become a problem someday, making up these wild, elaborate tales and misleading people into believing they were true. Sometimes she wondered if you believed them yourself. They were so detailed and told with such passion. But she just couldn't bring herself to crush your creativity, especially when it was coming from one so young. Me, let's just say if you were my child, I would have worn out that little ass of yours."

I swallowed hard. "That's why you never liked me much?"

The pain in her face was unmistakable.

"Oh, honey, there are no words to describe how much I love you. I love all of you kids. It was just that your mother and I disagreed about where boundaries needed to be set and what should happen if they were broken. It had nothing to do with how I feel about you. Take your father, for example."

"What about him?"

"Your father, well, if there was one thing we agreed on, it was how to handle your behavior. Your mother told me she and your father also fought about your wild imagination, but in the end, she won. You don't think he loved you any less because of that, do you? Your mother always won. That's just who she was. I'll let you in on a little secret. I used to be angry at your father for so long because I thought he stole my little girl away from me. The reality is that when my daughter made up her mind, no one could change it."

My grandma sat there in silence for a few moments, her gaze unfixed. But then she snapped out of her trance and focused on me again.

"I thought you had turned a corner after what happened to your brother."

Now I wish I had never brought us here and wanted to be anywhere else.

"So, I'm giving you one last chance to tell me what is going on with you. Understand, young man?"

"Yes, ma'am," I answered solemnly, tears welling up in my eyes.

Grandma Fuller leaned forward in her chair and reached out to place her hand over mine.

"So?"

I answered without hesitation, but with a slight quiver in my voice. "We need help to kill a demon we believe has possessed one of my sisters."

Grandma leaned back and picked up her tea.

"Get out of my house."

MOVING FEAR

Thirty-Two

Knox

Brodie pulled her car up to the curb in front of my house and shifted into park.

"You've been pretty quiet since we left your grandmother's," she said.

She wasn't wrong. I didn't know what I could say, having struck out with Ginny in such an epic fashion. I could say I was embarrassed, but that was fairly obvious. Our time was running out, and my one plan proved to be a fool's errand, leaving us no closer to coming up with a strategy to save my sister.

"I don't know what we're going to do," was all I could say as I stared at my hands in my lap.

"We'll figure something out," Lewis said from the backseat, the optimism in his voice almost encouraging. "We just have to put our heads together."

Brodie put her hand on my shoulder. "Lewis is right. The idea you came up with is a good one. Your grandmother just pointed out some obstacles, and we need to think about how we can overcome them."

"Right. Let's go back down to my basement and get started," Lewis added.

Minutes earlier, I didn't think I could have felt any worse, but Lewis and Brodie's enthusiasm was contagious. Still, the hill we needed to climb was steep, and the most favorable forecast was grim.

"I have to check in first with dad and Lorna," I said, showing them both a feeble smile. "I'll be over as soon as I can."

I climbed out of the car and watched the Honda head over and park in Lewis's driveway. I dragged my feet all the way to the porch and up the stairs, plastering an artificial smile on my face before entering the house.

"I'm home," I called out as I walked through the front door. I took one last look at the street before closing the door behind me. *Why wasn't Wilfred's red pickup anywhere to be seen? Where is he now?*

The reason I showed my face at home before heading next door was to reassure my parents that everything was okay after my imaginary visit to the police station, but I also thought I might need to intercept any calls from Grandma. She might try to give Dad the lowdown on the "craziness" we discussed, and that wouldn't be good.

"I'm in here," Dad called from the other room.

I stepped into the living room, where Travis was parked in his usual spot next to the couch, watching television. Dad was sitting at his desk.

"I see the TV is back to normal," I commented.

"Yeah, go figure," Travis replied, chuckling.

I began moving towards the den when the doorbell rang behind me. "I got it," I called out as I spun around and opened the front door. There stood Grandma Ginny.

"Grandma?" I said, a shudder of fear going up my back as I realized she was going to inform on me in person. "What are you doing here?"

"Do I need a reason to visit my grandkids?" she said gruffly, pushing past me and into the living room.

"There's my big man," Grandma said, giving Travis a mandatory hug. "Still enjoying school?"

"It's school, Grandma. It's not meant to be enjoyed."

The smile on her face dimmed when she noticed what was on the TV. "What are you watching?"

On the television screen, a news reporter was standing in front of our high school, recapping this morning's troubles.

"Just the news about the shooter at our school today," Travis said matter-of-factly.

"You haven't heard about our hero yet, Ginny?" Dad asked, swiveling around in his desk chair to face us as we approached.

Grandma looked at me. "I have no idea what you are talking about."

"I'm not a hero," I said, sticking my hands deep into my pockets.

"If saving a man from being shot isn't heroic, I'm not sure what is then," Dad said.

"He did what?" Grandma exclaimed, looking at me intensely now.

"Your grandson interrupted a woman who was trying to shoot someone at the school. It's all over the local news."

Grandma dropped into the wooden chair against the wall next to the desk. She stuck her feet out in front of her, letting her arms fall to her side as if she were exhausted.

Lorna appeared in the doorway leading into the kitchen, wiping her hands on a dish towel.

"Hey, Ginny. You look well."

"Evening Lorna. Looks like you've put on a few pounds."

Lorna let that go by and looked at me. "Were you able to identify the woman with the gun?"

"No."

Lindsey came down the stairs, stopping on the bottom step. "Hi Grandma, I thought I recognized your voice."

"Hi, honey," was Grandma's two-word response, which was the shortest sentence I could ever recall her using. My Grandma never lacked for words, but now they seemed to fail her. I couldn't figure out what she was up to. Was I in deep trouble or not?

But it wasn't my grandma I was paying attention at that moment. There was something about my sister that was different, something I couldn't put my finger on.

"You looked tired, darling," Grandma asked.

"Been studying. Big test tomorrow," was Lindsey's unenthusiastic reply.

Lorna tossed the towel over her shoulder. "Time for a break, then. Dinner is waiting on the counter. You're more than welcome, Ginny."

Lindsey stepped down off the stairs and headed towards the kitchen, and that's when I realized what was different about her. Mom's mood ring wasn't around her neck. The one piece of jewelry she never takes off.

"Where is Jadie?" Grandma asked.

"There's a basketball game tonight," Dad answered, a touch of sarcasm in his voice. We all knew that for any sort of social gathering, even if it involved a sport Jadie couldn't care less about, she would be there.

"That's too bad. Oh well. I really stopped by just to offer my services for everybody's annual checkups. I have time this weekend if you all want to drop by. That includes you and Lorna as well, David."

Grandma Fuller had been doing the family checkups for as long as I could remember, even after she officially retired three years ago. Every trip to Ox-Bow, no matter where we were stationed, always included a checkup from Grandma. She excluded Dad since he received military checkups. Lorna, being with the family for just a few short years, hadn't had the pleasure yet. But the timing of her reminder couldn't be a coincidence. Did this possibly have something to do with what I asked her?

"I'm fine, but thank you," said Lorna.

The smile on my grandma's face remained steady. "Do I need to tell you how many times during my career that I've heard those two words, and it turns out the patient is anything but? I'm afraid I'm going to have to insist."

"Insist all you want, but I'll find my own doctor."

It might have been my imagination, but I thought the temperature in the room was climbing.

"I'm going to pass too, Grandma," Lindsey said, standing behind Lorna, now with a plate of spaghetti and meatballs. "I'm old enough now that I should probably have my own doctor."

Grandma's smile faded.

"Lorna. Lindsey. Ginny is only trying to help," Dad said. The words sounded strange coming out of his mouth. Having Dad defend Grandma was weird. "You don't have to worry about wasting time in waiting rooms, and you can't beat the cost."

"Why can't I decide what doctor I see?" Lindsey whined.

"I'm just not comfortable seeing someone I'm not used to, David," Lorna said.

Grandma clasped her hands together. "Lorna, these children have lost one mother, and I just want to make sure I do everything possible to ensure it doesn't happen again."

"Because you did such a great job with the last one," Lindsey said, just before taking a bite of her food.

"Lindsey!" Dad barked, standing now. Even Lorna gave Lindsey a shocked look.

The doorbell rang.

Nobody moved to answer the door. Lindsey, Lorna, and Ginny were all locked in a three-way stare-down, and my father shifted his disbelieving gawk back and forth between all of them.

The doorbell rang a second time.

"I guess I'll get it," I said. I walked past Travis in the living room towards the front door.

"You need to apologize to your grandmother, Lindsey. Right now," I heard behind me.

I pulled open the door, and to my amazement, it was Wilfred, still dressed as a priest, with a light blue surgical mask covering most of his face.

"What's going on?" I whispered. "Why are you dressed like that?"

Wilfred leaned closer and answered in a hushed tone. "I'm sorry about the surprise. I use this priest disguise sometimes when I visit families. Otherwise, they would never let me in the door."

"Who was that girl who tried to shoot you? She was trying to shoot you, wasn't she?"

"We'll talk about that later. Right now, I need to speak to your parents."

I stood back and let Wilfred enter, and when he did, somewhere in the house a door slammed. Then another... and another. In rapid-fire succession, doors throughout the house closed with incredible force.

"What the hell?" Dad exclaimed.

I looked to Wilfred for reassurance, but he seemed unmoved by it. Both of us strolled into the living room together.

"Dad, somebody is here to see you," I said.

"I'm sorry for the facemask, everyone," Wilfred said to the room. "I just visited the infectious disease ward at the hospital, and I didn't want to pass anything along accidentally."

"You're the priest from the school," Lorna said.

Wilfred stood stationary in the living room; his hands folded in front of him at the waist. I watched the man's eyes scan the room, briefly hesitating when he spotted Lindsey, but he broke off quickly.

"I'm sorry to disturb your evening, Mr. and Mrs. Gidden, and I'm sorry we have to meet under such awkward circumstances, but I came here tonight because I felt compelled to warn you."

Wilfred's tone was so much different from when we first met, having adopted a softer, more conciliatory tone. He was playing a perfect priest.

"Warn us of what?" Lorna asked. "Why were you at the school this afternoon?"

"I had business at the school, but like your son, I happened to be in the right spot at the right time."

"I've practiced medicine and lived in Ox-Bow for over thirty years and know almost everybody in this town, but I've never heard of you before," Grandma chimed in.

Wilfred turned his attention to Grandma, the smile in his eyes unfazed.

"I'm sorry, we haven't met."

Dad did the formal introductions. "This is my mother-in-law, Ginny Fuller."

"I'm Reverend Wilfred Perkins, and I'm new to the area. I just started as the youth director at St. Augustine's Catholic Church, and I'm only now making acquaintances in town."

Up to that point, Wilfred's gaze had continued to wander around the room as he spoke, taking in the surroundings and the people—all except Lindsey. He seemed to be purposely avoiding looking in her direction.

I saw the opportunity to ask the question that had been bothering me all afternoon. "Why was that woman trying to kill you?"

"That's why I'm here, son. I'm not so sure she was aiming at me. I believe she might have been targeting someone else," Wilfred replied, looking squarely at Lorna.

"Us? Why us?" Lorna replied.

"I do not know. I caught a brief glimpse of the woman, but I didn't recognize her. I can think of no reason she, or anyone else, would want to harm me. You and your son were in the same line of fire, and when I saw on the news that the

252

police theory seemed to focus on the woman gunning for me, I felt it prudent to warn you as well."

"But why did you disappear before the police arrived, Reverend? They wanted to ask you questions," Lorna asked.

"I really didn't feel like I had much to contribute. Like I said, I didn't know the young woman, and the school was about to turn into a media circus, which would have brought negative attention to our church. So, I left, but with the full intention of going by the precinct tomorrow to give my full statement."

"But it doesn't make sense that someone would try to shoot any of us," Travis said from his chair. "We just moved here. Nobody knows us."

"I can't understand it either, young man. But I feel that all of us should be on alert."

The television volume, which Travis had muted, suddenly blared. Travis fumbled with the remote, trying unsuccessfully to lower the piercing voice of the narrator on the screen.

"It won't turn down," Travis yelled over the noise.

"Let me," Wilfred shouted, being the closest to the television. He stepped towards the TV when, suddenly, a blinding light, a loud pop, and the screen exploded outward. Shards of glass flew directly at Wilfred. He tried to cover his face with his arm, but he was a second too slow.

Thirty-Three

Knox

"Oh my goodness, are you alright, Reverend?" Grandma cried out as she and my dad rushed forward to catch the stumbling priest, his hands covering his face.
"I'm okay... I'm okay," Wilfred's muffled voice said. "None of it got in my eyes."
Grandma grabbed him by one elbow and Dad the other. Together, they guided him towards the nearest chair. "Sit down here and let me take a look. I'm a doctor."
Wilfred eased down and let Grandma pull his hands away from his face. From my vantage point, I could make out tiny streaks of blood and small pieces of glass sticking out of Wilfred's skin.
"It's not that bad. Do you have a pair of tweezers I can use?" Grandma asked to no one in particular.
"Lindsey, the upstairs bathroom," Dad commanded, sending my sister quickly out of the room and up the stairs.
"You don't need to do this. I can take care of—"
"Nonsense. This won't take a minute. Let me just take this mask off —"
"No," Wilfred exclaimed, reaching up to hold the mask in place. "I'd rather not."

"If you insist," grandma replied.

"I have some peroxide somewhere if it will help?" Lorna said.

"Peroxide can damage the tissue and slow healing. I just need some cotton balls, warm water and gentle soap."

"Knox, there are some cotton balls in the downstairs bathroom under the sink," Lorna issued directions without turning away from watching over Ginny's shoulder.

I sped to the bathroom and found the bag of cotton balls where my stepmom had said. I grabbed the whole bag and returned to the living room, where Lindsey had already returned with the tweezers.

A short time later, Wilfred's face was both glass and blood-free.

"Thank you for that," he said, smiling weakly.

"I can't understand how a television could do that," my dad said, looking at our destroyed television.

"It's a plasma, so it contains electrically charged ionized gases, but I've never heard of them blowing up," Travis offered.

Wilfred rose from the chair. "Do not worry about it. It was an accident, and I hold no ill-will."

"Are you okay driving home? You still might be in a bit of shock?" Grandma asked.

"I'm fine. Really. Thank you again," Wilfred said to Grandma, then looked at Lorna. "I'm going to be going now, but I want you to remember what I said. I'm almost certain I wasn't the intended target of that disturbed young woman."

"We will. Thank you, Reverend," Lorna said.

Wilfred's eyes smiled at everyone, avoiding Lindsey yet again, and then he pulled open the front door. He gave a start when he almost ran into Jadie standing there on the doorstep, doing something with her phone.

My sister looked up and said, "Hi."

I wondered if Wilfred had heard Jadie's greeting because the silence lasted for several moments before he finally responded with, "Hello."

Wilfred stood aside to let Jadie enter and watched as she moved next to Lindsey. He stared at the two of them momentarily, smiled at us all again, then left.

"Who was that?" Jadie asked, then her eyes grew big. "GRANDMA!"

My sister gave our grandmother a generous hug. It might have been my imagination, but I got the impression Grandma was trying to return the hug without actually touching Jadie.

When the two of them separated, Grandma gave a weak smile and addressed everyone. "Well, that's quite enough excitement for me tonight. I believe I'll be going as well."

I could feel the tension lift from my body as I realized Grandma wasn't here to rat me out about our earlier conversation.

Jadie pushed her lips out in a pout. "But I just got here," she pleaded as she watched Grandma give everyone parting hugs, except Lorna.

"I need to go, darling," Grandma explained. She retrieved her handbag from the entry table and gave Jadie the last hug. "David, call me in the morning if you decide to do the physicals tomorrow."

"I have reservist maneuvers this weekend, Ginny," Dad said, glancing at Lorna. "So, it will have to be some other time."

"Oh... okay. Well then, some other time." Grandma turned towards the door but didn't move. Then she said, "Knox, can I have a word with you in private before I go?"

Everybody looked at me without trying to hide their shock, and I couldn't blame them. It was the first time Grandma had ever called me Knox.

"Um... sure. You want to go to my room?"

"That's fine."

I headed into my room with Grandma right behind me, wondering what sort of blistering tongue-lashing I was in for. She closed the door behind us.

"I want to help."

I was stunned. "Huh?"

"Whatever it is you're mixed up in, I want to help you. I'm guessing it has something to do with a demon?"

All I could do was nod my head.

"Good. Why haven't you told your parents?"

"A combination of things. A lack of proof for one, a track record of not being able to tell the truth according to them, and I'm not one hundred percent convinced one of them isn't possessed."

"We'll figure something out. I need to know everything. The two friends you brought to the house, they're in on this as well?"

I nodded.

"Okay, then let's go someplace and you can tell me what we're dealing with."

When my tongue finally found a gear, I told her that Brodie and Lewis were waiting for me in Lewis's basement. She said that would work, even though Jules Bonvillain gave her the creeps.

"When I leave here, I'll head right over there. You make your way over in a few minutes. Okay?" Grandma said.

"Yeah, that's great. But—can I ask what made you change your mind?"

"My reasons are my own. You just have to know that I'll help you in any way that I can."

With that, she slipped out of the door. I heard her saying her goodbyes to everyone, and then the front door closed.

My mind was racing a mile a minute, but Travis wheeling into the room interrupted my thoughts. He shut the door behind him, then looked at me carefully.

"What the hell, Knox? That was some circus at school today, and some help this Wilfred turned out to be. What are we going to do?"

I stood up. "Travis, I really want to tell you everything, but I have to go next door and talk to Lewis first."

"Then take me with you. I don't want to be here by myself."

I gestured to Travis's wheelchair. "You know I can't do that. Mrs. Bonvillain had ramps and all that installed for you, but the only place we can talk without her hearing us is the basement or Lewis's room on the second floor, and they haven't worked out anything for either of those yet."

"You can carry me," he pleaded.

My brother's sad face was breaking my heart.

"I won't be long... promise, and I'll fill you in on everything when I get back. Stay here in the room or stick close to Dad. If Lorna asks where I went, tell her I'm working on a project with Lewis."

"On a Friday night? Like anyone would believe that. And she just finished making dinner."

I moved to the door. "Tell her I'm not hungry, and that's the truth. I'll be back soon."

I peeked out of our door and saw Lorna vacuuming the living room floor, her back to me. No one else was in sight. I quietly slipped out the front door and then sprinted over to Lewis's house.

The door opened before I even finished knocking.

Mrs. Bonvillain stood at the door, smiling. Over her shoulder, I could make out the outline of someone else.

"Hi, Mrs. Bonvillain," I said.

"Knox, what a coincidence. I was just standing here talking to your grandmother."

Mrs. Bonvillain opened the door wider and revealed my grandmother standing in the foyer, with a look that said *Get me out of here!*

"Why didn't you tell me your grandmother attended the same church as Lewis and me," Mrs. Bonvillain asked as she closed the door behind me.

"Oh, I doubt Knox knows where I go to church," Grandma said, placing her hand on my shoulder. "I've been trying to get their whole family to come out on Sunday, but I haven't had much luck."

"I expect you're here to see Lewis, right, Knox?"

"Actually, we both are," I said, putting my hand on top of my grandmother's, which was still on my shoulder.

"I was just about to explain that to you, Jules. The boys have asked for my medical expertise on a project they're working on," Grandma said.

Mrs. Bonvillain frowned. "And they made you come all the way into town instead of visiting you?"

"Oh no, this was my idea. It's better this way. I was already coming into town anyway to visit my grandchildren, so when I found out you lived right next door, I suggested we just meet here. I hope you don't mind?"

"Never. I'm glad you stopped by."

"Is Lewis downstairs?" I asked.

"Yes, he's down there with his friends. I'm surprised he hasn't come up. He's usually so attentive."

"Don't worry, Mrs. Bonvillain, I know the way," I replied as I started making my way down the hallway.

"Surely you're not going to take your grandmother down into that danky ole basement?" Mrs. Bonvillain called after us. "Why don't you meet around the kitchen table?"

"I don't mind, Jules," Grandma said over her shoulder. "Besides, the kids will be more communicative in their own environment."

"If you're sure, then?"

"Absolutely. We'll talk more afterward."

I led Grandma through the kitchen door and down the wooden stairwell. As I cleared the overhang on the way down, I could see Lewis and Brodie sitting in the matching beanbags, facing away from the wall of electronics and towards the back of the room.

Both of their faces were glum. That wasn't surprising, but neither of them seemed to react to my grandma's presence.

"I brought someone to help," I said as I reached the bottom of the steps.

"She can't help you," came a female voice from the back of the room. A young woman with short, trimmed, jet-black hair wearing a grey hoodie emerged from the shadows, pointing an old-fashioned six-shooter in our direction.

"No one can."

MOVING FEAR

Thirty-Four

Knox

"This is unexpected," my grandma said casually, accepting the appearance of a woman with a gun in stride. I was doing my best to appear unnerved.

"She was waiting for us when we got back," Lewis explained, talking fast. "I had to tell my mom she's Brodie's older cousin."

"You didn't have much choice with that gun in your back," Brodie added, her eyes burning holes through the stranger.

The young woman smiled, and then used the gun to motion to a spot next to Lewis and Brodie. "If you'll both take a seat, I'll put this away and then we can talk."

Grandma slowly moved between the woman and me. "Listen, Missy, whatever problems you're having, they will not get any better by—"

The woman pulled back the gun's hammer with her thumb. My heart skipped a beat. Maybe two.

"Don't even try, Granny. Just do as I ask. Take a seat, and nobody will get hurt."

Ginny put her hands on her hips. "Did you just call me granny?"

"Please do as she says and sit down, Mrs. Fuller," Brodie pleaded calmly.

When I could pull my eyes away from the gun, I recognized the woman holding it. She was the one at the school this afternoon who tried to shoot Wilfred. Given how conservative Ox-Bow was, she really stood out. She was in her early twenties, had a short bob hairstyle with the tips extending past her jawline, her right eyebrow was pierced, and sported dark eyeliner under her eyes. She had the look of someone I wouldn't want to mess with, gun or no gun.

"I don't think I will," grandma said, crossing her arms across her chest.

I could see where this was heading, so I took steps to defuse the situation before it got out of hand. Grabbing an old dining room chair from the corner, I placed it next to Brodie's beanbag, then locked eyes with my grandmother and silently willed her to sit in it. She did so, but with obvious reluctance. Then I positioned a beanbag next to her and sat down myself. When I settled, the woman slowly uncocked the gun and tucked it into the back of her jeans.

"Do you know this woman, Knox?" Grandma asked through gritted teeth.

"She's the one who shot off the gun at school today. And that gun looks familiar. I thought you left it behind at the school," I said.

"It's part of a pair that my father gave me, hero-boy. Thanks to you, I no longer have its brother. What's your name?"

"Knox Gidden, and this is my grandmother."

Grandma tilted her head back and stuck out her chin. "Ginny to my friends, but you can call me Mrs. Fuller."

"Who are you?" I asked.

"My name is Sierra. Sierra Pennington."

I looked sharply at Lewis, who must have had the same realization as I did.

"That's Wilfred's last name," Lewis said excitedly.

"Whose Wilfred?" Grandma asked.

"The priest you just met, the same one she tried to shoot," I answered.

"He's also my uncle," Sierra said flatly.

"Wait, you knew that priest before he showed up at your parents?" Grandma turned and asked me. I could see that she was becoming frustrated.

"He's not really a priest," I replied.

"If you're with Wilfred, why did you try to kill him?" Brodie asked Sierra.

Sierra looked defiantly at Brodie. "I'm not with him, and after you hear the complete story, you'll wish I had killed him. First things first. Let me make sure I understand everybody's part in this." Sierra turned and looked directly at me. "I know why my uncle has been following you, and I'm guessing you recruited Granny... sorry... Mrs. Fuller... to help, along with these two airheads."

Sierra motioned towards Lewis and Brodie, which prompted Lewis to return a muted smile.

"How did you know your uncle was following my family?" I asked.

"Because of the demon, ass-wipe. Don't play dumb with me."

"You know about Seraphim?" Lewis said.

"Whose Seraphim?" Grandma asked.

Sierra looked at the floor and shook her head. "This is worse than I thought. You shouldn't have gotten your friends involved. That was a bad move on your part."

"He didn't ask us. We volunteered," Lewis chimed in.

"That says a lot about how smart you **aren't**," Sierra shot back. "Look, I'm impressed that you know the demon's name, but this will go a lot quicker if you let me ask the questions. I'm guessing my uncle told you he was here to help your family get free of Seraphim?"

"The demon has a name?" Grandma said, looking more confused than ever. "I'm sorry, but I'm still playing catch-up."

"I'll explain it all to you later, Grandma. Yes, Wilfred told us he was here to help."

"And he told you about the visions?"

Three of us nodded.

"Well, I hate to burst your bubble, but he has no intention of helping you."

"Then why is he here?" Grandma asked, refusing to be relegated to the role of bystander.

"To assist Seraphim in any way he can."

The realization hit me like an icy wave. Suddenly, I couldn't breathe, and the temperature in Lewis' chilly basement seemed to have dropped fifty degrees. What had I done? I thought I had found an ally against this evil, but instead I had invited in the opposite. I felt like I was going to be sick.

"That's how he operates. He pretends to be a knight in shining armor to get close to the unsuspecting victims, telling them just enough to believe him, but all the while, he's manipulating things in Seraphim's favor. You should consider anything he's told you a lie. You cannot trust him. He will do anything to ensure that Seraphim has its feast."

"He's working with the demon?" Brodie asked, as if she couldn't believe what she was hearing.

"Then why did all the doors in my house slam shut and the TV explode in his face when he showed up at my house a little while ago? It was like the demon was pissed at him for being there," I said.

Sierra shook her head. "Seraphim doesn't control Wilfred. It barely acknowledges him. Wilfred is doing this on his own. He wants to get on the demon's good side. Seeking favor."

Lewis shook his head. "Why should we believe any of this? You could be the one helping the demon." I could tell he was channeling his doubting-Thomas role again, like he did with Wilfred. *Why didn't I listen to him then?*

"You're right to question everything. I would do the same if I were in your shoes. But I can prove to you I'm telling the truth. First, I need to give you a little more background. Have you noticed Wilfred always wears long-sleeved shirts with the neck buttoned to the top?"

"Yes," I answered.

"That's because his body is covered with tattoos pledging his allegiance to Seraphim and the demon realm. Many of his tattoos match the markings on the box. Did he tell you how the visions are passed down in our family?"

"Yes," I answered again.

"We call the person who can see the visions a *seer*."

"Of course you do," Brodie remarked, using her best snarky voice.

"Wilfred is my father's brother. Before Wilfred started seeing visions, there was only one Pennington per generation who could be a seer, and that was my father. When someone in the younger generation turns eighteen, they begin seeing the visions, and the previous seer stops receiving them. My father was older than Wilfred, and he became a seer when he turned eighteen. But two years later, when Uncle Wilfred turned eighteen, he started seeing the visions as well. Two seers. It had never happened before. Everyone considered it a sign. A sign we were gaining dominance over the evil with the gift of a second seer. Uncle Wilfred saw it differently.

"My dad said that when they were growing up, Uncle Wilfred was always a troublemaker. He despised school, had no hobbies or interests, and ran with the wrong crowds... or rather, they ran with him. When his visions started, he treated it as a contest—which brother could find the demon's victims before the other. But over time, Wilfred began to see the visions as something else. An opportunity. A chance to align himself with forces he thought would offer the best chance for ultimate victory and everlasting life. In short, he became a devil worshipper and turned into our family's sworn enemy. He is an outcast in the truest sense."

Grandma shifted in her chair. "Did something happen to your father?"

Sierra looked shaken by Grandma's question. "My uncle murdered him."

"I see."

"It happened in Portland, right after my father had rescued a family. Witnesses saw somebody matching my uncle's description running away from my father's hotel room. His throat had been cut."

"Bastard," Lewis blurted.

"That happened when I was seventeen, and he's been on the run from the police ever since. When I was eighteen, I had my first vision and became a seer. That's when I began my own hunt."

"And Wilfred still sees the visions?" I asked.

Sierra nodded her head. "Yes. My uncle and I see precisely the same thing. The visions only come to us during the brief time it takes for someone to be taken over. I saw an Ox-Bow church flyer in my vision when the person in your family was taken, and so did Wilfred, and that's how I knew he'd be here in Ox-Bow. I have a friend who knows a thing or two about computers, and he hacked the county's public school records to get me a list of newly enrolled students. It wasn't hard to find you after that."

"You said you could prove you weren't lying," Lewis said.

Sierra nodded and pushed herself away from the support beam. She took two steps closer to us.

"There's something else that happens to a seer when they begin having visions. We lose the ability to tell lies. Well, technically, we can speak an untruth, but our bodies give us away."

"How do you mean?" Brodie asked.

"That bean bag is green," Sierra said, pointing to the red bean bag I was sitting on. Then she stuck out her tongue.

It had turned pitch black.

"Ewwww," Brodie said.

Sierra drew her tongue back into her mouth, waited a couple of seconds, then showed it to us again. It looked normal now.

"There's your proof," Sierra said. "If anything I've told you was a lie, you would have known it."

I suddenly remembered something. "That night we first met Wilfred, I noticed something weird about his tongue, but I thought it was because of the poor light in his truck. And that's probably why he was wearing that surgical mask in our house. The son of a bitch has been lying to us."

"My uncle is extremely paranoid and cautious. After I watched him follow you to the school, I knew the person Seraphim possessed must be there as well. Then, when I saw the kids running out of the school, I knew he'd be drawn inside to see what was going on. He had to. It's a compulsion of his to watch the demon at work. So, I used the confusion to get the drop on him. It would have worked too if the boy hero here hadn't interfered."

Sierra tilted her head at me. All I could do was shrug my shoulders.

"Why was he dressed as a priest?" Brodie asked.

"He does that to gain the trust of the families Seraphim infects. People have a hard time saying no to a priest."

"Where's your mother?" Grandma asked.

Sierra blinked. Once again, Grandma's question had taken her off guard. "She's back home in Chicago. She's a schoolteacher."

"Does she know what you're up to?"

Sierra's expression hardened. "She knows I'm here doing what my family has always done."

"And she's aware that you are attempting to murder your uncle?"

That question went unanswered.

"You wouldn't have shot him," I blurted, letting a thought that had been bothering me spill out.

"Ummm... she did shoot at him, didn't she?" Brodie pointed out.

"The gun went off accidentally when I hit her arm," I said to Brodie. Sierra stood there with her arms crossed. I raised my hand towards her. "But I saw your face. There were tears in your eyes. I don't think you would have gone through with it."

Sierra gave me an unpleasant grin. "Don't be so sure of yourself."

"So... if I heard you correctly, you're not actually here to help Knox and his family?" Lewis asked. "You're in Ox-Bow after Wilfred."

"That's right."

"Then why are you talking to us?" Lewis said.

"I thought you ought to know who you're dealing with. Just in case I'm unable to stop him."

"You're still going after him, even though he knows you're here?" I asked.

"He killed my father."

Everyone fell silent, probably because, like me, nobody knew how to respond. I took the opportunity to consider everything we learned from Sierra, trying to plot a way forward. As I turned things over in my head, I kept coming back to the idea we pitched Grandma. In my gut, I knew our plan had promise, but then again, who was I but some fifteen-year-old kid thinking about taking on an unearthly demon?

I looked over at Ginny. When she looked back at me, I swear there was a glint in her eye. When a smile formed on her lips, the back of my neck began to tingle, and I knew what to do.

"What if I told you there's something you could do more satisfying than revenge?"

Sierra made a sour face.

"What if you could destroy Seraphim?" I asked.

Sierra shook her head. "It can't be done, and I have a thousand years of history to back that up."

I glanced at Ginny again, who nodded for me to continue. "I think it can be done. We just need to find a way to get that book back?"

Sierra's eyes narrowed. "What book?"

MOVING FEAR

Thirty-Five

Knox

"The book that your uncle made us put back, instead of burning it like I suggested. He must have been lying then, too?" Lewis asked, but I heard a distinct 'I told you so' in that tone.

"Hold on. I don't know anything about any book," Sierra said, her brows furrowed in puzzlement.

Lewis got up and went over to the table where a collection of papers was lying. He picked up a newspaper clipping and handed it to Sierra. We all watched and waited as she read the article.

"This is huge," Sierra said when she finished. "We never knew about a book."

"Can I read that?" Grandma asked, reaching out. Sierra handed her the article.

"There was never a survivor to tell anyone about the book before," I pointed out.

"But this changes everything we knew about how Seraphim operates. And my uncle knew about this?"

Both Lewis and I nodded our heads.

"Our family has always believed Seraphim's only link was through the box. I've never seen a book in my visions. No one has."

"Well, I've held it in my hands, and we need it for my plan to work," I said.

Sierra crossed her arms. "Tell me about this brilliant plan."

Brodie held up her open hand. "Before we go down that path, I want to again ask about getting a real priest involved," she said, then looked directly at Sierra. "Wilfred told Lewis and Knox that the church won't help us, but we know now that Wilfred was spewing lies left and right. What do you say?"

The dour expression on Sierra's face communicated the answer before she opened her mouth. "My uncle was telling you the truth about that. As soon as they hear the details about what has been happening, they'll run for the hills. But even getting to that point would take weeks, and you don't have that kind of time."

With Brodie's question answered, I spent the next several minutes outlining the broad strokes of our plan, how we would stop the heart of whoever was possessed, destroy the book once the demon had left their body, and then resurrect that person. At key points, Grandma would step in to explain how stopping and starting the heart would work.

"What do you think?" Lewis asked when I was finished.

Sierra shook her head. "It will never work. Seraphim will never let you close enough to put a needle in them."

"We got a demonstration of that at school today. But you agree, in theory, it might be possible to drive it out that way?" I asked.

Sierra started pacing again, as she had been doing nervously for the last fifteen minutes, her energy seemingly limitless.

"Based on what I've read about the woman in Arkansas, theoretically, yes. But you need to understand that it was a fluke. Even if we could figure out a way to make it happen without getting us all killed, which is a huge IF, there's the part of bringing your sister back to life... which even your grandmother admits isn't a given. And don't forget, if we fail and can't bring her back to life, we'll all be guilty of murder."

"Some demon hunter you are," Lewis said under his breath.

"Listen, nose-boy, all my dad ever taught me was how to locate the family in danger, grab as many as I could, and then run like hell. His exact words were, *"We don't do battle; we simply save who we can save."* What you're talking about here, well, it ain't that."

I looked into the eyes of Lewis, then Brodie. I knew what the smart thing to do was, the prudent thing, but I also knew I couldn't sacrifice one of my sisters. I couldn't let the demon have them. My two friends barely knew my family, and I couldn't ask them to put themselves in danger to help save one, but I had to be sure about one other person.

I looked at Ginny again. "Grandma, I can't just walk away, not if there's even a glimmer of hope."

My grandma leaned over and laid her hand on mine.

"You asked me why I changed my mind and decided to help. A long time ago, I faced a similar choice. I'm ashamed to admit that I wasn't strong enough... and I turned my back. I chose to run away instead. There was somebody I could've helped, and I didn't even try. It was probably my lowest point in this life. But not this time."

Ginny looked at everyone in the room. "I DO believe in demons, and I also believe you fail one hundred percent of the time if you don't try."

Ginny held out her hands, and I took hold of them.

"I failed someone once, but I won't fail my daughter's family this time."

Even if I could think of something to say, I couldn't say it with my throat choked up as it was.

"That's a sweet sentiment," Sierra observed. "But it may not be up to you."

For a long time, nobody said a word. It was my grandmother who broke the silence.

"My grandson's plan might have some holes, but I believe in him." Grandma looked directly into Sierra's eyes. "However, we need you for it to work."

I watched as doubt and uncertainty revealed themselves on Sierra's face.

"We're talking about killing a demon. Something that has never been done before," she said solemnly.

"Yes, I am. What do you say?"

Little by little, the uncertainty faded, replaced by narrow eyes and a clenched jaw.

"I'm in."

"You know I'm in," Lewis announced.

My heart sank as I turned to face my neighbor. "Lewis, you can't help us with this. There's a good chance it won't work, and I couldn't live with myself if something happened to you."

Lewis smiled and touched his glasses. "Knox, if this doesn't work, you won't have to live with yourself. You'll be dead. You're going to need my help."

I reached out and straightened his glasses. "You're the first friend I've made in a very long time... definitely best friend material, but—" I glanced at Grandma, "—this is a family matter."

Lewis appeared stricken. "But, Sierra's not family."

"No, but this is kinda her job. Her calling."

Lewis's head looked like it was on a swivel, swinging back and forth between all of us. "But... I... we... you can't—" he stammered.

"I know how much you'd like to help, but I just can't take the risk of—"

"We're helping," Brodie said, cutting me off. We all turned to look at her, standing off by herself with tears in her eyes.

"We may not be family, but in Lewis's and my experience, a family isn't always what it's cracked up to be. You know what is? Bonds formed by choice. Having each other's back. Doing something for another person, even when there's a real cost. You know... go big or go home... all in mentality? That's how Lewis and I feel about you, Knox. I realize you're trying to protect us, and that just makes us want to help you more. Make no mistake about it. We. Are. Helping."

My heart filled with so much emotion at that moment that I couldn't speak. Luckily, I didn't have to.

Ginny reached out and put a hand on both Lewis and Brodie's shoulders. "For someone who sucks at making friends, you sure snagged yourself a couple of good ones, Knox. So, how do we do this?"

"I think I know a way we can knock out Seraphim without getting too close," Brodie said.

"We're listening," I said.

"There's a boy in my calculus class, Tyler, I think his name is, his dad works at the Tulsa Zoo. He's one of the veterinarians there and takes care of the big cats. We could convince Tyler to sneak us one of his dad's tranquilizer guns and some empty darts."

"Convince him how?" Lewis asked.

Brodie rubbed her fingers together.

Lewis's eyebrows shot up. "Oh. Yeah, I could do that."

Brodie looked at Ginny. "Do you think that would work if we got one?"

Grandma reflected on that for a moment. "Yes, I believe it would. Even though it takes two injections, the first is a heavy sedative, and the second stops the heart. We could use the gun to deliver the first injection, which should incapacitate her and allow us time to administer the second."

Sierra rocked back and forth as she shifted her weight back between her feet. "It's a great idea, but you'll need to get her out of the house for a clean shot far enough away from her—just in case the tranquilizer takes a while to kick in."

"I'm just as concerned about the sedative as I am about stopping the heart," Grandma said. "If we get that dosage wrong, we could do serious damage. But I realize we have little choice. What about the school gym? It's wide open. There'll be no one there on the weekend. I can set up the other equipment I need to revive her, and since I've been doing the physicals for all the girls' sports teams for years, I have a key."

"Okay, the school gym then," Sierra announced. "How long will it take to get the drugs and the tranq gun? Remember, time is of the essence. You said your dad is away this weekend, so Seraphim probably won't do anything major while he's gone. It's better to wait until everyone is home so it can get you all. But the longer we wait, the greater the chance it figures out we're on to it."

Lewis looked at Brodie. "I think we can get the gun by tomorrow afternoon."

"Same with the drugs," added Grandma.

"Then Saturday afternoon," Sierra said, looking at each of us.

"Good idea. How do we get your sisters to the school? Maybe a better question is, how do we find out which one it is?" Brodie asked.

"I have that figured out, but we'll have to test them one at a time," Sierra said.

"Lorna goes grocery shopping on Saturday afternoons, so we'll do it then," I said. "I'll get Travis to sweet-talk Jadie into taking him to a movie, just to get them both out of the house in case something goes wrong. Then I'll tell Lindsey I need to go to the school because I left something in my gym locker that I'll need before Monday."

"Why Lindsey?"

"Let's just say I have a hunch."

"How will you explain getting into the school to Lindsey?"

"Lorna has a key. She keeps hanging by the fridge."

"Okay, so Ginny and I will wait at the school for the two of you," Sierra said. "You get there, join us in the gym, then when you don't come back out, she'll have to come in looking for you. That's when we'll zap her. But before we do this, I want to test her to make sure she's the one possessed. I don't want to kill the wrong person."

"How do you test her?" Brodie asked, taking a spot beside Lewis. "Is there a demon pop-quiz? With all these rules and things, isn't there some kind of book we can read? You know, like *Demons For Dummies*?"

I had to laugh at that, but Sierra's expression was unchanged.

"Actually, there is," she said. "My father's notebook. It was something else handed down from generation to generation. Pretty much everything we knew about Seraphim was in that book."

"Where is the notebook?" I asked.

"Wilfred stole it from my father when he murdered him," Sierra answered flatly.

This time, the silence that filled the basement seemed to have weight, and it was heavy.

Sierra reached into her backpack and removed a clear plastic water bottle.

"Holy water. One drop will immediately cause blisters on anyone possessed."

"I thought that was for vampires?"

"Never ran across any of those, but my dad said it works like a charm on people possessed by demons. Be careful though, you dare not use it until you're pretty darn sure you've identified who it is, because Seraphim will know instantly it's been found out and all hell will break loose. That's another good reason for doing this in the gym—a minimal amount of pointy objects or heavy furniture to be tossed around."

"We have the same problem, though—how to get close enough to use the holy water."

"You do what someone did to coach Rawlings last year," Lewis suggested. "You rig a bucket over the door to the gym so when Lindsey walks through, she gets doused. It's easy."

"So, we're going 1970s now?" Brodie said.

"The classics never die," Sierra replied, winking at Grandma, who didn't appreciate the humor.

"And if it turns out not to be Lindsey?" I asked.

"Then she just gets wet, and we do the whole thing again the next day with your other sister."

"Okay, but won't Lindsey tell Jadie what happened, and the demon will be on guard?" Brodie pointed out.

"My grandson is well-known for his pranks," Ginny said. "We can play it off as such."

"Okay then. We'll need the demon's book you talked about," Sierra said.

"Brodie and I can get that," Lewis spoke up quickly. "I know where it's hidden."

"What if the demon moved it?" Sierra said.

"I was with Knox when he searched his house for the first time. I know where to look if it's not there."

I patted Lewis on the back, secretly relieved to have him involved again. Still, I was going to make sure he and Brodie stayed as far away from the action as possible.

"Great," Sierra said with a nod. "Knox, you leave the door open for them, and as soon as you and Lindsey leave, they'll go inside, grab the book, and follow you both to the school. When your sister goes down, we'll have a brief window of time to burn the book and destroy this thing once and forever."

"How will we know when the demon is back in the book?" Grandma asked.

"My guess is that there will be some sort of disturbance, much like when the possession first took place. You described it as the light disappearing. It will be something like that, and we'll just have to watch for it," Sierra said.

"That's it then, we have a solid plan," Ginny said, putting her hands on her hips. "There's one more thing I think we should do before Saturday?"

"What's that?" I asked.

"Ft. Smith is less than three hours from here. I think we should pay a visit to the woman survivor to see if there's anything else we can learn."

"Will they let you in to talk to her?" Brodie asked.

Ginny shrugged. "I'll figure something out, but I think it's worth the trip."

"Then I want to go with you," I said.

"You can't, Knox," Sierra said. "Seraphim will know something is up if you disappear for the day."

"That's right," Brodie agreed.

"Then I'll go with you," Lewis suggested. "Nobody will miss me, and I probably know as much about what's going on as anybody else, except Sierra, of course."

Sierra returned Lewis's grin.

"Fine by me. We'll leave first thing in the morning. Should I come pick you up?" Ginny said.

"I'll drop him by your house," Brodie offered. "That way his mom won't be suspicious."

Ginny nodded her agreement. "Bring some church-going clothes to change into."

"Yes, ma'am."

A sudden thought struck me. "We forgot about something."

"What's that?" Sierra asked.

"Wilfred. He's not going to just sit around twiddling his thumbs."

We all thought about how to handle this not-so-minor detail.

"I'm not really needed at the school gym, so I can take care of him," Sierra offered.

"No way. You are needed at the school," I said, raising my voice. "I know you want to deal with your uncle, but there will be time for that later. You know this demon better than any of us, and if things go wrong, we'll need you there."

"If things go wrong, you won't need me. You'll need the marines."

"I know a way to distract Wilfred," Lewis said, drawing stares from everyone. "But it will mean breaking a law or two."

Thirty-Six

<u>Lewis</u>

Ginny and Lewis had driven most of the way to Ft. Smith in silence. Lewis was kicking himself for volunteering so quickly because Knox's grandma made him extremely nervous. She wasn't anything like the women he grew up around, especially his mother, so he didn't know how to talk to her. He really wanted to because he was curious. It wasn't until they had entered the city limit that Lewis worked up enough courage to ask the question he'd been dying to ask since yesterday.

"You knew that family the demon killed in 1979, didn't you? In Oklahoma City?"

Ginny's shoulders slumped, but her gaze remained fixed on the road ahead.

"How did you know?" she asked.

"I looked you up last night. You did your residency at the same hospital the family went to days before they..."

The tip of Ginny's lips lifted ever so slightly in the beginning of a smile, but that's as far as it went.

"You are a smart one," she said.

Lewis pushed his glasses up from the bridge of his nose. "You can find anything out on the internet these days."

Ginny nodded. "My medical career was getting started, which now seems like a lifetime ago. It was before I met Chace's grandfather. There was this one patient—a young woman. I had forgotten about her until Chace started asking me those questions. Maybe forgotten isn't fair. It was more like I blocked out the memory of her."

Ginny fell silent as she revisited old memories.

"At first I thought her husband was abusing her… but then… what I saw. I came face to face with something that day — maybe it was something like this Seraphim — who knows — but instead of helping her and her family, I ran. I was so scared. Please don't tell Chace and the others. I couldn't face them if they knew."

"I won't… but I don't think you could have done anything," Lewis said.

"Maybe not," Ginny glanced at Lewis. "The husband of that woman told me his wife had been docile except when he was marching her into the ER entrance. As an attending doctor, I rarely used the main entrance, so I went out to the lobby weeks later. I'm not sure why… but I did."

"And?"

"It was a gorgeous day, so I walked out the front doors and stood for a few minutes. I think I was trying to let the sun's rays burn off the dark feeling I had been carrying around with me. It had worked too because I could feel my mood improve just standing there. But then I turned around and saw it."

"It?"

"As soon as you walk through the doors of Mercy, they have this wall that makes you choose to go right or left. Mounted on that wall was a large, backlit cross."

Lewis thought about that for a moment. "That's interesting. Portals to interdimensional worlds or not, there is definitely a religious element to this."

The two of them dealt with their own thoughts until they pulled into the parking lot of their destination.

"Are you sure this is going to work?" Lewis asked, fidgeting with his tie.

"We'll know soon enough," Ginny responded before pulling open the building door.

Ginny had told Lewis earlier that she had learned who the primary care physician was for the woman they were going to see, a Dr. Pricilla Weatherstone, and had reached out to her. Ginny explained that she was a doctor herself and had her own patient who exhibited similar symptoms, though her patient hadn't harmed anyone… yet. She was requesting permission from Dr. Weatherstone to visit the patient, Evelyn Cole, in hopes of gaining insight into whatever was causing the unusual delusions. Dr. Weatherstone was surprisingly accommodating, probably because she doubted Ginny would gain much from the visit, since Evelyn Cole was still uncommunicative. Even still, Dr. Weatherstone would leave word at the facility where Mrs. Cole was being held to allow Dr. Ginny Alvarez access.

"How did you explain that I would be tagging along with you?" Lewis had asked.

"I didn't mention you."

After a couple of moments of listening to the car driving down the highway, Lewis said, "Ummmm… don't you think that's going to be a problem?"

"I have an idea about how to get you in, but we'll have to wing it, okay?"

"I'm not very good at winging it, to be honest."

"Don't worry. Worst case, you'll just have to wait in the car while I talk to this woman."

And now, as Ginny held the door open so Lewis could enter the lobby of the Arkansas State Hospital, his palms were sweating. Once they entered the building Ginny jerked her head in the direction of some chairs, and per her previous instructions, Lewis made a beeline for them and sat down. Ginny then strolled through the vast lobby and confidently up to the receptionist's desk,

"How can I help you?" the woman behind the desk asked.

"I'm here to interview Evelyn Cole. I believe Dr. Weatherstone made arrangements for me," Ginny said with hesitation.

The woman typed something into her computer terminal, and a few seconds later, she nodded.

"I have you checked in. If you'll take a seat in the chairs, someone will be out soon to take you back."

"Thank you very much," Ginny replied with a smile, then walked slowly over to the row of chairs where Lewis was currently sitting and took the one beside him.

Ginny turned to Lewis. "So good so far. Now, when they come to take me back, I want you to get up and follow me, but stay quiet. Let me do all the talking. And also, don't smile."

"Oh, don't worry," Lewis replied.

The two of them didn't have long to wait as an orderly dressed all in white stepped through a door at the end of a small hall and called for Dr. Alvarez.

Ginny and Lewis rose from their seats, and as they approached the orderly, he gave Lewis an inquiring look.

"Ummm…who's this?" the orderly asked, looking down at Lewis.

"This rascal is my grandson, Lewis."

The orderly's expression changed from puzzled to resolute. "He can't come back with you."

Ginny adopted an embarrassed smile.

"Listen…" Ginny's eyes darted to the orderly's security tag, "…Vince, I'm in a bit of a pickle. My daughter has an important job interview today… came up at the last minute… and she asked me to watch her son while she went."

"He can wait for you out here," Vince replied flatly.

Ginny took a few steps to the side, forcing Vince to follow. Her smile had now turned into a grimace. "I can't really," she said in hushed tones. "I'm embarrassed to admit that my daughter's family is... well... a shitstorm. My grandson, Lewis, is a bit of a flight risk. He's already run away from home twice. I'm afraid that if I leave him alone, he'll bolt. I'm doing what I can to help, but not everyone in the family is appreciative, if you know what I mean."

Vince glanced over at the unsmiling Lewis.

"Then you'll have to reschedule your appointment to see Mrs. Cole," he said.

Ginny shook her head. "I can't do that either. Come on, Vince, work with me here. You and I both know that this is a waste of time because Evelyn Cole isn't going to say a word. But I've promised another client's family that I would do this. Today is the only day that works for me, but I've got this sorry excuse for a grandson hanging around my neck. Let me take him back there with me, he'll sit in a corner and won't say a word, which is his usual mode of operation anyway, and I'll ask my questions to Evelyn and be done with it. How about it?"

Vince looked over at Lewis again, then back at Ginny, then stuck his hands in his pockets.

Ginny nodded, then reached into her coat pocket and pulled out five one-hundred-dollar bills.

"I forgot to give you our visitors' passes," Ginny said.

Vince quickly jammed the money into his pocket. "She's already in place in the interview room. Follow me, but he'd better not say a word."

Lewis did everything he could to keep the apparent look of shock off his face as he followed Ginny and the orderly down several hallways. He drew a curious stare from another orderly they passed, but nobody questioned his presence. They ended up in front of a door with a foldable chair leaning up against the wall next to it. The orderly used the set of keys hanging from his belt to open the door, revealing a brightly lit room where a woman was already sitting at a small metal table. Lewis could see that the small room had a two-way mirror on one wall and an old radiator with a pipe running along the baseboard.

The orderly took the foldable chair, opened it, and then set it against the wall opposite the mirror. He looked at Lewis and pointed to it.

Lewis sat down, but he couldn't take his eyes off the woman on the other side of the table. What he could make out through the black hair hanging in front of her face was that she was extremely pale with dark circles under her eyes. She was wearing loosely fitting, well-worn maroon scrubs. The way she was sitting in the chair —head bowed, shoulders slumped —made him think she might be asleep.

Ginny took the seat opposite Evelyn Cole, placing the palms of her hands flat on the table in front of her.

"Just give a knock on the door when you're finished," Vince the orderly said, then closed and locked the door behind him.

Ginny motioned with her head for Lewis to take the seat beside her, but he didn't move.

"Lewis, she's not going to hurt you."

Lewis still didn't move.

"My mom was in a place like this, wasn't she?" Lewis finally said, his eyes dropping down to stare at the hands in his lap.

Ginny's expression drooped. "Oh, honey. No. The help your mom received was voluntary. She didn't commit a crime, just lost her way for a bit. Where she stayed was nothing like this, I promise."

Lewis rubbed his thumb with the other.

"Come sit next to me, and let's see if we can get Evelyn to talk to us."

Lewis shuffled over and sat next to Ginny. When they both looked across the table, they were shocked to see Evelyn Cole staring back at them. Her attention seemed focused on Lewis.

"You... your name is Lewis?" Evelyn's raspy voice asked.

Lewis nodded slowly.

"My boy's name was Louie."

Lewis glanced at Ginny, who nodded with her encouragement.

"That's a nice name. My dad wanted to call me Louie, but my mom said I looked more like a Lewis."

"Louie's dead," Evelyn said. Her head was still raised, but her gaze had dropped to the table. "I killed him."

"That's not true, Evelyn," Ginny said. "You didn't kill Louie, or anyone else. Something that was using your body did."

Evelyn's eyes locked on Ginny. "You know?"

Ginny nodded. "We know. You opened a box and let loose an evil that destroyed your family."

Evelyn straightened her back and seemed more alert. "You must know Wilfred."

Ginny and Lewis exchanged a surprise look.

"You met Wilfred?"

"He came to see me. Told them he was my priest. He knows about the box and the demon. He said he was trying to help others so they wouldn't go through what I did."

Ginny sighed. "Evelyn, Wilfred is not who he claims to be. He is not trying to help you or anyone else."

Evelyn appeared confused. "I don't understand."

"Wilfred is working with the demon," Lewis explained. "He tricks people by pretending to help them."

Evelyn stared first at Lewis, then at Ginny, raised her arms, and brought her fists crashing down. When her fist collided with the tabletop, the mirror on the wall behind her splintered but remained intact, causing both Lewis and Ginny to jump in their seats.

After a couple seconds of silence, Ginny said, "I... uh...I mean, Lewis and I know someone who is currently being possessed by this same demon." Ginny's eyes were still drawn to the splintered mirror. "And we need your help. Can you tell us anything that might help us, Evelyn?"

Evelyn relaxed her fists and let them fall into her lap. When she answered, her voice sounded tired and defeated. "All I remember is opening the box, seeing a book, then waking up soaking wet with my sister hovering over me. I don't remember any of what I did."

Lewis thought to himself how that was probably a blessing.

"How many others has this happened to?" Evelyn asked.

"This has been going on for centuries, so it's hard to say," Lewis answered.

"You may not know, but was your heart actually stopped before your sister saved you?" Ginny asked.

Evelyn stared at a spot between Lewis and Ginny, thinking.

"I recall someone afterward saying that I had no pulse."

"Thank you, that's helpful," Ginny said.

"That same person joked that they couldn't give me the death penalty because I already died once."

"I'm sorry," Lewis said instinctively.

Evelyn leveled her gaze at Lewis. "I'm the one who's sorry. Somebody you know is going to die soon, and there isn't anything you can do about it."

"I think we'll be going now," Ginny said.

Thirty-Seven

<u>Knox</u>

All the pieces were in place.
    Outside my window, the sky looked bruised. The weather had been threatening rain all day, but all it had really delivered was blustery winds. The tree branches lining the street waved back and forth as Mother Nature set the stage for nastiness sure to come. What a perfect day for what we had planned. I only hoped the storm would hold off long enough for us to execute our plan.
    I glanced at the clock for the hundredth time, then went to the closet, pulled out the oversized towel and photo album I had placed there earlier, and set them on my bed.
    I was ready.
    Grandma had just texted, informing me she and Sierra were at the school. Lewis and Brodie were a block away in Brodie's car, waiting for me to leave. Lorna was doing her shopping, and my brother was at the movies with Jadie. I was alone in the house with Lindsey... and the demon. It was now or never, and in this case, *never* meant condemning my sister to certain death.
    The choice was obvious: Now.
    I glanced at the clock by my bed again. Six fifty-five.

I took a deep breath, then walked out of my room.

When I last checked, Lindsey had been dividing her attention between the television our dad had brought down from their bedroom and her tablet. Now the TV was turned off, and she was nowhere to be seen. The house was eerily quiet.

I made my way down the hallway to the kitchen, expecting to see her grabbing a snack or drink, but it was empty as well. Where could she be? I would have heard her footsteps on the stairs if she had gone to her room. I stepped over to the door leading into Dad's study, but she wasn't there either.

"LINDSEY," I yelled.

"Yes," came a calm voice from behind me.

I spun around so fast I almost tripped on my own feet. I gathered myself and stood face to face with my sister.

"Jeeeez... you scared the crap out of me," I admitted.

Lindsey placed her hands on her hips. "Why are you so jumpy?"

"I'm not... unless someone sneaks up on me."

"I wasn't sneaking up on you. I followed you here from the living room."

"I was looking for you. Can you take me to school? I need to get a book out of my locker?"

Lindsey turned around and headed toward the refrigerator. "When Lorna gets back, she can take you."

"But it's really important, I need it now."

Lindsey stopped and turned back to look at me. "The school is locked, nimrod."

"Lorna keeps a key on the hooks. I can let myself in and be out in two minutes."

"You need a schoolbook now, on a Saturday afternoon?"

"Lewis and I have plans to go fishing tomorrow, and I know I won't have time to do it then, so I'm trying to finish it now. If I don't turn in this assignment on Monday, the first grade I get in Social Studies will be a zero."

Lindsey continued her slow walk to the refrigerator door, with me trailing behind. She reached in and came back with a can of Diet Coke. "You know what Dad would say. 'That's not very responsible of you.' Maybe we should make this a lesson and have you just accept the poor grade?"

I half-expected this. "I don't think Dad would want me to take a poor grade just to learn a lesson. Besides, if I don't turn in this assignment, then I'll have to do make-up work after school for a week, which means somebody will have to come pick me up every day."

Lindsey stared at me for a long time before saying, "Go lock the front door."

I ran up the hallway, pretended to lock the door, then ran back. Lindsey pulled her key-strap off the serving counter, then watched me as I grabbed Lorna's school key from the hooks. My smile showed my readiness, and I followed her out the back door.

Pulling out of the driveway, I nonchalantly looked down the street at the red pickup sitting in the shadows.

MOVING FEAR

Thirty-Eight

Lewis

Lewis slapped Brodie's thigh and pointed out the windshield of her Honda. "There they go."

"I see them," Brodie answered, her voice a calm contrast to Lewis's excited one.

Lindsey's car headed straight at them, then turned south and disappeared around the corner. Brodie twisted the ignition of her car, shifted it into drive, then gunned the accelerator. Within seconds, they pulled into Knox's driveway and parked.

"Don't forget to leave the keys in the ignition," Lewis instructed.

"I will."

"And you have my mom's keys, right?"

"For the hundredth time, yes! You just make sure you take care of my car," Brodie said.

Lewis climbed out of the Honda, resisting the urge to turn his head towards the red pickup down the street. He and Brodie went up the steps and tried the door. It opened without resistance.

They both stepped inside, closing the door behind them, then went directly to Knox's bedroom. Once there, Lewis picked up the oversized towel from Knox's bed, wrapped it around the large photo album, then clutched the bundle to his chest.

"Gotta wait a couple minutes to make it seem real," he said to Brodie, who was watching him from the doorway.

The two of them stood silently for a minute, Lewis bouncing back and forth with excited energy, Brodie looking at him with concern.

"Next time I suggest you make friends with your neighbor, slap me," she said.

Lewis's broad smile hid his nervousness.

Brodie wiped some dust from the top of Knox's dresser. "Lewis... I have to tell you something... before we do this," she said hesitantly.

"What?" Lewis replied, his attention focused on something outside the bedroom window.

"My mother... she..."

Lewis redirected his gaze to Brodie, but she wasn't saying anything and appeared anxious.

"Your mother what?" Lewis prompted.

"She... she was the woman your father left your mother for." Then after a brief silence, she added, "I'm so sorry."

Lewis scrunched up his face. "What for?"

Brodie looked like she was about to burst into tears. "Because she ruined your life."

Now Lewis appeared confused. "First off, my dad did that, not your mother. And secondly, I don't consider my life ruined. I have you, Knox, and a boatload of money, which all seems pretty awesome to me. Even so, why are you sorry?"

Brodie began pacing back and forth. "I don't know... I just am. She's my mother."

"Brodie, our parents are always trying to dump their baggage on us, but that doesn't mean we have to carry it."

Brodie stood still and regarded Lewis. "That's good."

Lewis smiled. "I think my therapist told me that. Or maybe I heard it on one of the talk shows my mom always watches."

Now it was Brodie's turn to smile. "So, you don't hate me?"

"Pssh. Like that could ever happen," Lewis replied before looking out the window again.

"You know, when the time is right, you need to pass on that nugget of advice to Knox."

Lewis glanced back. "True dat. Listen, you have to remember that after I leave, the real book is in the luggage underneath the bed in the room directly over this one. You'll know it when you see it."

"Please be careful, Lewis."

"Don't worry about me. I'll be fine."

"I'm not talking about you. It's my car I'm worried about."

Lewis fake-frowned before heading for the front door. He paused before opening it, looking back at Brodie once more.

"Showtime," he said, and was out the door.

MOVING FEAR

Thirty-Nine

<u>Wilfred</u>

He'd been watching the house for hours, using the time to plan out his next move and ponder recent events. Sierra showing up wasn't a complete surprise, but trying to kill him certainly was. And using one of the same guns he had given to her father years ago? That was a nice touch. He loved the irony of the Gidden boy saving his life, but he needed to be extra careful now. Although Sierra had lost the element of surprise, he knew she was highly motivated and resourceful.

The Gidden boy and his sister had just taken off in their car. He debated following them, but chose to stay put and watch over the book instead. That turned out to be the right decision because a few minutes later, the big-nose neighbor kid showed up with some girl, and Wilfred watched them walk through the front door like they owned the place.

"Something's not right," Wilfred said aloud to himself.

That neighbor boy—Lewis—had been suspicious of Wilfred's story from the start, despite Knox's gullibility. Maybe the kid was taking matters into his own hands. Wilfred couldn't take a chance that the boy would accidentally mess things up. He swung open his door and then froze.

The neighbor boy burst out of the house holding something wrapped in a towel and tucked under his arm. *It had to be the book!* The boy jumped into the car and whipped it out of the driveway, peeling the tires as it sped off down the street.

Wilfred slammed his door shut, fired up the truck, and pulled a hard U-turn. He couldn't let some reject from The Breakfast Club screw things up now.

Forty

Knox

I slid the key into the lock and opened the door to the teacher-designated entrance. Before entering, I glanced back at Lindsey, still sitting behind the wheel of her car in the handicap parking spot.

"I'll just be a minute," I lied, then disappeared inside.

I ran down the dark hallway, paused at the first corner to check and make sure Lindsey wasn't following me, and then sprinted for the gym. As I turned the last corner, I could see Sierra sticking her head out of the first push-door leading into the gym. When I got closer, she opened the door wide enough to let me slip inside.

"Your granny's not back yet," Sierra said as soon as she shut the door. There was tension in her voice.

"Back? Where'd she go?" I asked, matching Sierra's volume. "I thought the two of you were together?"

"We were. But not long after we got here, Ginny told me she had to run a quick errand. I don't know where she is."

"She got the tranq gun from that kid, right?"

Sierra nodded. "He liberated it from his dad, no sweat."

"How long has she been gone?"

"At least thirty minutes, maybe more."

"Crap!"

"We gotta call this off and try it another day."

"Another day may not—"

The gym door flung open, and Grandma hurried inside. She was wearing Grandpa's old fishing vest, the one with multiple pockets across the chest. Slung over her shoulder was a very old rucksack, and in her arms was a rifle, very similar to the paintball guns I had used before. The gun was made of forest-green tubing, with a black trigger guard, a black barrel, a telescopic sight, and a silver cylinder screwed into the trigger guard below the barrel.

"Where have you been?" I asked.

Grandma handed the rifle to Sierra. "I had something to do. Don't worry, we're fine."

Sierra stood the rifle up against the wall and pulled a small rubber doorstop out of her pocket. She placed the doorstop in front of the door to keep it ajar, then reached for a long wooden board propped against the wall next to the rifle.

"Give me a hand with this," she said, extending the board for me to take a side. The two of us lifted it and balanced it atop the two recoil arms attached to the automatic closers on either side of the dual doors. When the board was in place, she reached for a small plastic bucket filled with water and placed it on the board, centered on the partially open door.

"I sure don't miss high school," Sierra said as she surveyed our handiwork.

"What if it doesn't spill on her?" Grandma asked.

"Even if it doesn't land directly on her, it will splash, and one drop is all it will take."

Sierra reclaimed the rifle, and I followed the two of them, making our way through the dimly lit gym to the other side of the folded bleachers. I recalled what had taken place the last time I was in the gym, and it made my skin crawl.

When we reached our position, a medical kit that looked like an oversized fishing tackle box and a red plastic box shaped like a lunch pail were already there.

"What's in the red box?" I asked.

"The school's portable defibrillator. Just in case."

Sierra positioned her body up against the bleacher and raised the tranquilizer rifle to adjust the sights. I took up a position behind her, positive that everyone could hear the thumping of my heart in my chest.

"How far can that thing shoot?" I asked.

"From what I read, its range is a hundred yards, but only really accurate to fifty."

I measured the distance to the gym door in my head. I estimated it was about 50 yards.

"She should be coming anytime now," Grandma said behind us, a slight flutter in her voice. It was the first time I recall hearing her sound unsure of herself.

My phone vibrating in my pocket startled me. I pulled it out quickly and looked at the caller ID. Brodie.

"Are you on your way?" I answered.

"The book isn't where you and Lewis said it was. I've gone through everything underneath your parents' bed, and there's no book."

"Shit!" I exclaimed.

"What is it?" Sierra asked.

"The book isn't where we found it before. Lindsey must have moved it."

"Shit. Now Brodie will have to search the entire house to find it," Grandma said.

"Tell her to look in the basement," Sierra interjected. "The demon has always favored dark, musty locations. The murders have often occurred near them, and there's usually been evidence of some sort of disturbance in them afterward."

I passed the message along, and all I heard was a weak, "okay." Then the line went dead.

"How long can we keep Lindsey unconscious before we have to give her the second shot?" Sierra asked.

"For a normal person, with this dosage, she should be out for hours," Grandma said. "But we're not exactly dealing with normal, are we?"

"Maybe I can stall by telling her I grabbed the wrong book—".

"Chace?" came a muffled cry right outside the gymnasium.

"Too late."

Forty-One

Lewis

By his count, he had now run three stop signs, two red lights, and exceeded the speed limit by at least 20 mph in spots, but the chipped paint hood of the red Dodge pickup was still on his tail. He really thought such reckless driving would have drawn the attention of at least one police officer by now. He was going to have to resort to Plan B.

He jerked the wheel to the right, squealing the Honda's tires as he made a sharp turn onto Mulberry Drive. In the rear-view mirror, he saw the red pickup match his maneuver by swerving into the oncoming lane, drawing horn blasts from cars forced to jam on their brakes.

Just four more blocks, and he'd be home free. He didn't care if Brodie was worried or not; this was the most fun he'd had since... ever. No video game or computer simulation could rival this experience. He was darting back and forth between lanes to avoid slower traffic and using the passing lane to bypass congestion. His heartbeat had to be going a mile a minute, and there were times he had to remind himself to breathe. If he could, he'd keep this going all night, but he needed to distract Wilfred and get to the school with the rest of them. Brodie was probably there by now, so it was time to end this.

He blew through yet another stop sign, and up ahead, he could make out the soft glow of the theater marquee. He had read online that a new horror movie was due out today, *Saw Infinity*. The theater would be packed, and people would be mingling everywhere. There were always patrol cars working the crowd on the weekends, so all he had to do was zoom through the parking lot, with the red pickup close behind, and hope they'd catch Wilfred first.

When he turned into the parking lot, it was full of cars, vans, trucks and SUVs as expected, but no people. Glancing at the time on the dashboard clock, he knew why. It was 7:15 and the movie probably started at 7:00. Everyone was inside already. And to make matters worse, there were no police to be seen.

Dammit! Where was a cop when you needed one?

Lewis had to slow down to wind his way through the cramped space. He still felt safe, though. There was nobody around, but this was a high-traffic area, and surely Wilfred wouldn't…

His head jerked back sharply when the red truck plowed into the back of Brodie's car.

Forty-Two

Knox

"Chace, are you in there?"

Grandma and I shrank further behind Sierra, who was now aiming the tranquilizer rifle at the gym door.

"Chace?"

"I'm back here," I called out, improvising.

Time seemed to stretch out forever as nothing happened. *Did she hear me? Is she headed in this direction? Has she sniffed out our trap?*

The gym door abruptly swung open. As it did, the recoil arm retracted until the board was no longer supported, causing both the board and the pail of water to topple forward. The board struck Lindsey directly on the top of the head while the bucket impacted the gym floor just in front of her, throwing most of its contents onto her body.

For a few seconds, the only sound we heard was that of the wooden board clattering on the ground.

The primal scream that followed reverberated throughout the entire gymnasium.

Forty-Three

Lewis

He was dazed.

The deflated airbag was sitting in his lap, along with the two halves of his glasses. They must have snapped when his face impacted the airbag. He could hear steam hissing from somewhere. A sharp pain radiated from his nose and eyes, and he felt something warm and wet rolling across his lips. When he reached up to find out what it was, he found blood on his fingertips.

The driver-side door flew open, and a beefy fist grabbed a handful of his shirt, yanking him from the car.

"Here, let me give you a hand."

Lewis couldn't get his feet underneath him, and if it wasn't for the hands pulling on his shirt, he would have probably fallen. He felt himself being tossed, bouncing off the rear of a nearby SUV, and falling onto his hands and knees. When his head cleared, he could make out the front end of Brodie's Honda, smashed against a light pole, sandwiched by a red pickup that was barely damaged. Wilfred was leaning into the Honda through the driver's door.

"Damn jerk weed kid, just what do you think you're up to?"

Wilfred was talking more to himself than anyone else as he pulled back out of the car and turned around. He was holding the bundled towel from the passenger seat in one hand, and what looked like Lewis's cell phone holster in the other. A look of satisfaction beamed from the man's face. Lewis reached for the spot on his hip where his phone should have been. Empty.

Wilfred took the cell phone and hurled it to the ground, watching it explode into pieces, then tore off the cloth to reveal the photo album beneath. The look of satisfaction on his face disappeared.

"What the hell?" Wilfred stared at the album in disbelief. The man's nostrils flared when he looked back at Lewis, his eyes cold and hard. He threw the book at Lewis but missed, bouncing harmlessly off the SUV. Wilfred's face now radiated pure anger.

"What are you up to?" the white-haired madman growled at Lewis. In one long step, he was on top of Lewis, grabbing him by the shirt again and snatching him to his feet. "Dealing with Sierra was one thing, but I will not let some runt like you spoil my chance at absolute power."

Fear froze Lewis, and he now felt a pounding pain across his entire face.

He never saw the slap coming. It caught part of his cheek and most of his ear, which was ringing loudly. Tears filled his eyes. Suddenly, memories he devoted years to bury deep in his psyche came rushing back, awakening a familiar terror. Sweat formed on his brow, his heartbeat quickened. The deeper his breathing became, the more out of breath he felt. His ears rang with echoes of his own past screams.

Fun time was over, and now he didn't want to be part of this anymore. All he wanted was to have his mother wrap her arms around him and squeeze the breath out of him.

"I asked you a question, boy. What are you and your friends up to?" Wilfred screamed at him.

Lewis opened his mouth to say something, but he didn't know what it would be.

"You left your girlfriend alone in the house? What's the matter? You don't have the balls to do what's necessary?" The tone in Wilfred's voice was an equal mixture of pleasure and menace. "Too bad for her."

Then, from somewhere else in the parking lot, Lewis heard somebody call out to him.

"Hey, Villain."

Forty-Four

Knox

"Shoot!" I yelled, wondering why Sierra hadn't pulled the trigger already.

Lindsey's drawn-out scream was just subsiding, the echoes of it still bouncing off the gym walls. My sister was standing just inside the doorway, her hands pressed to the top of her head.

"Goddammit, Chace!" Lindsey screamed.

Sierra unexpectedly lowered the rifle. "Oh, shit."

"What's the matter? Why don't you shoot?"

Sierra turned to look at me and Grandma, panic on her face.

"It's not her. She's not the demon."

"What?" I exclaimed, not believing what I was hearing. "But she's not wearing mom's ring."

"What? What ring?"

"Oh no," Grandma said.

Sierra turned and bolted towards the doorway, me right behind her, and Grandma doing her best to keep up. As we approached Lindsey, her eyebrows squished together, and her expression changed from anger to confusion.

"Grandma? What are you doing here? What the hell's going on?"

Sierra bent down and examined Lindsey's wet pants. "It's definitely not her."

"Then it has to be Jadie," I said, pulling my phone out of my pocket. "I need to call Brodie and tell her to leave the book alone."

My sister stood there with her arms held out to her sides, water dripping everywhere, looking like she had just come in from a rainstorm.

"What's going on, Grandma? You helped Chace do this to me?"

Grandma pulled a cloth out of her backpack and held it out for Lindsey. "It's only water, darling. Don't be such a drama queen."

Lindsey tentatively reached for the cloth, but she missed the exchange, and it fell to the floor, where it immediately began soaking in the pool of water at her feet. She ignored the fallen cloth, her attention instead locked on the rifle in Sierra's hands. "You were going to shoot me?"

"Well," Grandma answered. "It's complicated."

While I was listening to their conversation, Brodie's number had gone straight to voicemail for the second time. "She's not answering."

A voice from behind startled everyone.

"What's going on here?"

Lorna was standing in the doorway, blocking our only way out of the gym.

Forty-Five

Lewis

Tug and three of his burly friends came walking up from the back of the parking lot. Two of them wore all-black bandanas to match their black leather jackets. Another wore a wool cap pulled down so far that you could barely see his eyes. Tug was wearing his same old Cubs cap.

Leave it to Tug to be late to the movies, Lewis thought to himself.

"You have yourself a fender-bender, Villain?" Tug asked, eliciting chuckles from his cohorts.

Gripping Lewis's shirt, Wilfred dragged the boy behind him.

"We're working it out. Thanks," Wilfred said through smiling teeth.

Tug opened his mouth to say something, but hesitated, his eyes narrowing. He seemed to notice Lewis's face for the first time. The playfulness in Tug's demeanor disappeared.

"Is there something wrong, Lewis? This guy bothering you?" Tug asked, his voice deeper now.

"Do we care?" the tallest of Tug's companions asked, continuing to walk on.

"Like I said," Wilfred explained, "we're just working out the details, so we don't have to get the police and insurance companies involved. So why don't ya mind your own business?"

Tug's friends also came to a stop, waiting for him.

"Lewis?" said Tug.

Lewis struggled against the steely grip, stretching out the neckline of his shirt to poke his head around Wilfred. "Help," is all he squeaked out.

The transformation in Tug was almost immediate. He puffed himself up to appear more imposing, and his eyes became dark and steely. Although Tug was the same height as Wilfred, the white-haired man had twenty pounds and years of experience on him. Yet Tug strode up confidently until he was a couple of feet from Wilfred, turned his hat around so it faced backward, then balled up his hands into fists.

"Let him go right now, you Malfoy wannabe."

"Listen, boy, you don't want to get messed up in this. Just run along to your movie and don't trouble yourself."

"I'm not going anywhere without him."

"Son, I will squash you like a bug."

"Yeah, well, I hope you have quick feet because I have a whole posse to your one puny foot."

Lewis was grateful to see that Tug's pals had taken up position on either side of him, and even better, they all looked willing.

Wilfred considered the four of them carefully. Finally, he released his grip on Lewis's shirt, and the boy stumbled backward until he caught himself on the SUV. Wilfred took a step forward, ignoring Lewis altogether.

Wilfred reached into his back pocket, and when he pulled it back, he flicked his wrist, snapping the serrated blade in place on the six-inch knife. "I tried to warn you," he growled.

Lewis knew he couldn't stand there and let Tug or his buddies be hurt for trying to help him, so he looked around for anything he could use as a weapon. On the ground next to him was the photo album. What was it that Knox advised him to do when dealing with bullies?

Lean into it.

Lewis reached down, grabbed the album in both hands, and swung it with every ounce of strength his body could muster. Years of pent-up rage and fear struck the back of Wilfred's head squarely, stunning the white-haired man and causing him to stumble forward, right into Tug's left-handed haymaker. Tug's fist caught Wilfred square on the temple, and the man went down like a robot that had its battery pulled, thudding heavily on the pavement.

They all stood there for a moment, silently staring down at the immobile white-haired man.

"You okay?" Tug finally asked without taking his eyes off Wilfred's prone body.

"I'll live," Lewis answered shakily.

Tug turned to face Lewis, grimacing when he looked at his nose. He reached out and grabbed the bandana from the head of his nearest companion and handed it to Lewis.

"What's this guy's deal?"

"It's a long story… one that I don't have time for right now," Lewis said, putting the bandana to his nose. He walked over to Brodie's car, reached in, and took the keys. "I need a huge favor."

"I may be wrong, but I think I just did one for you."

"Good point. Then I need one more."

Tug turned his back to Lewis and started walking away. "My limit for favors is one a day. I'm maxed out."

"What if I promised to do your homework for a month, and all you have to do is keep this guy occupied for a couple of hours?"

Tug stopped in his tracks but didn't turn around. "What subject?"

"You name it. I'll even do it for all three of you."

Tug turned on his heels and walked back to where Lewis stood.

"They don't go to school anymore," Tug said in a hushed tone, gesturing with his thumb towards his companions. "But I could use the help. Every subject—until the end of the semester."

"Deal."

"Okay. What do you want us to do with Malfoy?"

Lewis pulled out his wallet and handed Tug a hundred-dollar bill. "Why don't you take him to a movie? My treat."

The slightest trace of a smile appeared on Tug's lips. "What are you going to do?"

Lewis glanced at the unconscious white-haired man, then ran towards the red pickup. "I'm going to steal his truck."

Forty-Six

Knox

"Lorna. What are you doing here?" was all I could think to say.

"I could ask you the same," Lorna replied, crossing her arms in front of her chest. "Ginny, do you want to tell me what's going on here? And why is Lindsey soaked?"

"Knox, back away," Sierra said calmly from behind him.

"What for? It's not her. It's gotta be Jadie."

"And who was it that told you it was one of your sisters?"

"Wilfred. Remember, I told you he saw one of them carrying Travis to the pool."

"Wilfred, the man who's been lying to you since you met him? And who did you think it was before Wilfred changed your mind?"

An icy chill started creeping down my back. Out of the corner of my eye, I could see Grandma digging around in her rucksack.

"What the hell are you talking about?" Lorna asked, her brow furrowed and eyebrows raised. "Someone took Travis to a pool?"

"We thought Lindsey did," I said, taking a step backward. There was nowhere to run. All the other doors into and out of the gym were padlocked shut.

"What?" Lindsey cried. "Why on earth would I carry Travis to a pool? Look what they did to me, Lorna. I'm drenched."

"Why does that girl have a rifle, Ginny?" Lorna asked, nodding in Sierra's direction.

"Lorna, how did you know we were here?" Grandma asked instead, taking Lindsey by the hand and pulling her backward. Grandma still had her right hand inside her rucksack.

"What are you doing, Grandma?" Lindsey asked but didn't resist.

Lorna dropped her arms to her sides. "Why are you all acting so weird?"

"Just answer the question, Lorna," Grandma said. "How did you know we were here?"

"I was driving by the school and recognized Lindsey's car in the lot. Imagine my surprise when I see you here with the woman who tried to shoot us."

"What do we do, Sierra?" I asked, dropping all pretenses. If we were going to survive this, we needed another plan, and quick.

I watched as Sierra raised the rifle on her hip and pointed it at Lorna. At this distance, it would be almost impossible to miss.

When Lorna took a step further into the gym, things seemed to happen around me all at once. Grandma turned and began running in the other direction, pulling a confused Lindsey behind her. Sierra dropped to one knee and swung the rifle from her hip up to her shoulder. I remained glued where I was, torn between the instinct to flee and wanting somehow to help Sierra.

Then Lorna bent over and picked up the soaked cloth from the gym floor.

"We need to leave," she said. "None of you should be here. I can lose my job."

It hit me like a ton of bricks. "Oh god, Brodie."

MOVING FEAR

Forty-Seven

Lewis

The bad feeling located somewhere between the pit of Lewis's stomach and his racing heart grew ten times worse when he pulled the red pickup into Knox's driveway. Everything was a blur without his glasses, but he could still make out his mom's car in their own driveway. That meant Brodie hadn't left yet. To make matters worse, Knox's sister's VW was here now, meaning she and Travis were back early.
Things definitely weren't going as planned.
What he needed to do was call Knox and find out what he should do, but his phone was in pieces back in the theater parking lot. Lewis looked around the inside of the truck, and his heart leaped when he spotted an old-style flip phone jammed in a storage hole in the dashboard. He grabbed the phone and dialed Knox's cell number.
"Hello?" came Knox's voice on the line.
"Knox, it's Lewis. Is Brodie with you?"
"Lewis," Knox responded, stress evident in his tone. "Lindsey wasn't the demon... it has to be Jadie... we're on the way back to the house."
"Where's Brodie?"

"We haven't heard from her and she's not answering her phone. She called earlier to say that the book wasn't under my parents' bed, so we told her to search in the basement, but you—"

Lewis dropped the phone and was out the door. He made his way toward the front porch with purpose. He kept his watery eyes trained on the windows, looking for any sign of movement inside, but he couldn't see much. Even if his glasses hadn't broken in the wreck, he wasn't sure he'd be able to wear them now. The radiating pain from his broken nose was excruciating.

A rainy blast of wind momentarily disoriented him. He turned his shoulder into it and lowered his head, working blindly toward the porch. When the onslaught of unsettled air died down, Lewis's attention returned to the inside of the house. At the living room windows, he noticed a blurry shadow moving. He hugged the left railing of the porch stairs, trying to prevent being seen by anyone in the living room. Once he was on the porch, he moved to the wall and began inching his way toward the bay windows.

When he reached a point where he thought he could safely peek inside, he paused. He heard a car driving down the street. A gray Toyota drove in front of the house from the left, two adults and two small children inside. One child, a small boy, was looking directly at him while the car rolled past his own house on the right. Lewis imagined what he must have looked like to the boy—some strange teenager with a stream of dried blood trailing from his nose, probably two black eyes, hugging the wall on somebody's front porch, with a storm threatening outside.

Lewis turned his head and pushed off the wall far enough so that he could peer inside. Through his blurry vision, he could see that the house was dark. No lights anywhere. He could make out the destroyed television with a second smaller one sitting on a stool in front of it. Stepping farther away from the wall, he could see the rest of the living room and the study behind it, but nobody was occupying either room.

Lewis made a quick decision. If Brodie had been down in the basement when Knox's brother and sister showed up, she might still be down there, and it bothered him that she wasn't answering her phone. He had to go help her. She was down there because of him, and if anything happened to her, he didn't know what he would do. So, he opened the front door and eased his way in.

There should have been at least three people in the house making noise, but there was nothing but silence. Lewis lowered his head, pretended he was invisible, and made his way directly to the kitchen. He could see that the basement door was cracked, and a light was coming from downstairs. Without pause, he opened the door and descended.

As he cleared the bulkhead, he could see that the Giddens' basement was nothing like his. First off, the stairs started down towards the front of the house to a landing midway and then continued in the opposite direction towards the rear of the house. The basement was unfinished, with wooden posts joined to overhead support beams. The long, rectangular-shaped room was cut in half by a partially completed wall of two-by-fours and more wooden slats. Bland concrete blocks surrounded the whole thing. A single 100-watt light bulb hanging from the low overhead ceiling was the only source of illumination, casting shadows everywhere.

When Lewis reached the bottom of the stairs and turned to face the open room, he noticed a water heater to the left on the other side of the stairs, next to an empty metal shelf unit. His first thought was that there was nowhere to hide anything, much less a book the size of a photo album. He walked further into the room. The musty smell of unventilated air was thick in his nostrils, as his eyes probed the corners for any hiding spot.

He came to the wood-framed wall and was about to step around to the other side when he saw something that made him freeze. Strewn across the floor leading back to a power box in the middle of the partial wall was a bundle of exposed wiring. He relaxed when he saw that the main breaker switch was in the down position. He was about to continue his search when, out of the corner of his eye, he detected movement.

"What are you doing down here?"

Forty-Eight

Lewis

Lewis turned and saw Knox's sister standing halfway up the stairs. He didn't get a good look at what either of the twins was wearing earlier, so he could only assume the girl standing before him was Jadie. Lindsey was supposed to be with Knox and Sierra at the school. Wasn't she?

"Knox told me the acoustics of your basement would be perfect for recording our project, and he wanted me to come over and see it." Lewis was never very good at lying and especially terrible at it when he had to make things up on the fly.

Jadie made her way down the rest of the stairs. Lewis's blurry vision could barely make out her printed dress and a thin red belt.

"Where are Knox and Lindsey?"

Lewis stepped away from the framed wall into the middle of the room, directly underneath the light bulb. "He forgot a piece of our assignment in his locker at school, so Lindsey ran him out there to get it. I thought you were taking your brother to the movies?"

Jadie stood uncomfortably at the bottom of the stairs, seemingly afraid to touch anything.

"I got a stomachache. Just what kind of project are you working on that you have to record in a dingy old basement?"

"Oh, it's a horror story. We're acting out an old-time radio show. It's a story that Knox wrote."

"Knox wrote? My brother Knox? That's a laugh. What's it about?"

"It's about this strange box that suddenly appears in this family's home and starts wreaking havoc."

Jadie's body stiffened, and her eyes narrowed, telling Lewis that Knox's sister didn't appreciate the topic of his story. She walked around the room, feigning interest in the surroundings.

"Really? Sounds corny to me."

"I think you'd be surprised. It's riveting listening to Knox tell it. "

"Are there characters in this story?"

"Several. A dad and stepmom, two brothers, and twin sisters. I'm going to be the voice of the brother."

Jadie stopped her meandering and looked directly at Lewis now.

"Well, I certainly hope his story has a happy ending."

"I can answer that," said a voice from the stairs.

Lewis and Jadie turned at the same time.

"I can guarantee," Travis answered, *standing* at the bottom of the stairs, "that a happy ending is nowhere in sight."

Forty-Nine

Knox

"Crap, Wilfred's here," I said when I spotted the red pickup in our driveway.

"Who's Wilfred?" Lindsey asked from the seat behind me, sniffling.

I turned my head to look at my sister, sandwiched between Lorna and Grandma. A steady stream of tears was still flowing down her cheeks.

"He's the priest who was at our house last night," I said. "Except he's not really a priest, and he's here to help the demon."

"This can't be happening," Lorna repeated. It was probably the fiftieth time she had said it during our drive from the school.

"It's got to be a mistake," Lindsey said tersely. "I know my sister, and she's not this demon you're making her out to be."

Grandma turned her head from looking out the window to Lindsey.

"Buck up, both of you. You need to be strong for your family. You can't be anything less right now."

As our car drew closer to the house, I could make out another car in the driveway. "Oh no," I exclaimed softly.

"What is it?" Sierra asked from behind the wheel.

"That's Jadie's VW. She and Travis must be there as well."

"Shit," said Grandma.

"Listen, we can still do this," Sierra commanded. "Knox, you and your grandmother go in the front door. I'll go in the back with Lorna. Lindsey, you stay in the car. All you need to do is distract it long enough for me to get off a shot."

"When you say *it*... you mean Jadie, right?" Lorna asked.

I couldn't help but notice the genuine worry in Lorna's voice. "We're gonna get her back," I said with fake confidence, trying to bury the fear I was feeling. "I promise."

"Here we go," said Sierra, as the car came to a stop in front of the house.

After four of us exited Sierra's Explorer, Grandma and I waited as Sierra, tranquilizer rifle in hand, made her way with Lorna down the driveway and disappeared into the backyard. Off in the distance, thunder rumbled, signaling that the promised rain would arrive soon. Grandma and I, complete with her rucksack filled with life and death chemicals draped over her shoulder, marched straight to the front door and walked inside.

The house was still and dark. I forced myself to take deliberate steps into the living room, my eyes darting to every corner of the room that might serve as a hiding place. Where was everyone? Upstairs? In the basement? That's where Sierra had instructed Brodie to look for the book, but going down there now would probably be suicide. It was too compact a room and certainly too dark for Sierra to get off an accurate shot. No, this room was our best bet, with the little light coming in through the windows and its open setting. I had to draw the demon here.

I summoned every ounce of courage I could muster. "JADIE," I yelled.

The whipping wind outside was my only answer.

"JADIE... or whatever you call yourself... I'm waiting for you."

"That's funny," a guttural voice from overhead replied. "I've been waiting for you."

Startled, I lurched backward and tripped over the ottoman, tumbling onto the carpet. I heard my grandmother gasp, and I followed her eyes up to the ceiling, where several dark shapes seemed to hang like a cluster of enormous spiders. As I raised myself into a sitting position, one form dropped from the ceiling and landed upright between the coffee table and the televisions.

It had been so long since I'd seen my brother standing upright that I almost didn't recognize him. All the clues I had missed suddenly fell into place.

He was the one who spent the most time alone with the box.

He was ten feet away when my bed shook me awake at night.

He had killed his own pet.

He purposefully jumped into Lewis's pool to throw off suspicion.

He intentionally hid the book in Lorna's stuff.

He was in the school gym when all shit broke loose during the pep rally.

The demon had possessed Travis all along.

Silhouetted against the bay windows, I could barely make out my brother's facial features, but the one thing I couldn't miss was the muted glow in his eyes.

My grandmother had backed up against the hallway wall. "Oh, Travis."

"Hello again, Doctor Alvarez," the demon grunted, looking in Grandma's direction. "So nice to see you again."

The color drained from Grandma's face, and her eyes went wide.

"You ended up keeping our little secret, didn't you?"

As I got to my feet, the demon's dead eyes found me again.

"Here to rescue the sister and girlfriend, are we?" the demon said, glancing towards the ceiling. I could barely understand its voice. The words sounded more like they came from a ninety-nine-year-old man who had smoked for years, choking as he tried to speak.

I followed the demon's gaze upward into the shadows. I could see Jadie, Lewis, and Brodie suspended in the air. They all appeared to be in a trance.

"And Travis," I answered as I rose from the couch. "I'm here for my brother as well."

Something that could be considered a chuckle came from the demon. "Why would you want to risk your life for someone who despises you?"

"You're lying. Travis doesn't hate me," I answered back.

"You're right, he doesn't hate you. Hate isn't a strong enough word for how he feels towards the person who robbed him of his legs. I can't tell you what a joy it's been sharing his body and soaking up that rage. This family has certainly been different, but in a good way. So much mistrust. It's such a shame it has to end so soon. I was just getting started."

"I will not let you put our names in your book."

The demon moved slightly to its right, its motions very smooth, predatory. Like a snake stalking its prey.

"Your pitiful existence is less than that of a fly's larva to me, boy. You have no say in what happens here, any more than the ant can stop the foot from crushing it. I must thank you, however."

"Why's that?"

The demon raised its arm and pointed to the rear of the house. There was a yelp and Sierra's body came flying through the room towards us. Her limp figure slowed to a halt and hung suspended in the air a few feet from the demon. I could see her eyes were wide open, conscious of everything happening to her, but she was unable to speak.

"You brought this one to me," the demon said. "Her clan has deprived me of prizes far too many times. Her death will be lovely indeed."

I don't know what I was thinking. In fact, I'm pretty sure I wasn't. Instinct seized control of me. I lunged forward and threw myself at my brother, stretching out my hands and arms for his neck. But the demon raised his other hand, and I froze in mid-air, my body going numb. I felt encased in some sort of invisible foam, squeezing my entire body hard enough to drive the air from my lungs. Just like Sierra, I hung in the air, unable to move, listening to the agonizing sound of my grandmother screaming in the background.

MOVING FEAR

Fifty

Knox

Panic consumed me, constricting my throat and lungs. My heart was pounding inside my chest. Our great plan had fallen apart so quickly. How could we have ever thought it was going to work? Sierra was caught in the web, just like I was. Lewis and the girls dangled from the ceiling like sides of beef. Somewhere in the back of my mind, where optimism once existed, I hoped Dad would walk through the door and give us a fighting chance. That his weekend maneuvers might have been canceled, maybe because of the weather, and he'd come to our rescue.

But that stuff only happened in the movies.

Then something whizzed past me and struck the demon in the head.

We all fell to the ground. Lewis landed perfectly on the couch, and Brodie bounced off the recliner onto the floor, but Jadie crashed hard on the carpet between the coffee table and the television. The demon was shrieking like a banshee as Sierra and I back-crawled away. It was clawing at its face, red blisters rising all over it.

I looked over my shoulder in the direction the object had come from, and there stood my grandmother with her open rucksack in one hand... and a second water balloon in the other.

"I thought we might need backup."

Brodie was the closest to me, so I sprang to my feet and helped her up. She was dazed, but was quickly regaining her senses. I pushed her towards the front door and turned for Jadie, but then I heard the front door slam shut.

"YOU WILL SUFFER FOR YOUR—"

The demon's roar ended so abruptly that I had to turn to see what had happened. My brother was standing there, staring down at a silver dart with a red, fluffy tail, embedded in his chest. Within seconds, the demon collapsed to the floor.

I turned to the study where Lorna was holding the tranquilizer gun—still pointing towards the demon.

"Get the second injection!" Sierra yelled. Grandma set the water balloon on the floor and began digging in her rucksack.

Lorna dropped the rifle and ran to Travis's crumpled body. She fell to her knees beside him. I kneeled down on the other side.

"Is he going to be okay?" Lorna asked before biting down on her bottom lip, tears pooling in her eyes.

"He's got to be," I answered. I watched Brodie and Lewis rush over to Jadie, who was still motionless on the floor.

Grandma slid in next to me with her medical kit in one hand and the portable defibrillator in the other. I stood up to give her better access to Travis, watching as she hurriedly opened the case.

"Is this going to work?" Lorna asked.

"I don't know. The dosage in the tranquilizer was based on Lindsey's body weight, not a small boy. He could be dead already," Grandma informed us as she worked.

"Wait!" Sierra shouted. "We need the book."

"WHAT THE HELL IS GOING ON?" Lindsey screamed hysterically, standing right inside the front door.

"The basement," I said, ignoring my sister and already on the move. Lewis was right behind me.

"I didn't see anything down there," Lewis said as we made our way through the kitchen.

I flipped on the basement light and the two of us clattered down the steps.

"You take that side," I said, pointing to the right. I checked around the water heater, behind the metal shelf, and then moved further into the room, where the shadows made seeing difficult. Between the two of us, we covered every inch of the basement, and still no book.

"Where else could it be?" Lewis asked, desperation in his voice.

"I don't—" I started to say when a thought struck me. Peering up into the rafters where strings of thin wire held insulation in place, I scanned the ceiling quickly until I saw an area that looked crooked. I stepped over to it and there it was. Propped between two beams was the book.

"Lift me up," Lewis instructed. I grabbed my friend by the waist and raised him readily off the floor, where he pulled the book from its perch.

I lowered Lewis. "Hurry," I said, but he was already racing towards the stairs.

When we returned to the living room, Brodie was still attending to Jadie, and Sierra was clearing away the furniture close to where Travis had fallen. Lorna was holding a bag of clear liquid with a tube leading into Travis's arm. Grandma was busy taking my brother's blood pressure. Travis was flat on his back with his t-shirt pulled up to his chin, exposing his chest. Two white adhesive pads were stuck to the upper and lower sections of his ribcage, each attached to the portable defibrillator box.

"We found it," Lewis said as the two of us entered the room.

I watched as Sierra reached into her back pocket and pulled out a can of lighter fluid. "Give it," she said. She took the book from Lewis, covered it with the can's contents, then tossed the empty container aside and pulled a lighter from her hip pocket.

"Let's do this."

My grandmother was on her knees next to Travis, a stethoscope hanging around her neck. Grandma looked up at everyone in the room.

"Here we go," she said. My heart, already racing from the exertion of retrieving the book, went into overdrive. My body was shaking from a combination of adrenaline and panic.

Sierra stepped away from the rest of us and then dropped to her knees. She placed the book on the floor in front of her.

Grandma took a syringe from her medical kit and injected its contents into Travis's arm, then put the stethoscope in her ears and placed the circular tip over his heart.

Seconds felt like an eternity as we waited until Grandma finally proclaimed, "His heart has stopped."

I almost jumped out of my skin when a booming thunder shook the house, and the skies opened up outside, releasing the rain that had been storing up all day. Buckets of water started coming down, pounding on the house, the sound of it filling the silence inside.

The living room grew even darker than before. Suddenly, a cyclone erupted. A whipping wind circled the room, knocking me onto my backside. The force sent books, magazines, lamps, pictures, and plants flying everywhere. It felt like being trapped inside a twister. I struggled to reach Brodie and help her shield Jadie.

The whirlwind caused the black book to slide away from Sierra. She lunged after the evil manuscript and just as she pinned it down a powerful explosion of force, originating from the book, knocked everyone down and sent Sierra flying across the room and through the front window, shattering the glass.

"Knox!" Lewis yelled. "You have to burn it now."

I didn't have a lighter. I looked to where Sierra had once kneeled, but there was nothing there but the black book. Following the track where she had flown, I spotted the lighter resting at the base of the window. I scrambled on all fours, scooped the lighter off the floor, then scrambled to the book. Flicking the lighter, I got no result. I flicked it a second time and the flame shot out, but the punishing wind quickly snuffed it out.

"Hurry," Lewis yelled.

I shook the lighter, did my best to shield it from the wind, then flicked it once more. It fired to life. I lowered the flame to the tip of the book when a second forceful blast sent me sliding across the floor until I slammed against the wall.

Squinting at the center of the room, my heart soared when I saw that the fire had taken hold and the book had become engulfed. The blaze reached towards the ceiling, forming a vortex of white flames. The fiery tornado spun faster and faster, completely consuming the book, growing brighter and brighter until it became impossible to look at. I buried my face in my arms and felt my ears pop as the roar became deafening.

Then it was gone. Flying debris dropped to the ground.

I raised my head. The only sound was the steady rain falling outside. I looked to where the book had been, but there was nothing. No ashes, no scorched carpet, nothing.

"Bring him back, Grandma," I cried.

Grandma and Lorna righted themselves. My grandmother reached into the medical kit for another syringe. This one possessed a needle three inches long. She inserted the needle straight into Travis's chest, pressed the piston down, then extracted it.

"Lewis... oxygen," Grandma commanded.

Lewis grabbed the slim tube connected to the clear mask Grandma handed him. He twisted the knob to start the oxygen flow and placed the mask over Travis's nose and mouth.

Grandma placed the tip of her stethoscope over her grandson's heart and listened.

Outside, I saw Sierra rise from the porch, brush broken glass from her body, then focus on the activity around my brother.

Grandma reached over to the defibrillator and, before she pushed the button, cried, "Clear."

Travis's chest rose and fell. Grandma placed her stethoscope back over his heart and listened again, her expression unreadable.

"Ginny?" Lorna asked. "Is he—"

"Nothing yet. Make sure the oxygen is flowing, Lewis."

Lewis leaned over and listened to the clear mask. "It's working."

"Here we go again," Grandma said. "Clear."

My brother's chest convulsed again. As soon as it settled, Grandma placed the stethoscope back over his heart.

"I've got a heartbeat."

Fifty-One

__Knox__

I couldn't remember a time from my past when I felt this good.

I felt weightless in the passenger seat next to Lindsey, who was driving the four of us back from Grandma's house. Continuous chatter came from the backseat between Brodie and Lewis. The two of them were comparing battle scars from the last twenty-four hours, and my sister was sprinkling in sarcastic remarks at opportune moments to stir the dispute.

After we brought Travis back to life, everyone went out to Grandma's house so she could give him... and everyone else... complete examinations. Everyone except Sierra, that is. She wanted to stay behind to keep an eye out for Wilfred, who we learned had given Tug and his friends the slip.

I turned sideways in my seat to play along with the teasing, drawing mock annoyance from both Lewis and Brodie, along with round after round of laughter. It had been a long time since I'd felt so upbeat, so playful. Even my sister and I were laughing at each other's jokes again.

"Oh, I almost forgot," I heard Brodie say from the back. I turned my head and watched as she dug through her front pocket for something. She produced a silver chain with a ring at the end. A mood ring.

Brodie extended her arm over the seat back and dangled the necklace in front of my sister, which brought about a shout of glee.

"My ring! I thought I lost this," Lindsey cried out, snatching the chain from Brodie's hand. "Where did you find it?"

Brodie shot Lewis a look before answering. "Let's just say I accidentally borrowed it."

When the car turned the corner, I smiled as our headlights illuminated Sierra sitting on the steps of the front porch. I was glad that she hadn't ridden off into the sunset and deprived me of the chance to thank her for everything she had done for us.

After Lindsey parked the car in the driveway and everyone exited, Sierra rose from her seat.

"How's your brother and sister doing?" Sierra asked.

"Jadie's got a mild concussion, and Travis is doing good," I answered. "He's been drifting in and out of sleep, but they're both well enough that Lorna and Grandma are bringing them back home. They're a couple of minutes behind us."

"Why didn't your grandmother take him to the hospital?"

"She said that the drugs in his system would have raised questions we couldn't exactly answer."

Lindsey reached out her hand. "We haven't officially met. I'm Lindsey, and I understand we're standing here right now because of you."

"Nonsense," Sierra said, shaking Lindsey's hand. "We all played a part."

Lindsey pointed to the smashed bay window. "Some more than others. I bet you're a little sore."

Sierra smiled and shrugged her shoulders. "Nothing a hot bath won't cure."

"That goes ditto for me," said Brodie as she reached out and pinched Lewis's ear. "But before I take my bath, a certain someone has to take me car shopping."

Lewis made a face somewhere between a grimace and a smile. "My first accident, and it wasn't even my fault."

"But I'm the one who'll probably get a ticket for leaving the scene of an accident, and that's not even considering the hot water I'll be in with my dad. You are going to pay through the nose for it all, mister! I told you to take care of my car."

"Okay... okay."

Brodie released his ear, and he began rubbing it.

"No sign of Wilfred?" I asked Sierra.

She shook her head. "Nada."

"What did you do with his truck?"

"I left it at the park about a mile from here."

"What do you think he's up to?"

"Oh, he's probably hanging around somewhere. Sulking. That's why I'm gonna stick around for a few more days to make sure he doesn't bother your family."

"You don't have to do that, but it'll be nice to get to know you better."

Everyone else nodded their agreement.

"Whatever," said Sierra, the hint of a smile on her lips.

I bounded up the stairs to the front door. "Why don't you come inside and wait until the rest of the family gets here? I'm sure they'll all want to thank you as well."

As we all entered the house, I stopped momentarily to stare down the dark hallway at a wide-open back door. Then I remembered we had all left in a hurry, leaving the doors as they were. Lindsey flipped on the light switch, and we stood in the foyer looking at the destruction we used to call the living room.

"It looks like a frat house," Lindsey said. "How about we get things cleaned up before everyone else gets here?"

I looked at all the glass from the shattered window covering the floor. "We're going to need a broom. Lewis, do me a favor and grab the one out of the hall closet."

As we set about straightening up the furniture, Lewis stopped on his way to the closet and looked down. He reached out and picked up a red water balloon.

"This thing saved our lives. Who'd have thought... holy water-balloons? Look what your grandmother wrote on it," he commented, starting towards me.

One of Lewis's feet caught the corner of the overturned stool, causing him to stumble forward. Sierra was standing directly in his path, but instead of grabbing him and breaking his fall, she jerked back out of the way, allowing Lewis to stagger clumsily before catching himself.

Sierra's behavior struck me as odd, so I kept watching as her eyes darted around the room, checking to see if anyone had noticed her reaction. I glanced at Lewis, wondering why Sierra would avoid him like that. The red water balloon was still clutched in Lewis's hand, and when my gaze returned to Sierra, she was staring directly at me.

That's when I knew.

"Oh, shit!" I said before I could stop myself.

"What's the matter?" Brodie asked as she placed a lamp back on a table.

Sierra was just inside the framed archway leading into the room. Lewis was between her and me, having just recovered from his stumble. Our only escape would be through the study, then out the back door in the kitchen.

"It's still here," I said, my eyes still locked on Sierra.

Everyone stopped what they were doing and looked at me.

"What's still here?" Lindsey asked.

Letting my sister's stupid question slide, I answered the obvious. "Seraphim."

They all followed my gaze to Sierra.

"She touched the book after we stopped Travis's heart and drove it out."

Sierra's head and shoulders dropped forward, hanging limp as if she had suddenly fallen asleep on her feet. Then slowly, her head pulled back slightly, just enough so her eyes peered out from under her bangs.

"Peek-a-boo," the evil hissed.

My feet were glued to the floor, unable to answer my instinct to run.

The demon tilted its head to the right, and the front door slammed shut, followed closely by what must have been the back door. Raising its arms out to the side, the shards of glass on the ground first fluttered, then rose and floated around Sierra like a crystalline halo.

The demon looked right at me when it said, "I'm tired of you." Then it snapped its arms toward me.

I backpedaled as the glass fragments flew at me like tiny missiles, raising my arms against the impending skewering. My feet caught on the step leading into the study, and I fell over backward just as the projectiles passed inches over my head. I hit the ground while glass embedded itself in the far wall.

"THE BACK DOOR!" I yelled, adrenaline allowing me to overcome my shock. I scrambled to my feet and grabbed the lamp Brodie had just put on the table, hurling it in Sierra's direction. I broke for the other room. Lindsay and Brodie were already moving, and I ran to catch up. The contents of the bookshelves flew off the shelves at us. The barrage knocked us off stride and forced me to raise my arms to shield my face. I pushed on the backs of the others, keeping us moving forward, even as the second bookcase emptied its contents at us.

Just when the three of us burst into the kitchen, we collided with Lewis, who had come sprinting down the hallway.

Before anyone could pry open the back door, the oven door dropped open and a fireball exploded into the room. We dove behind the serving island in time to avoid shooting flames that roared over our heads and engulfed the far wall.

With the back entrance blocked and Sierra creeping toward us, our options were limited.

"The basement," I shouted.

I was last through the door, slamming it shut behind us and reaching for the lock, only to discover it only locked from the other side. Scanning the room, I frantically looked for a way to barricade it shut. A shriek from the bottom of the stairs caused me to abandon my search, and I jumped down to the landing several steps at a time. I found Brodie and Lewis staring at something in the middle of the room. Lindsey had her face covered with her hands.

Hanging from the ceiling, a noose wrapped tightly around his neck, was Wilfred.

Fifty-Two

Knox

The rope around Wilfred's neck was so taut that his eyes bulged from their sockets like an over-inflated blow-up doll. His stiff, purplish tongue protruded from his open mouth, now being used as a landing pad for the flies that had already gathered. The white-haired man was dressed in his priest's outfit, arms hanging limply at his sides, his body twisting ever so slightly from side to side. Someone had ripped the front of his shirt open, revealing a chest full of tattoos.

Also dangling from the rafters on either side of the body were seven additional nooses.

As awful as the sight of the devil worshippers' body was, I couldn't afford to linger on it. I had to find something to fight with —anything —and we had little time. I scanned the basement. There were two pieces of PVC pipe lying on the ground, both approximately four feet long, but nothing else I could use as a weapon. My eyes kept searching, first passing over and then coming to rest on the electrical box located on the partially framed wall. I dashed over and looked at the bare-lead wires leading from the box to the ground at my feet. The red tip power switch was off. I grabbed the wires and manipulated them so they draped chest-high over the top of the box, then reached for the power switch and pushed it upward.

When I turned around, Lindsay was beside me.

"Why did you lead us down here, Chace?" she asked, her voice quivering from fear. "Now we're trapped, and that thing is coming."

"This was the only place we could go," Lewis said.

"But what do we do now?" Brodie asked, her eyes pleading with me to find a solution.

I tried to think of something reassuring to say, but I didn't want to lie. I stared at the others, and that's when I noticed Lewis was still holding the water balloon filled with holy water. An idea began to form.

I removed my outer t-shirt, leaving the plain white undershirt. "I have a plan," I said, which was partially true. "We don't have much time. This is what we're going to do."

As I laid out my plan, Lewis took a step backward and shook his head.

"I can't do that."

"Lewis, yes, you can. You have to."

"Why can't somebody else do it?"

"Honestly, because the demon will pay the least amount of attention to you."

"But —"

Brodie moved directly in front of Lewis and placed her trembling hands on either side of his face. "Lewis, I have faith in you."

The door on the landing above crashed open.

"Move!" I yelled.

I tossed my t-shirt to Brodie and watched Lewis run to the back corner where the water heater stood. Brodie and Lindsey took up positions on the right side of the room, against the wall. Brodie held my t-shirt behind her back. I grabbed one of the PVC pipes off the ground and stood on the other side of the room, the electrical box between me and the girls.

The stairs creaked as Sierra descended.

I heard Lindsey begin sobbing.

"Don't worry, Sis, we got this," I called to her, doing my best to sound convincing.

Sierra turned the corner, her movements eerily fluid. I found it almost mesmerizing. Her head and shoulders were still hunched over, her eyes peering up at us with the same otherworldly glow I had seen in Travis's eyes earlier.

The demon came to a stop beside Wilfred's body, twisting its head to regard its former worshiper.

"This one may have had his uses—despite being so pitiful—but now that I'm trapped in this body, I can't afford to have anyone know the truth."

The demon studied us again, its glowing eyes pausing on Brodie a few seconds longer than everyone else.

"I should consider myself fortunate. Fragile as it may be, this body is an excellent specimen to spend eternity in, now that you've destroyed my ledger. I can use this vessel with the freedom I've not previously known, spreading my will in so many more ways. And I find the irony so rich, don't you? By taking this one and her uncle, I also end the clan's bloodline. There won't be anyone else like them left to disturb my work. Through her, I will reap the very prizes their clan dedicated their pathetic lives to saving."

"I wouldn't count on that," I said, doing my best to keep my voice steady. "You're not leaving this basement."

Sierra leveled her gaze at me now and smiled. The corner of her lips seemed to fold backwards and touch her earlobes. It was one of the worst things I had ever seen.

"Do you know how pathetic you sound with your heroic, grandiose statements? Your brother was right in despising you as much as he did."

"Screw you."

"And so articulate also. By the way, your mother says 'hi'."

I could feel my ears turning red as white-hot anger surged through my veins, replacing the fear in me.

"You're lying," I screamed.

"Don't listen to her, Knox," Brodie said.

"I know she's not in your world."

"You'll find out for yourself soon enough."

"We'll see about that," Brodie shouted.

Seraphim tilted its head at Brodie. "Brave words from a girl whose mother is a home wrecker. Aren't you even a little ashamed, taking advantage of the boy your mother left fatherless?"

Brodie's eyes went wide, and her mouth half-opened. She looked towards Lewis. Lewis came running out from behind the water heater, anger on his face, the red water balloon in his right hand cocked to throw.

"LEWIS… NOT YET," I yelled.

But before he even got the chance to release the balloon, the demon turned on him and, with a flick of its wrist, sent him flying. He landed several feet away, his limbs splayed in different directions, and then rolled several times before coming to a stop. The busted water balloon dangling from his limp hand.

"LEWIS!" screamed Brodie, and she drew back her own arm to throw my shirt. The demon anticipated her move as well because it swiftly pointed its finger in her direction, slamming both girls up against the wall.

With the demon's attention diverted, I lunged and jabbed the PVC pipe into its midsection, pushing with all my might. I had caught it off-guard, allowing me to force the beast backward towards the electrical box. Then its head swung back in my direction, the glowing eyes now a pair of white-hot coals. I felt myself lifted off the ground, and kicked my feet wildly in search of something solid. It slammed my shoulders up against the rafter a few feet from Wilfred's lifeless body, stunning me. I lost my grip on the PVC pipe, and it drop to the ground. I felt the noose hanging closest to me begin crawling over my head like a snake.

"LET HIM GO YOU BITCH!" I heard Lindsay cry.

"You'll get your turn soon enough," Seraphim croaked. "You all will."

I struggled unsuccessfully to free myself from the force holding me. As the rope slid across my forehead and started covering my eyes, I felt more pissed than scared. Just when I was finding a purpose in life, some otherworldly demon was going to get the better of me.

Suddenly, Sierra shrieked, and I toppled to the ground. I looked up in time to see Lewis with his hand pushed up against the demon's face. The hand was still wet from the busted water balloon.

With a swipe of her arm, Seraphim sent Lewis flying again, colliding with the far wall with a sickening crunch. His limp body fell in a heap at the base of the wall.

I reached for the PVC pipe, but before I could grab it, I felt myself lifted off the floor again and flung up against the wall next to Lewis. Colliding with the wall drove the air from my lungs, causing me to desperately gasp to force air back in. Instead of falling, I remained pinned upright by the invisible force. I could only watch as the PVC pipe floated into the air and pointed at my midsection.

"This has grown tedious," Seraphim growled. "Goodbye, Knox."

"NO!" came a scream from the other side of the room. Lorna came running at Sierra, ramming into the demon's midsection, driving them both into the electrical box on the wall.

The light bulb on the ceiling burst into a shower of sparks, and I collapsed into the darkness. Wasting no time, I scrambled to my feet, my eyes struggling to adjust to the sliver of light still being provided by the open basement door. I could barely make out Lorna and Sierra's bodies in a deathly embrace against the electrical box, convulsing violently, the smell of burnt flesh filling my nostrils. I picked up the PVC pipe and brought it crashing down on the power switch. Both women fell lifelessly to the ground.

    A few seconds of stillness passed. All I could hear was the faint sound of flames burning from upstairs. Suddenly the room filled with deafening screams, forcing me to clamp my hands over my ears, and dropping me to my knees. The shrieks surrounded me, coming from every direction and no direction, so loud that my entire body vibrated. I tried to open my eyes, but there was only blackness. What little light that had been there before had disappeared, along with the heat. I felt my nose hairs freeze as I breathed in the frigid air. Even though I couldn't see a thing, it felt as if the room was full of movement—a swirling swarm of something terrifying. A sense of dread filled me, and I knew I didn't want to see what was stirring around me. Somewhere, I thought I could hear Brodie and Lindsey crying out. The ground shook beneath me, and the screams became so loud that it sounded like the roar of a jet engine. I balled myself up into a fetal position and screamed at the top of my lungs.

    Just when it felt like I couldn't stand another second, the only sounds left in the room were our own screams.

    "Chace?" came my grandmother's voice from the top of the stairs.

    I opened my eyes. Brodie was already using the light on her cell phone to make her way to Lewis. Lying a few feet from me in the dim light were Lorna and Sierra's still bodies. My heart sank.

    "Grandma, grab your defibrillator. Lorna and Sierra need your help," I yelled as I moved to the two women.

    I checked their pulses as my grandmother had shown me, but neither woman had one. I rolled them both onto their backs, just when Lindsey joined me at my side.

    "You do CPR on Sierra—I'll do Lorna," I instructed my sister.

The two of us began the chest compressions and forced breathing, just as our grandmother had drilled into us during every visit to Ox-Bow. In the back of my mind, I worried about the sobs I heard coming from Brodie where Lewis had fallen, but I couldn't allow myself to get distracted.

I heard loud steps coming down the steps, and then my grandmother was there by my side with her medical kit and the defibrillator.

"How long?" my grandmother asked as she opened her medical kit.

"Just over a minute," Lindsey responded, out of breath from the exertion.

Grandma went to work quickly, dropping next to the closest woman, who was Sierra. She began cutting open the front of Sierra's shirt.

I listened to my grandma and Lindsey working on Sierra while I continued compressions on Lorna. Once, then twice, I heard the defibrillator being used followed by the most comforting words I'd heard in a long time - "I have a pulse."

I smiled to myself. One down, one to go. Against the far wall, the light of Brodie's cell phone illuminated a dazed Lewis. He was sitting up and clutching his arm to his chest.

"Dammit," Grandma said under her breath.

"What's wrong, Grandma?"

"I'm not sure there's enough juice left to revive Lorna."

The realization of what she was saying hit me like a sucker punch to the stomach. My mind filled with worry and thoughts about my stepmother, combined with more than my share of guilt. I had been crappy to her since the first day Dad introduced us, and now I could see that all she ever did was try to fit in as best she could.

"No, no, no," Lindsey cried. "She saved us."

"You've got to make it work, Grandma," I said. "Please make it work."

"Stand clear, Lindsey," Grandma said in the calm voice of a seasoned professional. "Here we go."

MOVING FEAR

Fifty-Three

Knox

I pushed open the hospital room door to find Lewis sitting up in bed, taking a massive bite from a sub-sandwich. His mother was in the chair on the side of his bed closest to the door, and Brodie was in a seat opposite.

"Well, I see your mom is already taking good care of you," I said.

"My son's stomach won't see one bite of this hospital's food," Mrs. Bonvillain said bluntly.

"I guess it's a good thing he'll probably go home tomorrow morning," said Brodie, her eyes remaining on me as I moved to the foot of the bed.

"How long will you have to be wearing that?" I asked, motioning to the dark-blue cast running from Lewis's wrist to his shoulder.

"Eight weeks," he answered through a mouthful of sandwich.

"And during those eight weeks, all three of you will come to church with me every Sunday," Lewis's mother said as she pointed to each of them. "I give you a little bit of freedom and look what happens. No more horseplay, especially on Sunday."

"But, we told you, Mrs. Bonvillain, it wasn't horseplay," Brodie said. "Lewis was helping Knox put out the fire and slipped on the water."

Lewis's mom's eyebrows raised, and she tilted her head. "This mysterious fire that his sister started in the kitchen?"

"Mom, it was just an accident," Lewis said.

"Don't give me that, or the 'boys will be boys' excuse. You scared me to death, and I'm collecting my eight weeks."

"That's fine, Mrs. Bonvillain. We'll be happy to go with you and Lewis to church," I said, looking at Brodie.

"It's settled then."

"Well, I just dropped in to see how you were doing. I'm going to head next door."

"I'll come with you," Brodie said, rising. "I'll be back in a minute, Lewis."

"Say 'hi' for me," Lewis said before taking another bite from his sandwich.

"Bye, Mrs. Bonvillain." I held the door open for Brodie.

"Bye, darling."

In the hallway, Brodie grabbed my hand to prevent me from walking down the hall.

"Well?"

I looked up and down the hall before I answered.

"It's done. Dad and I took care of it last night."

"What did you do?"

"Wilfred and his truck are at the bottom of Lake Vista."

Now Brodie scanned the empty hallway.

"The lake? Really?"

"We couldn't call the cops. There was no way to explain how a guy pretending to be a priest hung himself in our basement. Best thing to do was to make him disappear altogether."

"But I swim in that lake."

"Don't worry, Dad knew a remote area where no one ever hangs out."

"And he's okay with keeping that secret?"

"Don't get the wrong idea. He's still really pissed that I didn't tell him what was going on. I think he's probably more upset with Grandma, but he understands, and he'll keep quiet. But speaking of keeping uncomfortable secrets," I put my hands on her shoulders. "What did Lewis say about your mom?"

Brodie dropped her head and stared at my shoes.

"He already knew, even before I confessed to him. Turns out his mom told him a while back. She had been suspicious of me from the get-go. When she learned who my parents were, well, she thought Lewis deserved to know the truth. He said he couldn't care less."

I rubbed my hands down the sides of Brodie's arms. "He's something special."

She looked into my eyes and wrapped her hands around my neck. We hugged for a long time. I wished that we could stay like that forever.

"You are too," she said over my shoulder.

When we broke apart, I took her hand in mine, and together we walked to the next room.

My grandma occupied the chair closest to the door. Lindsey was in the chair on the far side.

Lorna lay in the bed, asleep.

Grandma put a finger to her mouth, to which I nodded my understanding. Brodie and I stood at the foot of the bed, staring at the sleeping woman.

"Is she okay?" I whispered to my grandmother.

"She's fine. A couple of cracked ribs and she's still running a weak fever, but I think she'll be right as rain. Needs rest is all," Grandma whispered back.

"Dad was finishing up boarding up the front window when I left. He'll be here soon."

"Is he still mad?" Lindsey whispered from across the bed.

"What do you think?"

"I have some pretty wonderful news?" Grandma said.

"We can use some of that," I said.

"Jadie called from my house. She's doing fine, but that's not the news." She was having a hard time concealing a smile. "Travis is awake, and—he has movement in his legs."

"What? That's wonderful," Brodie said, grabbing my arm.

"Whatever that thing did to him, it must have healed his vertebrae. We have to do some tests, of course, but I believe he might walk again."

I didn't know what to say, because truthfully, I was torn. Of course, this was a good thing. The possibility that Travis might walk again was fantastic. But how it came about was concerning to me. Could the remnants of the evil Travis bore inside him have really left behind such a wonderful gift?

There was a knock on the door, and it opened just enough for a head to stick its way in.

Sierra smiled awkwardly when she saw everyone in the room.

"I just wanted to make sure your mom was okay."

Habit almost made me correct her mistake, pointing out that Lorna was my stepmom, but I decided against it. This time, it felt right.

"She's doing great," I said instead. "In fact, everyone is great."

"Well, I'm going to go. I just wanted—"

I moved to the door and motioned for us to talk outside. As I stepped into the hallway, Brodie and Grandma followed right behind me.

Grandma lifted one of Sierra's eyelids, looking for something in her eye. "You should be in a hospital bed, young woman. I still can't believe how quickly you've recovered. Your body experienced a tremendous shock and needs to be monitored in case there are complications."

"I appreciate your concern, Ginny, but I feel fine, and I need to make myself scarce as soon as I can. Remember, I'm the loony who tried to kill someone at the high school."

"What are you going to do? Where will you go?" I asked.

Sierra smiled. "A long vacation is first up on the agenda, then I'm not really sure. Somehow, I have a feeling that my family's calling didn't die with the demon. And if that's so, then I plan to be ready."

"Good for you," Brodie said, embracing Sierra in a tight hug.

Grandma did the same, then placed her hands on the sides of Sierra's face and kissed her forehead.

When Sierra turned to me, her eyes were glistening. I moved in for a hug of my own, and as I did, I whispered in her ear so that no one else could hear.

"If you ever need any help, just call."

When we broke apart, the tears were now rolling down her cheeks. She gave us all an awkward smile and a wave, then headed off down the hallway.

When Sierra turned the corner, Grandma casually returned to the room, leaving Brodie and me standing alone in an empty hallway.

"I'm going back to be with Lewis," Brodie said.

"Okay, I'm gonna wait for Dad in Lorna's room. But don't go anywhere without coming to get me."

The smile Brodie gave me warmed my entire body, as did the peck on the cheek that followed.

"Promise," she said and strolled down the hallway, gifting me with another smile before stepping into Lewis's room.

When I re-entered Lorna's room, her groggy smile greeted me. She was awake and surrounded by Grandma and Lindsey, standing on either side.

"Knox, did Ginny tell you about Travis's legs?" was the first thing that Lorna said.

"She did," I said as I took a spot at the base of the bed. The memory of her throwing herself into Sierra and the two of them convulsing as a deadly electrical charge passed through their bodies flashed through my mind. "How are you feeling?"

"A little sore. A little tired. Nothing I can't handle."

"I don't doubt it. Listen, I'm thinking it's time I drop this whole Knox thing and just start being Chace again."

Out of the corner of my eye, I saw Grandma grin.

To my surprise, Lorna shook her head.

"If you don't mind, I like it the way it is. Your mom had Chace—and that's something I would never, ever try to impose on. But Knox—that's between you and me. Whatever anyone else calls you, you'll always be Knox to me."

I didn't think my smile could be any broader.

"Deal."

Epilogue

Tug tried the combination on his locker for a third time, irritated with himself for not being able to remember what the last number was. When the dial aligned with his latest guess, the lock dropped open, and he breathed a sigh of relief. He wouldn't have to go to the office to get a new lock... again.

He banged open the door, as was his custom, and immediately he noticed the small white box sitting on top of the books he hardly ever touched. Displayed on the end of the box was a silver outline of an apple. He checked the outside of his locker to make sure he had opened the right locker, then picked up the box. As he did, a note fell off the bottom and tumbled to the floor. Tug picked up the letter and read it. Twice. Then grinned.

It simply read:

This is just in case you ever get AirPods... and you inevitably lose them.

Your Friend (so you'd better get used to it),

Villain

Acknowledgments

I always struggle with this part.

Numerous people have been instrumental in my development as an author along the way, so I feel it is only right to mention them in every book I publish. Their influence, however slight, has contributed to who I am as a writer today. I always fear leaving someone out, so if I unintentionally do that… please accept my apology.

I'll start with the folks who took the time to read my drafts… regardless of what book I was working on… and provide insight into how to improve. Critique Partners, Alpha Readers, Beta Readers, Friends, the list goes on and on. Their efforts over the years have molded me into what you see today. Thank you, all! In alphabetical order – Angela Brown, Patricia Burroughs, Lindsay Carlson, Alexia Chamberlyn, Crystal Collier, Julie Dao, Patti Downing, Melissa Embry, Elise Falson, Chris Fries, Sierra Godfrey, Christy Hinz, Donna Hole, Liz Larson, Lori Lopez, Laura Maisano, Linda Masterson, Alex Perry, and Nancy Williams.

In one way or another, each of the following individuals has kept me moving in the right direction and boosted my self-confidence when I needed it most. A most heartfelt thanks to

Brianne van Reenen, Lisa Regan, Dianne Salerni, Barbara Poelle, Sarah Negovetich, and Tina P. Schwartz.

Special recognition is reserved for everyone who contributed specifically to MOVING FEAR. Hijabi, Samantha Hansen, Brad Willis, Jennifer Fox, Amy Vidmar, Karen Hullander, Stefanie Gutierrez, Kendra Lynece, and Amber Nystrom. Each one helped me shape this book into something that I'm extremely proud of. Thank you ALL for the guidance!

And then there is my wonderful editor and cheerleader extraordinaire, **Shelly Stinchcomb**. This is the fourth book of mine that she has edited for me and I continue to bask in her knowledge and expertise. I would not be where I am today without her guidance and support. Thank you, Shelly!

I again used a service called Kickstarter (a way to fund the expense of publication by finding backers willing to take a chance on it…and me…ahead of time) and these are the individuals who helped me fund the book, for which I will be eternally grateful. They are: Amy Buzard, Brinda Berry, Brandie Black, Melissa Burns, K. L. Busick, Davia Chroniewski, Cassidy Darin, Matthew Dawson, Cheryl DiFiore, J Lenni Dorner, Taylor Elizabeth, Zack Fissel, Jennifer Fox, Stefanie Gutierrez, Greg H, Samantha Hansen, Karen M Hullander, Katie Hunsaker, Kimberlee M Kelley, Krista Kennedy, Tristan Lane, Samantha Lane, Caryn Larrinaga, Sarah Lummus, Jessica M, Stacy Mitchell, DeeAnn Myres-Magboul, Karen Nelson, C. Niehot, Rolexia Pittman, Kristy Ryan, Kelly Schroeder, Becky Seely, Valerie Anne Sizemore, Melodie Simard, Mandy Simon, Angel Stout, Kelsie Weber, Brittney Willingham

Last, but most assuredly not least, are my family—my children—Cody, Jaime, and Casey—and especially my best friend and wife, Kim. She has always owned the first read, the last word, and my heart. Thank you for believing in me and allowing me to pursue this dream. It means the world to me. Love you all!

Oh… wait… there's one more! You, my faithful reader. I can't forget about you. Thank you for choosing this book and keeping me firmly seated on this rollercoaster ride. Stick around… there's more to come.

    Much love!

A Letter From DL

I want to say thank you for choosing to spend some of your hard-earned income on MOVING FEAR. If you want to keep up with my future plans, as well as some keen exclusive material, consider signing up for my newsletter at the link below. I also use my newsletter to recruit ARC (Advance Reader Copy) readers for future releases, so if that's something you'd be interested in, you're one click away. Your email address will never be shared, and you can unsubscribe at any time.

https://dlhammons.com/

Also, if you enjoyed this book then I'd really appreciate it if you'd leave a review or recommend it to a fellow booklover. Reviews and word-of-mouth recommendations are CRUCIAL for authors, especially Indie Authors, and the best way to introduce new readers to one of my books for the first time. No joke. These things make a difference. It doesn't have to be much. Even something like This book ROCKS is enough.

I'd also like to hear from you. You can usually find me hanging out at one of the social media places below, as well as my website listed above. Tell me what your reading experience was like, or just say HI. I don't bite (unless you're covered in caramel – then all bets are off).

https://www.facebook.com/DL.Hammons
https://www.goodreads.com/DLHammons
https://www.instagram.com/dl_1956/
https://www.tiktok.com/@dl_books4us

www.ingramcontent.com/pod-product-compliance
Lightning Source LLC
LaVergne TN
LVHW010307070526
838199LV00065B/5471